Praise for
USA TODAY bestselling author
RaeAnne Thayne

"A story of love, forgiveness and healing. Once again, Thayne proves she has a knack for capturing those emotions that come from the heart."
—*RT Book Reviews* on *Willowleaf Lane*

"Thayne pens another winner by combining her huge, boisterous cast of familiar, lovable characters with a beautiful setting and a wonderful story."
—*RT Book Reviews* on *Currant Creek Valley*

"Thayne, once again, delivers a heartfelt story of a caring community and a caring romance between adults who have triumphed over tragedy."
—*Booklist* on *Woodrose Mountain*

Praise for *USA TODAY* bestselling author
Marie Ferrarella

"Ferrarella's engaging romance takes a sad occasion and turns it into joy. The characters are fascinating and will leave readers eager to hear their stories."
—*RT Book Reviews* on *Innkeeper's Daughter*

"Crisp storytelling combines with sympathetic, genuine characters for an entertaining, heartwarming read."
—*RT Book Reviews* on *Cavanaugh on Duty*

Praise for *USA TODAY* bestselling author
Leanne Banks

"Banks'...holiday story, featuring two authentic and memorable leads, is both heart-wrenching and heartwarming."
—*RT Book Reviews* on *A Maverick for the Holidays*

"Banks's prose sparkles with energy and heart... the story strikes a true vein of gold."
—*Publishers Weekly* on *Some Girls Do*

RAEANNE THAYNE

finds inspiration in the beautiful northern Utah mountains, where she lives with her wonderful family. Her books have won numerous honors, including four RITA® Award nominations from the Romance Writers of America and a Career Achievement Award from *RT Book Reviews* magazine. RaeAnne loves to hear from readers and can be reached through her website at www.raeannethayne.com.

MARIE FERRARELLA

earned a master's degree in Shakespearean comedy, and, perhaps as a result, her writing is distinguished by humor and natural dialogue. This RITA® Award-winning author's goal is to entertain and to make people laugh and feel good. She has written more than 240 books for Harlequin and Silhouette Books, some under the name Marie Nicole. Her romances are beloved by fans worldwide and have been translated into Spanish, Italian, German, Russian, Polish, Japanese and Korean. Visit Marie's website at www.marieferrarella.com.

LEANNE BANKS

is a *USA TODAY* bestselling author with over sixty books to her credit. She has won many awards and accolades, but she is most thrilled to hear from readers when they enjoy her books. Leanne lives in Virginia with her family and her little muse, a four-and-a-half-pound Pomeranian named Bijou. You can learn more about Leanne on her webpage, www.leannebanks.com, and on Facebook, www.facebook.com/leanne.banks.

RaeAnne Thayne
Marie Ferrarella
Leanne Banks

Island Promises

HARLEQUIN® ANTHOLOGY

ISBN-13: 978-0-373-83783-0

ISLAND PROMISES

Copyright © 2014 by Harlequin Books S.A.

The publisher acknowledges the copyright holders
of the individual works as follows:

HAWAIIAN HOLIDAY
Copyright © 2014 by RaeAnne Thayne

HAWAIIAN REUNION
Copyright © 2014 by Marie Rydzynski-Ferrarella

HAWAIIAN RETREAT
Copyright © 2014 by Leanne Banks

Recycling programs
for this product may
not exist in your area.

Printed in U.S.A.

H HARLEQUIN®
www.Harlequin.com

CONTENTS

To Dan, Angela, Odell, Terri, Everett
and Val for all the fantastic island memories.
Mahalo nui loa!

HAWAIIAN HOLIDAY

RaeAnne Thayne

CHAPTER ONE

MEGAN McNEIL WAS already exhausted.

By the time she'd herded two wildly excited seven-year-old girls, three carry-on bags, two backpacks, a wheelchair, a walker and a small cooler of medications that had needed to be hand-screened by security at O'Hare, she only wanted to curl up somewhere and take a nap.

It didn't help that she really, really didn't want to be here in the first place.

"We're going to Hawaii. We're going to Hawaii," her daughter Sarah chanted in a singsong voice.

Grace added her own verse. "We're gonna swim in the ocean. And I can't wa-ait."

A few passersby smiled at the identical twin girls and their exuberance.

"Yes, we are," Megan said, trying to tug her shoes on again and stuff all their stray possessions—hoodies, cell phone, laptop—back into the carry-on bags. "It's going to be wonderful fun, isn't it?"

But first, they had to survive the nine-hour trip.

When everything was carefully stowed again, Megan hung Grace's bag on the back of her chair, helped Sarah into her backpack, grabbed her own carry-ons and checked their gate assignment one last time. Of course, it *would* be the farthest one from their current position. Nothing about this trip was likely to be easy.

"All right, let's go catch an airplane," she said to her daughters.

"I'll push," Sarah insisted—as she so often did on the rare occasions when Grace's moderate cerebral palsy tired her so much she needed the chair for distances. Sarah moved behind her twin's wheelchair to do the honors.

"Thank you, sweetheart. We're looking for Gate 21. Can you watch for that?"

"I'll find it, Mommy," Grace offered, ever helpful. They made their way, weaving and dodging around other travelers until they finally found the right gate. Even if Megan hadn't seen the sign, she would have figured it out by the preponderance of brightly colored Hawaiian shirts

"Look! There's Daddy," Grace exclaimed, clapping her hands. She and Sarah both gave vigorous waves and Sarah called out to Nick.

He and Cara stood surrounded by family members, but when he heard Sarah he immediately hurried over to them.

"There're my girls. I was starting to worry you wouldn't make it!" He hugged Sarah tightly and kissed her cheek, then bent down to do the same for Grace.

After he had greeted their daughters, he turned to give Megan a warm hug.

"Thank you so much for doing this, Megs. It means the world to both Cara and me."

She hugged him back, gave him a kiss on the cheek and then stepped away. He looked good, she had to admit—smiling, relaxed and far happier than he had ever been during their short-lived marriage.

"The girls are both over the moon," she told him. "The beach and their dad's wedding all in one trip. What could be more fun? I don't think either of them slept a wink last night. I went in after midnight and had to put Sarah back in her own room or they would have giggled all night."

She didn't add that she wasn't looking forward to a nine-hour flight with two tired girls. She could only hope they would nap a little on the way.

Before Nick could respond, his fiancée, Cara, approached them. She glowed with happiness. If she didn't like the other woman so much, Megan might have been seriously annoyed at how great she looked, considering her own chaos of the last hour.

Cara hugged her. "You're here! I was worried you would miss the flight."

"We made it. No worries."

She was happy for Nick and Cara. She really was. The two of them made a beautiful couple, the handsome firefighter and his blonde, lovely bride. They were deeply in love and it was obvious to everyone who knew them.

Nick had never looked at *her* the way he did Cara. Theirs hadn't been a romantic destination wedding with all their closest friends and family, but rather frightened, hurried vows exchanged in her hospital room. She'd been on strict bedrest to avoid going into extremely premature labor with the twins.

Megan and Nick really had barely known each other, had dated for only a few months—and had slept together exactly twice. While she had liked Nick, and had been lonely and a little lost at the time, they never really generated much spark.

By mutual consent, they had both begun dating other people when Megan discovered she was pregnant, despite the condom Nick had used. As he was the only man she'd slept with in more than a year, she knew he had to be the father.

More than eight years later, she could still remember her stunned devastation when that pregnancy test turned positive. At the time, she was still a year away from graduating with her RN, living on scholarships and financial aid and the carefully parsed-out proceeds of her parents' life insurance policies.

She could barely take care of herself, forget about another human being—and then came the further shock when an ultrasound revealed twin girls.

She and Nick had considered giving the girls up for adoption. That had seemed the logical decision for two people who had no real foundation to build a life together—and never really wanted to take that step in the first place.

But when she went into labor eighteen weeks early, everything drilled down to a fight for their daughters' survival.

They had decided to marry so she and the girls

could be covered by his medical insurance policy as a Chicago firefighter. It had seemed the logical, wise decision.

They'd never been in love, though they tried to pretend otherwise through the frightening weeks she'd been on hospital bedrest, each moment tense and anxious, then the long weeks while their girls were in the neonatal ICU, and afterward, when their life had become a blur of medical appointments and tests.

Eventually, they couldn't pretend anymore. By the time the girls were two and Grace had been diagnosed with prematurity-related cerebral palsy, both of them had realized they made better friends and coparents than husband and wife. Megan had always considered their divorce the very definition of amicable.

Friendly or not, Megan still didn't feel she belonged at this wedding.

Grace's medical needs were complicated, though, between her overnight gastric-tube feedings, her medications and her breathing treatments. Megan couldn't put her on a plane and send her away with just anyone. While Nick and Cara were experienced enough to handle any complications, and Nick's mother, Jean, was comfortable caring for her, all of them would be focused on the wedding, not on a needy seven-year-old girl.

The hard reality was that Grace couldn't go to Kauai unless Megan went along to take care of her, and Sarah—sweet, loyal, loving Sarah—wouldn't attend her father's wedding unless her sister could go, too.

So here Megan was, swallowing her social awkwardness at feeling like an interloper and focusing instead on her genuine happiness that Nick had found someone as wonderful as Cara to be stepmother to her twins.

"We should have thought to help you through security," Cara exclaimed. "Was it a nightmare?"

"Not too bad," Megan lied.

"The good news is, the plane is on time. They should be boarding in twenty minutes or so. Let's find you a place to sit. Looks like there's room over by my brother. I'm so excited you finally have the chance to meet him. He's fantastic. You'll love him."

Cara led them over to a row of chairs with a few empty seats on the end and a convenient spot to park Grace's wheelchair. She could see a tall guy with dark hair, but she couldn't see his face—he was turned away, speaking with an elderly woman she guessed was a grandmother.

"He can help you carry all this stuff onto the plane. Shane, this is Megan, Nick's first wife, and these are their gorgeous daughters, Sarah and Grace. Girls, this is my brother Shane. I guess he'll be your new step-uncle."

Her brother turned around with a smile…and Megan's stomach did a somersault.

It was him. Sexy ER Guy.

Oh. She only needed this to ratchet the fun factor into the stratosphere. She felt as if she'd just thrust her face into a hot, steamy sauna and her vague sense of awkwardness at being here for Nick's wedding suddenly nosedived into excruciating embarrassment.

She saw startled recognition flash in his blue, blue eyes before he smoothly hid it.

"Hi, Megan. Nice to meet you," he said. Oh, how could she have forgotten that delicious voice? It had been one of the first things she had been drawn to a month ago during their brief ER interaction.

"Um, hi," she mumbled.

"Sit by me," Grace demanded of her sister, and Sarah dutifully plopped onto the aisle seat next to the wheelchair, which only left the spot right next to Cara's extremely sexy brother.

Despite the heat still burning through her cheeks, she stood frozen with indecision. Oh, could this day possibly get any *worse?*

Nick's mother, her former mother-in-law, Jean, came over just then. She brushed her cheek to Megan's before greeting her granddaughters. "Hello, my darlings!"

Since their grandmother was there, Megan seized on it as a ready excuse to escape for a moment. "I need to go talk to the gate attendants about stowing the wheelchair when we board. I'll be right back," she told the girls.

They barely heeded her, happy to be surrounded by people fussing over them. She walked quickly away, feeling Shane's gaze on her retreating back.

The gate attendant had her fill out a claim ticket

for the chair, which would be stowed in cargo during the flight and would be waiting for them when they made their connection in Los Angeles. To her vast relief, he also told her those with special needs would be boarding in only a few moments. At least she wouldn't have long to endure the torture of sitting next to Cara's brother, whom she had treated abominably.

With deep reluctance, she returned to her daughters and sat down beside him, aware of his heat and strength. What could she possibly say to him that would explain her actions of a month earlier? She didn't know where to start.

She was further relieved when he spoke first. "Your daughters are adorable," he said. "How old are they?"

"Seven," she answered. Her voice came out a little on the ragged side, so she tried again. "They're seven."

"How long have you and Nick been divorced?" he asked in an undertone, after a careful look to make sure the girls were busy with a couple of coloring books their grandmother had brought along.

She wondered at the hard note in his voice. "Five years now—which, incidentally, is about three years longer than the marriage lasted. Just in case you were wondering or anything."

He glanced between her and Nick, who was holding hands with Cara. Shane's sister. Megan forced herself not to squirm. She had long ago accepted that she and Nick had tried as hard as they could to make a marriage work that never should have happened in the first place.

Still, right now she would rather be anywhere else on earth than waiting to board a plane for her ex-husband's destination wedding—alongside an extraordinarily great-looking guy she was fiercely attracted to. Especially when she'd acted like a stupid, immature girl around him the first time they'd met.

"How's the shoulder?" she asked. As much as she'd like to pretend they were strangers, it seemed pointless.

He rotated his left arm reflexively. "Good. I get a little twinge here and there, but it was only a through-and-through, like the ER docs said. I was back on the job just a few days later. I'll have to be a little careful body surfing while we're in Hawaii, but other than that, I'm good."

"Did they ever catch the guy who shot you?"

"Yeah. He's in custody now. He was only a stupid kid trying to earn a little street cred by shooting at a cop. I'm still not sure he meant to hit me."

"I'm glad you're okay." She might as well say it, just come out and apologize and clear the air, but the gate attendant's voice suddenly came over the loudspeaker, inviting those with special boarding needs to come forward.

She stood. "That's us, girls," she said.

"We get to go on first?" Sarah's eyes widened, as if someone had just offered her a free puppy.

"Aren't we lucky?" Megan said dryly. To her,

boarding a plane early only meant more time sitting in one spot, waiting to be jostled by other passengers trying to stow their luggage.

She grabbed their bags and started pulling one while trying to push the wheelchair with her other hand.

"Let me help." Before she could protest that she could handle it, Shane grabbed the bag from her and started tugging the other one.

She reminded herself to be grateful. One of the first things she'd learned when she had twins—one with special needs—was to take whatever help was offered, even when her pride bristled.

The girls handed their boarding passes to the agent with excited flourishes that made the woman smile.

"Do you need further assistance aboard?" she asked.

"No. Thank you.

"We're going to have to leave the wheelchair here for them to stow," Megan told Grace at the door to the aircraft. "Do you want me to carry you?"

"No. I can walk," she insisted.

Despite the stress and turmoil of the day, she wanted to hug her brave, wonderful, independent daughter who had come so far. Grace stood up from her chair and moved with her careful, stiff-hipped gait down the aisle.

"Look for Row 14, and seats C, D and E," she said to Grace.

"There's a coincidence," Shane said behind her. "I'm in Row 14 as well. Seat F."

The jet had two aisles, with two seats by the window, four in the middle and two more across the other aisle. She and her daughters and Shane were assigned the middle seats.

Since the girls didn't like to be separated, she took the aisle for herself and settled Grace beside her, with Sarah on the other side next to Shane. At least the girls would provide a little buffer between them.

It was a good plan, in theory—until their grandmother boarded and settled into the seat across the aisle from Megan.

"Grandma, guess what?" Sarah said. She leaned across her sister and Megan to launch into a story about her soccer game that week, all while other passengers filed past.

"You'll have to wait to finish your story," Megan told Sarah, when she saw her daughter growing frustrated at each interruption.

"Why don't you change seats with her, my dear?" Jean suggested. "It's a long flight, and you surely won't be able to entertain the girls by yourself."

She wanted to argue, but knew she'd sound ridiculous explaining that she couldn't spend the four hours until their Los Angeles connection sitting by the brother of the bride.

She forced a smile. "Sarah, do you want to sit by your grandmother?"

"Yes!" her daughter exclaimed. Aware of Shane

watching the interaction with interest, she and Sarah traded places.

"I think we're settled now," she said, after swapping Sarah's backpack for her own tote bag. "Sorry for the chaos."

"It's fine. You must be a brave woman to trek nine hours to Hawaii for your ex-husband's wedding."

She was fiercely aware of him beside her, edgy and uncomfortable, which didn't bode well for the long flight to LAX.

"Nick's a good father and our girls love him," she said. "It didn't seem fair to deprive them of the chance to see his wedding just because it would be hard."

The flight attendants made an announcement about boarding quickly and storing luggage. She could see Grace and Sarah both growing increasingly nervous about the flight. By necessity, she turned her attention to calming her daughters while the flight crew prepared the cabin for takeoff.

A short time later, they were in the air. "There. You made it, girls. That was fun, wasn't it?" She forced more enthusiasm than she really felt, since she wasn't all that crazy about flying herself.

"I forgot how it made my tummy tickle when we went to Disney World," Grace said.

"I like it!" Sarah exclaimed. "Can we do it again?"

"You've got four more takeoffs before we're done—one more today and two on our way home."

The flight attendant came on a few moments later

and announced that it was now safe to use electronic devices. Sarah immediately asked for Megan's tablet.

"Hey, Grace, want to play a game?"

Grace was always willing to play, and soon the twins were engrossed in the game, blonde heads close together in concentration. Megan pulled out a magazine from her tote, still strongly aware of Shane beside her in the cramped space.

She was going to have to talk to him, to explain and apologize for her actions. Why not do it now, while her daughters were distracted? She opened her mouth but he beat her to it.

"So, for the last hour I've been trying to figure everything out. Was it because of your daughters?"

She could feel heat rush to her cheeks. "My... daughters?"

He made a face. "I called that fake number you gave me three times, hoping each time I'd made some kind of mistake dialing. The elderly-sounding gentlemen on the other end of the line was *not* amused, by the way."

Oh, she had been such an idiot. If she could go back and relive any moment in her life, it would be that night in the ER. She *hated* working a shift on the night of a full moon. Everybody acted out of character, including her.

"I'm sorry," she said softly. "I was so stupid."

From the moment he walked in with a gunshot wound—not on a stretcher but on his own two feet—she had known the handsome police officer in the bloodstained uniform was trouble. He'd been charming and sweet and obviously interested in her. Something about the late shift and the crazy night and the way he looked at her had her acting completely unlike herself. She'd been fun and flirty, laughing and teasing him.

And then he'd asked for her phone number and reality had crashed back down. She couldn't go out with him. She didn't even know the man, and he certainly didn't know the real her, the stressed-out, overscheduled mother of twins.

Then she'd been called into a trauma, and in a panic she'd scrawled a fake number.

"So?" he asked now. "Did you brush me off because of your daughters?"

"If it's any consolation, at the moment I did it I felt terrible," she admitted. "As soon as the trauma crisis was over, I went back to give you my real number, but by then you'd been discharged."

Under other circumstances, she might have been tempted to look up his information but that would have violated privacy laws and she could have been fired.

"You could've just told me you weren't interested," he said. "I'm a big boy. I can handle a little rejection—but for the record, I prefer outright rejection to that kind of sneaky thing."

She winced. "I know. You'd think I was in high school or something. All I can say is, I messed up. I'm really sorry."

CHAPTER TWO

SEEING THE EMBARRASSMENT in her gaze, Shane wasn't sure what to think about Megan McNeil.

She was either crazy or had considerable grit to show up for her ex-husband's wedding to another woman. He wasn't sure which yet.

Even a month later, her rejection stung.

He had really liked Megan. Okay, he might have been a little woozy from pain medication—even a through-and-through round from a .38 hurt like hell—but he could have sworn they'd forged a connection.

His mind replayed their interaction. While she'd helped him out of his uniform she had been sweet and solicitous, a beacon of warmth on a bitter winter night that had turned to hell.

When she asked if he wanted her to call someone for him, he had floundered. His parents weren't in Chicago, Mom was on one coast, Dad on the other. Having them at the hospital would have been a nightmare of drama and accusations. He could have called Cara, of course, but this was only a minor injury and he didn't want to bother her.

When he told Megan he didn't need her to call

anyone, she had become even more solicitous and kind. He'd noticed she wasn't wearing a ring and at some painkiller-induced moment had asked if she was dating anyone. She'd blushed in a way that had completely charmed him, and said that she was divorced but she didn't have time to date.

He'd never thought to ask if a couple of cute twin girls were the reason she was so busy.

"Was it something to do with hospital policy?" he asked now. "Are nurses not supposed to date patients?"

"I wouldn't strictly be breaking any rules. But that wasn't it. Not really."

She glanced briefly at her daughters—the smaller one with the twisted limbs and her active, inquisitive sister—and then back at him. "As you've probably figured out, my life is…complicated. I haven't dated anybody seriously since the divorce. I'm out of practice and, I'll admit, I panicked."

He shifted his long legs in the uncomfortable space, surprised at her candor. "I can be a scary guy, I guess. That's not necessarily a bad thing when you need to get information out of a perp, but it has its disadvantages when it comes to the dating scene."

A hint of a smile peeked out at him. "You didn't scare me. I liked you. A little too much," she confessed.

"I felt the same way," he answered. "Which is why I hounded some old guy in Irving Park three times, hoping I'd only misdialed."

She sighed, and he saw more of that entrancing

blush seep over her soft features. "Please, can't we start over? I'm so embarrassed about the whole thing. It would be great if we could pretend we only met at the gate before boarding the plane. I really don't want to have to spend the whole wedding trying to avoid you."

After a moment's thought, he stuck out his hand. "Hi there. I'm Shane Russell, brother of the bride."

She gave him a relieved smile and held out a small, capable hand. "I'm Megan McNeil. I, er, used to be married to the groom."

They shook hands briefly, before her attention was diverted by a question from her daughter.

Shane picked up his book again, aware of a strange mix of relief and disappointment. While his ego was a little appeased to know he hadn't been completely wrong about the attraction that had simmered between them, it was more than a little disappointing to discover that attraction was doomed to die a fruitless death.

As much as he was drawn to her lush mouth, those blue eyes, those lovely, sweet features, he wouldn't do anything about it. A month ago, he might have, but she was right. Her situation had just become too complicated.

THE FLIGHT BETWEEN Chicago and Los Angeles was far easier than Megan expected. The girls were both relaxed and comfortable. She read to them for a while, they watched a movie, they played a game or two, and before she knew it, the flight crew announced they were preparing to land.

"What can I do to help?" Shane asked as they taxied to the gate.

While Nick was a great father, she handled most things on her own these days. The chance to lean on someone else was as novel as it was welcome. "If you could help me with the bags, that would be great. It might take a while, though. I'm afraid we'll have to wait for the wheelchair to be brought up from the cargo hold."

"I don't mind."

He traded knock-knock jokes with the girls while the rest of the passengers filed out. When they left the plane, the wheelchair was waiting for them.

"This is quite a complicated procedure," Shane said, as Megan pushed Grace into the terminal.

"I guess you can see why we don't travel much. The kids and Nick and I went to Disney World a few years ago, but that's as brave as I've ever been with them. Car trips are actually much less complicated than flying."

"Except we can't drive to Hawaii," Grace offered. "Grandma said so."

"Unless you're a really good swimmer," Shane said. "Or know how to ride a dolphin."

"I rode a horse, once," Sarah chimed in. "It was brown and had a black tail and mane. It was super fun, but we didn't go swimming."

He grinned at her daughter, and Megan's stomach started whirling as if *she* were riding a dolphin in wild circles. He really was gorgeous, with sun-streaked brown hair and eyes the deep green of a mossy forest. Add to that how sweet and charming he was with her daughters, and she was in serious danger of making a fool of herself.

They made it to their gate just in time to board the connecting flight that would take them to Lihue.

He again stepped in to help her stow their bags in the overhead bin and settle Grace into her seat.

"Looks like I'm behind you a couple of rows for this leg of the trip. If you need my help on the flight, I can see about trading with someone to be closer."

Megan told herself she wasn't sorry for a little space to catch her breath, regain equilibrium. "You've done more than enough already. Thank you for all your help. I would have been sunk without you. Girls, can you tell Cara's brother thank you for helping with our bags?"

"Thank you," Grace said, her voice soft but her smile genuine.

"Thanks!" Sarah held out a little fist to give him a bump, something she did with Nick all the time.

He chuckled and obediently pressed his knuckles against hers, then added a complicated little side twist and top pound that made Sarah grin.

"Safe flight," he said, before moving a few seats behind them to allow the other passengers to board. She did her best not to feel a little bereft.

"He's nice, Mom," Grace said. Her eyes drooped with fatigue, and Megan hugged her close, making room for her daughter to rest her head in the crook of her arm.

"Yes. Yes, he is."

To her relief, Jean again sat near them to help entertain the girls on the long flight. By the time the captain turned off the seat belt sign, though, it was obvious the excitement and anticipation of the day were taking their toll on the girls.

They started to become petulant and cranky with each other and with her. The mood might have shifted quickly into frustration if she hadn't pulled out their story again, ducked her head to theirs and read quietly to them. After only a few pages, both girls' eyelids grew heavy. They fell asleep at almost exactly the same moment, as they often did.

She decided to follow their lead and steal a moment to close her eyes while she had the chance. When she awoke, she found the girls playing quietly with their Barbies, and she realized they would be reaching Lihue in only an hour.

There. Like so many other things in her life, the reality of a transoceanic flight had turned out to be far less painful than she'd imagined.

Still, by the time the plane landed, she and the girls were more than ready to escape the tight confines of their seats.

"We're going to Hawaii." Sarah started chanting her little song again.

"We're gonna swim in the ocean," Grace added.

"We're not going to Hawaii anymore," Megan told them. "We're here!"

"Can we go swimming in the ocean *today?*" Sarah asked.

"I don't see why not. But we have to make it to our hotel first."

They were again last to leave the airplane. She was deeply grateful when Shane stopped to help them.

"You made it!" he said to the girls.

"Finally!" Sarah said with an exaggerated, long-suffering tone that made him smile.

They walked down the concourse to find Nick and Cara waiting for them with magenta-edged flower leis. "Welcome to Hawaii, girls!" Nick said. He put one over each of their necks with a kiss on the cheek and then added one for Megan, too.

"Thanks again for dragging them all the way out here. You're the best ex a guy could ever want."

She rolled her eyes as the heady scent of plumeria drifted to her. "I do my best."

The bride and groom were distracted by others in the wedding party, and Megan began heading toward the baggage claim area.

"Oh, look at all the flowers. It's so beautiful," she exclaimed as they moved through the open-air terminal.

"Is this your first trip to Hawaii?" Shane asked.

She nodded. "You've been before, I take it."

"A few times. Only once to Kauai, when I was a kid."

He waited and helped her retrieve their checked luggage, and even carried the bags outside for her into the sweetly scented air. "You're staying at the resort with everyone else, right?"

"Yes. That's the plan. Cara made all the arrangements for us."

"I'm renting a car. I can give you a lift to the resort."

"Nick and Cara have arranged for a wheelchair taxi to pick us up. Thank you, though."

"I'll see you there, then. Girls, aloha." He made the hang loose sign.

"What does that mean?" Grace asked.

"That's called a *shaka*. It's a Hawaiian greeting that kind of means hello, howzit, thank you, aloha. All that stuff."

Sarah caught on immediately and did the same gesture back to him, twisting her wrist back and forth with delight, but Grace struggled with the fine motor skills necessary to stick her thumb and pinkie out at the same time.

"That's not right," Sarah told her sister, and Grace huffed a little with frustration.

"Here, like this." The big, rangy cop bent down to her level and took her little hand in his to help her make the gesture.

"There it is. That's it. Perfect."

She beamed at him, and he grinned right back and kissed her on the forehead. As Megan watched them, something warmer and sweeter than the Hawaiian breeze settled in her chest.

Off the airplane, the girls seemed to gain a fresh wave of energy. All the way to the resort, they chattered excitedly with their driver, Pete, a big, warm native Hawaiian who was delighted to show them around his beautiful island.

"There it is! There's the ocean," Sarah said every time the road to their resort passed through the dense trees that opened up to that impossibly blue water.

The resort was beautiful, lushly landscaped with fringy palm trees, banyans with tangled, twisting trunks, bright explosions of colorful flowers. Megan had never seen anything as exquisite.

"You girls have a great time, now," Pete ordered them after he helped them out and handed their bags to a waiting bellhop. "I'm gonna be checking to make sure you are."

Sarah and Grace giggled at him and did their best *shakas,* which earned a wide grin and the gesture in return.

"*Shootz.* That means I'll see you lateh."

"Shootz," both girls chorused at him with delight.

Megan had a feeling they were going to have a very interesting vocabulary before this trip was over.

By the time they checked in with the helpful hotel staff and caught a small wheelchair-adapted golf cart to their cabana, her own words failed her.

"Wow! The ocean is in our front yard!" Sarah exclaimed.

The ocean *was* their front yard. Their small cabana was perhaps twenty-five feet from the surf, with a wide lanai featuring a plump upholstered wicker settee and two chairs overlooking the water.

Inside, the cabana had two bedrooms, a small living area and kitchen, and a comfortable, wheelchair-accessible bathroom. The cabana's location and size were luxuries she was completely unaccustomed to.

She needed to unpack, but while the girls were exploring their temporary home, she leaned against the lanai railing and watched baby breakers ripple to the shore. She was aware of a vague sadness, a melancholy emptiness. The cabana was beautifully romantic, the sort of place meant to be shared with someone special.

"It's so blue," Sarah exclaimed softly from beside her, and Megan forced herself to shake off her mood. She *had* someone special to share it with. Two incredible daughters. She was truly blessed.

"I want to swim in the ocean, Mom. Can we?" Grace asked.

"Yes!" Sarah exclaimed. "Can we go now?"

"Don't you want something to eat first?" she suggested. "We can order room service and swim after an early dinner."

"No. Swim now, then eat!" Grace said.

In that moment, Megan resolved to savor this. She might feel out of place watching her ex-husband marry the love of his life, but they were here in one of the most beautiful places on earth, with a vast ocean in front of them. She wouldn't waste a moment feeling sorry about all she didn't have. Instead, she would focus on her many gifts, starting with these two wonderful daughters.

"Let's do it," she said, gripping two hands in hers. "I think I know just where to find our suits."

CHAPTER THREE

Yeah. He could get used to this.

After settling into his cabana, Shane grabbed one of the cold beers in the refrigerator—thoughtfully arranged by his sister, he guessed, and headed out to his oceanfront lanai.

He stretched his legs, which still felt achy and cramped after a long day of trying to cram six feet, two inches of height into a space obviously designed for juvenile pygmies.

He took a sip of beer just as his sister walked up the steps.

"Hey there," he said. "How's my favorite bridezilla?"

She made a face. "Admit it. I've been amazingly bridezilla-free."

"You have," he agreed. "You picked a great place. The resort is beautiful."

She smiled. "Better than the pictures online. All the reviews were right."

"Don't you have wedding plans to arrange?"

"Not right this minute. I came to check on you. I'm sorry I didn't have much time to spend with you on the flight."

"That's what happens when you fly first class. No time for the little people."

He gave a mock wince when she socked him and she gasped. "Oh! I forgot all about your shoulder injury. I'm so sorry. Did I hurt you?"

Cara had always been too tenderhearted for her own good.

"Not at all," he answered. "I was shot in the other arm."

His teasing earned him another smack on the same shoulder, which made him smile.

She didn't smile back. Instead, she sank down beside him on the rather uncomfortable settee, her features troubled. She twisted her fingers together on her lap and gazed out at the lovely setting, tension radiating from her.

He waited for her to tell him why she had really come. When she didn't say anything, he finally spoke up. "Okay, what's wrong?"

She glanced at him, her eyes a murky green. "Have you heard from Dad?"

He and their father tended to avoid each other whenever humanly possible.

"Not lately," he answered.

"I had a voice mail from him when we landed. He's coming to the wedding, after all. He'll be here tomorrow and he's bringing…wait for it…wife number five. Sherri or Sharon or something like that. The message was a little garbled, but I figured out they were married last weekend in Reno. Isn't that great?"

He listened to her listless tone and wanted to

punch something. Trust Hal Russell to do whatever he could to screw things up if at all possible. He didn't know how to answer her and had to take a few deep breaths to keep from spewing anger that had absolutely nothing to do with her.

"Oh, Cara."

"Mom is arriving tomorrow, too. She's going to flip when she finds out."

"She can deal," he answered sharply, determined to make sure of it. "Don't worry, kid. This day is about you and Nick, not about Dad and his wedding *du jour* or Mom and her drama. I won't let either of them ruin your big day."

"Do you really think you can stop them?" she asked.

"I'll figure something out, even if I have to handcuff them in their cabanas."

She laughed at that. "I would love to see that."

He smiled. "Let's hope it doesn't come to that. I only brought one pair, though I could probably round up a zip tie somewhere. Don't worry, I'll talk to both of them, make sure everybody keeps things civil."

Their parents despised each other, which had certainly made for an interesting childhood.

Cara leaned her head against his shoulder. "I love you, Shane. Have I told you that lately?"

He threw an arm around her, wishing, as always, that he could do more to make things easier for her. Though four years younger, Cara had been about the only stable thing in his tumultuous childhood. By necessity, they'd clung together to survive the storm-tossed seas of divorce, remarriages, custody battles, family court hearings.

"Love you back, kid."

They sat that way for a few moments while the sea whispered against the sand. Finally Cara sat up, looking up the beach toward a few of the other cabanas.

"Oh, look. Megan's taking the girls swimming."

He followed her gaze and found Megan wearing a hip-skimming, pink swimsuit cover-up, carrying Grace on her back. Sarah skipped along beside them holding a basket full of beach toys.

The late-afternoon sunlight glowed in her burnished hair. A few feet above the wet sand mark, Sarah threw out a towel and Megan carefully lowered Grace onto it.

The scene touched a soft chord inside him, for reasons he couldn't have explained.

"She's pretty awesome, isn't she?" Cara murmured.

"I just met her," he lied. "She seems to be." He spoke in a guarded tone, not liking the note of insecurity in his sister's voice.

"I'm not jealous of her, I promise. You can get that worried look out of your eyes. I like her too much. I know both she and Nick tried hard to make their marriage work. They care about each other, but I don't think they were ever really in love. The marriage was shaky from the beginning, and just never recovered from the stress of the girls being so sick at birth. It's just…I want to be a good stepmother, and I'm not sure where to start, especially when she's so great with the girls. Why would they need me?"

"They strike me as pretty easy girls to love. That's about all they need from you, isn't it?"

She sighed. "I hope that's enough. I'm going to be a stepmother. I'm suddenly feeling bad for the rotten way I treated wives two, three and four. I can't feel guilty about Sherri or Sharon or whatever her name is, since I haven't met her yet."

"You have nothing to be guilty about. None of them wanted to be bothered with us. You, on the other hand, already care about Grace and Sarah, and they like you." He'd figured out that much, hearing them talk about the wedding. "Don't worry, you'll be fine."

She leaned her head on his shoulder again for just a moment before rising to her feet. "In the interest of saving my sanity and my nerves, I'm going to choose to believe you about that. I love Nick too much to back out now. Thank you. A bunch of us are going to dinner later, if you're interested. Around eight."

"I might be. I'll let you know."

After she left, he took another drink from his beer, listening to the light music of the girls' laughter on the trade winds.

They were having the time of their lives playing in the waves, and he suddenly wanted to be out there with them.

So why wasn't he?

He battled indecision for another minute before he hurried into the cabana for his board shorts.

"IT'S SO WARM!" Sarah exclaimed, trailing fingers through sea water. "Remember how cold Lake Michigan was last summer?"

Megan shivered at the memory, which seemed a distant lifetime ago. "Yes. I think my teeth only stopped chattering last week."

Sarah giggled, bouncing a little on a wave that rolled past them. They were in only about eighteen inches of water, barely to the girls' chests when they were sitting on the sandy bottom.

"What about you, Gracie?" she asked.

"I *love* it," she declared, beaming and wiggling her legs. In the water, Grace enjoyed a freedom of movement she didn't have elsewhere. She had more control over her muscles, somehow able to countermand the disrupted neural pathways created by the hypoxic brain bleed that had caused her cerebral palsy shortly after birth.

"I think a fish just nibbled my toe!" Sarah exclaimed.

She flopped onto her stomach and stuck her face straight into the water, emerging a moment later with wide-eyed delight on her dripping features.

"It did! I saw four little fish! They're silver and orange. Can you see, Grace? Can you?"

Grace might have been able to move better in the water, but she'd never mastered her fear of submerging her face.

She peered a few inches above the softly rippling water, straining hard to see into the depths. "I can't see anything but water," she complained.

"They're right there. Try harder."

"What are we looking at?" a male voice called out and Megan jerked up from her own scrutiny of the depths to discover Shane wading toward them, a pair of board shorts hanging low on his hips.

His shoulders were broad and muscled, and her toes suddenly tingled as if a whole school had started nipping them.

"There are fish down there," Grace announced, with all the wide-eyed glee of someone declaring the clouds had suddenly turned rainbow colors.

He smiled down at her with a soft tenderness, and Megan's stomach fluttered. "Is that so?"

"Yes. Sarah felt one bite her toe. They didn't bite mine, though."

"Lucky."

"I wanted one to bite me. I don't like to put my face in the water, so I can't see them, but Sarah said they're there."

"I saw them," Sarah declared. "Look, there's another one."

Shane obediently lowered his face to the water. "Oh, I see him. You're right."

He lifted his head, only inches away from Megan's. That fluttering went into double time.

"You know, there are boogie boards with snorkel windows on them," he informed her. "Grace could lie on the board and look right down into the water."

Sarah snickered. "You said boogie."

Grace giggled, too, and Megan had to hide a smile as Shane rolled his eyes at her.

He pulled the board out from under his arm. "For your information, missy, this is called a boogie board. It helps you ride the waves."

He turned to Grace. "Want to try it?"

Grace gave a little nod, though she looked apprehensive.

He held the wide board steady in the small waves while Megan helped Grace stabilize on it.

"Hold on to the sides. That's it," Shane said. He supported the board and angled it to take best advantage of the waves. A slightly bigger one rolled to shore and she laughed when she rode up and down on it.

"That made my tummy tickle like the airplane!" she said.

He grinned. "It can do that."

Megan really tried not to notice how sweet he was to entertain her daughter—or how gorgeous he looked doing it.

All the headaches of traveling with children, especially one with special needs, seemed to float away on the tide as she watched her daughter's joy at riding the waves.

"Go Gracie!" Sarah yelled, clapping her hands. After a minute she turned to Megan. "Do you think I could have a turn when Grace is done?"

"You'll have to ask Shane."

He overheard. "Sure you can. Just give us a minute."

After a few more waves, he tugged Grace back

to Megan, lifted her off, then helped Sarah onto the board.

While Megan and Grace sat in the warm, shallow water, he tugged adventurous Sarah out to where the waves were slightly bigger.

Grace, in Megan's arms now, gave a little yawn that for just an instant made her look like a fragile baby bird.

When Shane returned Sarah to Megan, he held out the board to her. "Do you want a turn now?"

She ordered her stupid hormones to calm down.

"No. Thank you, though. I need to get these little mermaids onto dry land for dinner and bed. We're still on Chicago time, I think. It's been a long day today, with more fun planned tomorrow."

"If you take the board, I can carry Grace up to the house for you."

He knelt down in the water, offering his broad, comforting back. "Hop on, Ariel," he said over his shoulder.

Grace and Sarah both giggled, clearly infatuated with him. Grace threw her arms around his neck and he stood easily, wading through the waves and sand toward their cabana.

"Outdoor shower first, girls," Megan said, following along with Sarah's hand in hers. "We need to wash all this sand off out here."

He lowered Grace to the little bench beside the shower. "Thanks for the boogie boarding," Megan said, trying not to stare at all those gleaming chest muscles, or the small, puckered red scar on his biceps from the gunshot wound.

"No problem. I'll see you all later."

His fingers brushed hers as he grabbed the board. His smile encompassed her and her daughters, then he turned around and headed back into the waves. He waded a little ways, then dove in with quick, sure movements, heading for deeper water.

"Mommy?"

Sarah's tone indicated that wasn't the first time she'd tried to get her attention, and Megan jerked her focus away from Shane and back to her daughters, where it rightfully belonged.

CHAPTER FOUR

SHE SLEPT WITH the windows open and the sound of the sea lulling her to a deep and dreamless state…and awoke to pearly dawn splashing across the white and red hibiscus embroidered on her Hawaiian quilt and the quiet, endless murmur of waves licking the sand.

For one disoriented moment, she couldn't think why she had brought the girls' sound machine into her bedroom, then she realized that it wasn't some kind of white noise sleep aid, it was the actual ocean.

She and the girls were in Hawaii, staying in a beautiful ocean-side cabana. Nick and Cara were getting married the next day.

She stretched and sat up. Though the clock on the bedside table read barely five-thirty, she was abruptly wide awake.

She loved working the night shift at the hospital for the flexibility it gave her with her daughters' schedules, but as a result her body had become conditioned to odd hours and quick transitions from sleep to full consciousness. She wasn't very good at sleeping in.

The ceaseless rhythm of the waves seduced and

entranced her. Was it as beautiful as she remembered here?

She climbed out of bed and padded through the
silent house to the lanai. Yes. In the pale pink predawn light, the water looked a mysterious, alluring
green. Palm fronds rustled in the breeze, and the
air was heavy with the scent of ocean and flowers.

She felt as if she were the only one awake this
early, as if she had the entire Pacific to herself. A
sudden, fierce urge to stand at the water's edge to
greet the sunrise washed over her.

Why not? How many chances like this would she
have?

She hurried back to her room and threw on the
first thing she grabbed in the closet, a soft, loose sundress the color of newly ripe peaches. She quickly
pulled her tangled hair into a loose ponytail and
picked up the video baby monitor she sometimes
still used when Grace was sick, grateful for the impulse to pack it at the last minute.

A quick check of the screen told her the girls were
still sleeping soundly, so she unplugged the little
monitor and slipped it into her pocket, then walked
out into the quiet.

The sun hovered just below the horizon, the puffy
clouds glowing orange and pink and pale lavender in
the gathering light. She could hardly take her eyes
off it as she turned to walk down the ramp of the
lanai to the sand.

Only then did she notice three boogie boards

propped next to the front door. Two of them had little clear windows for looking beneath the surface.

She stared. What in the world?

A note was attached to the biggest one, written
on resort stationery that flapped in the breeze. She
pulled it off, knowing instantly who had left these
on the porch.

"We can't let Gracie miss the fish," Shane had
written in bold, masculine handwriting.

She pressed one hand to her mouth as she reread
the note, warmth spreading through her like baby
breakers reaching the shore.

She couldn't believe he'd gone to so much trouble
on their behalf. She ran her fingers along the smooth
curve of the largest board.

If she wasn't careful, she could be in very grave
danger of falling for a man like him.

She'd have to use extreme caution over the next
few days. She couldn't afford to risk her heart, not
when she had two girls who depended on her to be
strong.

After tucking the note in her pocket with the monitor, she walked barefoot down the steps. The sand
was cool and soft between her toes as she walked to
the water's edge, the warm, sweetly scented trade
winds rippling the cotton of her dress around her
legs.

Shorebirds walked on gawky legs in the froth,
and a few more wheeled and called overhead. She
headed back to the dry sand and sat down, knees to

her chest, to watch them as the sun inched higher and painted the clouds with more vivid color.

She was alone with the birds until she spied somebody jogging in her direction from the far edge of the beach.

She knew who it was even before she could make out his features in the pale light. She recognized the breadth of those shoulders, the brown hair glinting with streaks from the sun. Of course, the faded gray Chicago Police Department T-shirt was a bit of a giveaway.

The instant he spotted her, he changed course and headed in her direction.

"You're up early this morning," he said when he was close enough to speak without yelling. "The time change must be messing with you, too."

"I decided a Hawaiian sunrise was too rare an event in my chilly Chicago life to miss."

"The girls are still asleep?"

She pulled the monitor from her pocket and held it out for him to see.

"That's handy."

"It has a range of a hundred-fifty feet. I can be back in the cabana in a second."

To her discomfort, he plopped down beside her, all those hard muscles just inches away. Again, she had to force herself not to stare, focusing instead on his kindness to her and the twins.

"Thank you for the boogie boards. That was a lovely thing to do."

He shrugged, his expression embarrassed in the

glowing sunrise slanting over his features. "I only rented them. I figured, what are you going to do with boogie boards back in Chicago?"

"It's still wonderful."

"It was a complete whim. I headed into Lihue last night for dinner and there was a surf shop open right next to the restaurant, advertising board rentals. It seemed like fate."

"The girls will be thrilled. I was tempted to wake them up for a test run the minute I saw them on the porch. Fortunately, I came to my senses in time and decided to enjoy five minutes of quiet."

His mouth twisted into a smile. "Until I came running along to disturb the peace."

He definitely disturbed her peace, but not for the reasons he probably thought. She wasn't about to tell him otherwise, though.

"What are you three planning today?"

She pointed to the water. "Sand, surf, sun. That about covers it."

His low laugh sent nerves shivering down her spine—which only intensified when he shifted closer to her, stretching out long legs covered in dark hair.

"Are you interested in a drive around the island a little later? I wouldn't mind playing tour guide. We could go see a couple waterfalls I know, visit some quiet beaches, maybe head up to Kailua."

The invitation both thrilled and terrified her. Spending a few hours in a car with the man likely wasn't the best way to protect her heart.

"I don't know," she stalled. "Things can be hard

with Grace's chair. She can use the walker most of the time, but we would have to take the wheelchair along in case she gets too tired."

"I rented a big Jeep. There should be plenty of room for the chair and walker in the back, and I can easily lift her in and out."

She should say no. The word hovered on her tongue. But the girls would love to see one of the plummeting waterfalls the island was known for and a little more of the island than this stretch of beach outside their cabana.

She supposed she could always arrange for a rental car and venture out on her own, but spending time with him was much more appealing. The twins would certainly love it, given how drawn they were to him.

"That could be fun," she finally allowed, though she wanted to call the words back the moment she said them.

"Great. Shall we say noon? That'll give you time to play around in the water for a while. And I know the girls have a hula lesson this morning, too. We can grab lunch on the way somewhere and still be back for the rehearsal dinner tonight."

Ah, yes. The rehearsal dinner. Nick and Cara wanted the twins in the wedding party. They had to practice their role, which meant Megan wouldn't be able to manufacture a convenient excuse to skip it.

"Sure. Okay. That would work."

From the monitor, she heard a little cough that her maternal instinct told her came from Grace. She pulled it out to check and saw that both girls were still sleeping, cough notwithstanding.

"Everything okay?"

"For now. They're pretty sound sleepers. I think I'm still safe for a few more moments."

She turned her face back to the sunrise, which exploded with color now above the horizon.

"It must be hard, on your own with twins."

She flashed him a look and saw his expression was compassionate, not judgmental. "Some things are hard. I won't lie about that. Two parent-teacher conferences, two sets of homework every night, two girls nagging me in the store to buy them a treat. Most of the time they're a joy, though. I wouldn't trade our life for anything."

"Do you ever wonder if things might have been easier if you had…" His voice trailed off, as if he had suddenly reconsidered what he'd been about to say.

"Stayed married?" she finished for him.

His expression turned rueful. "Sorry. That was a rude question and none of my business."

She bumped his shoulder with hers. "My ex-husband is marrying your sister in roughly thirty-six hours. I'd say that makes it a little bit your business."

"There is that."

She wrapped her arms more tightly around her knees while the breeze lifted strands of hair that had escaped her ponytail. "I care about Nick. I always will. But we've both discovered we're much better as coparents than we ever were as a couple."

"I can see that. The girls seem very happy."

"That's the important thing, as far as I'm concerned." She glanced over at him. "What about you? Have you ever gone through this?"

"What? Marriage? Not me. On the morning of my mother's third marriage, when she was stuffing me into yet another tuxedo for another trip down the aisle with her, I decided that when I get hitched, it will be forever. I think this was a year or so after my father's fourth wedding. I was about thirteen by then."

She'd guessed something of the sort from what Nick had told her about Cara's family. Sympathy squeezed her chest. She couldn't imagine that. Her own parents had been deeply in love until the day they were killed together in a car accident when she was in nursing school.

Sometimes she thought their dying together had been a gift, as neither would have been able to live well without the other. A gift to them, anyway. As an only child who had always had a particularly close relationship with her parents, the loss of them both at the same time had been a devastating blow.

She'd figured out a long time ago that her grief after their deaths was one of the reasons she'd hurried into a relationship with Nick. She'd been lonely and adrift, seeking a connection that had never really been there.

"For the record," Shane murmured after a long moment, "I like Nick. He makes my sister happy. But I'm beginning to question his sanity to let someone like you slip away."

Heat seeped through her at his words, and she gazed at him with startled eyes. It seemed natural and perfect—there, alone with the sunrise and the water and the few shorebirds pecking across the sand—when he leaned forward and kissed her.

CHAPTER FIVE

HER BREATH CAUGHT and she froze, his lips warm and delicious on hers. Oh, it had been so long. She had really, really missed kissing, the slide of mouth against mouth, skin against skin, the wild flutter in her stomach.

The breeze swirled around them and the ocean whispered and she didn't want this lovely moment to ever end.

She kissed him back, her hands curled into the cotton of his T-shirt. Since her divorce, she had focused only on being a good mother, a good nurse. The unleashed heat of Shane's mouth and tongue and hands reminded her she'd lost something along the way. She had forgotten that, at her core, she was still a woman, with needs and desires she'd worked hard to suppress.

He eased away from her a little, breath ragged and blue eyes glazed with hunger.

"Yeah. Nick is definitely crazy," he said, his voice gruff. He leaned in for another kiss, his arms around her, pulling her against his hard chest.

They kissed for a long time, while the sun rose higher in the sky. She didn't want to stop, but a muffled cough from the monitor in her pocket acted like a cold splash of water.

Oh.

What was she doing here, wrapped around Shane Russell like some kind of tropical vine?

This close, she could see his irises, speckled glints of silver in the blue. She could also see a certain light reflected there that looked suspiciously…tender.

An answering emotion flooded through her. Yes. She could fall in love with him very easily. She thought of his help and care on the long flight, and how sweet he was to rent boogie boards for her and her daughters.

He could break her heart like the tide washing over a sand castle.

Hearing a sleepy little huff from the monitor, she gathered all her strength and wrenched away from him, her heart pounding.

"I…need to go," she said, feeling flustered and off balance, rocked to her core by the kiss. "The girls will be up, and I don't want them to wonder where I am."

"Right." His voice was still rough, his expression dazed. She supposed it was small consolation that he'd been just as affected by their kiss.

"I'll see you later."

She fled back to her cabana before he could say anything else.

SHANE WATCHED MEGAN hurry into her little house as if she were being chased by reef sharks.

His head still swam from the dizzying shift in emotions, but one clear thought rose above the rest.

He shouldn't have kissed her.

He was intensely attracted to her. Something about those big green eyes, her delicate features, that small, curvy body just did it for him.

Not only that, but he greatly admired her caring and concern for her daughters. She obviously loved them deeply. It showed in everything she did, from her attention to their comfort on the flight over, to her delight last night playing in the water with them, to the video monitor in her pocket this morning.

He couldn't even imagine the guts she must have needed to drag her twins across the ocean for their father's wedding to another woman. He couldn't help but respect that.

Yeah, he liked her—way too much. He gazed out at the endless rows of breakers. Despite his attraction, both physical and emotional, he knew she wasn't for him.

He'd made a vow a long time ago, after years of seeing the chaos his parents created in his life and Cara's, that he wouldn't drag other children through that kind of turmoil. Kids had a rough enough time making their way in the world. They didn't need new people moving in and out of their lives, the stress of separate visitations, the drama of being forced to adjust to a different family dynamic.

He had a strict no-kids policy and he intended to stick to that.

No matter how difficult it was.

"Tell me the truth. Is this uncomfortable for you?"

Megan glanced over at Cara, stretched out on a beach towel next to her in a cute blue bikini, soaking up sun.

"Uncomfortable? No. Unfair, absolutely. We're roughly the same age and you look tanned and buff while I look like a pasty-white cream puff."

"Spray tan is a truly wonderful invention. But you know that's not what I mean. I'm talking about this whole destination wedding thing. While I was dreaming and making plans, I should have thought things through and realized how difficult it would be for you to haul Grace and Sarah all the way out here."

"They're having the time of their lives. Look at them."

Cara and Megan both shifted to watch Nick haul a giggling Grace around on the boogie board Shane had provided. A few yards away from them, Sarah was busy building a sand castle masterpiece, tongue lodged firmly between her teeth.

Her daughter must have felt them watching her. She looked up briefly. "I'm almost done. See, this is the princess's bedroom. When the bad guys come to take over her kingdom, she's going to jump out that window to her horse so she can fight them. And then she's going to Hawaii to get married."

Megan blinked a little at the explanation but she couldn't fault the spirit behind it.

She and Cara grinned at each other as Sarah jumped up to get more water in her bucket.

"I won't lie," Megan said as she watched her. "The

trip here was hard work, but I would've hated for the girls to miss seeing their dad get married. You know I'm happy for you both, right?"

Cara gazed at her, a little teary-eyed, then reached out and squeezed her fingers. "You're about the most amazing person I've ever met, Megan. You know that?"

Megan rolled her eyes, though she couldn't help being touched. "You should know better than that by now."

"I'm serious. I can't believe I'm so lucky to have you and the girls in our lives. Before I met you, I was so afraid you would hate me. My mom has hated every single one of my dad's subsequent wives, including the one he's bringing to the wedding. And she hasn't even met her yet."

"I don't hate you, Cara," Megan assured her. "Nick and the girls both love you, and that's more than enough for me."

Cara squeezed her fingers again before flopping over onto her back. "See how lucky I am?"

Megan didn't have an answer to that, so she just rested her cheek on the rough weave of the towel and watched Sarah put the finishing touches on her castle.

A few moments later, nerves jumped in her stomach when she heard Shane's voice.

"So this is where everybody's hanging out."

She looked up to find him standing near his sister, again wearing board shorts that bared all those delicious muscles.

Feeling at a disadvantage stretched out at his feet in a skimpy bathing suit, she rolled over and sat up.

"Oh. Hi."

"Hey! Hi." Sarah beamed, delighted to see him. She offered up a *shaka,* which he returned with a grin. "Look at my castle. Isn't it awesome?"

"Truly spectacular. You did all that yourself?"

"Well, my dad helped a little, but I did most of it."

"Looks like that parapet is tilting a little. Do you mind if I help you with it?"

She frowned. "I don't see any parrot pet."

"Parapet," he said with a smile. "It's that tower thingy there."

He plopped down on the sand by Sarah's creation and straightened one angle with deft motions. "There you go. Now it won't fall down when it's attacked by hermit crabs."

Sarah giggled. "Not hermit crabs. The bad guys are coming to take over the castle from the princess but she's going to jump out the window onto her horse and fight them and she's going to chase them into the ocean."

He blinked a little. "Okay, then. Good plan."

Cara stood up. "I think I'll take one more dip before I go in and shower. Sarah, do you want to come with me? We can look for more fish out there."

"Okay!" Eager for more time in the water, Sarah dropped her sand shovel and hurried to pick up her boogie board.

Only after they took off together did Megan realize this left her alone with Shane. She wanted to chase after them but couldn't figure out a graceful way to pull it off, especially when all she could think about was his exploring mouth, his tongue sliding against hers, the strength in those muscles as he'd held her.

She flushed, not quite sure what to say to him.

He was the first to break the silence. "Look, I'm sorry about what happened this morning. I shouldn't have kissed you. I promise, it won't happen again."

Though she agreed in theory, his words still sparked a little pang. "It wasn't your fault," she finally said. "I didn't exactly push you away. It's easy to get carried away by this romantic setting."

"The romantic setting," he repeated.

She shot him a quick look. "Sure. Sunrise, beach, palm trees. Paradise makes people lose their heads."

"It is beautiful," he agreed. He gazed out at the water for a moment before turning back to her. "I would still love to take you and the girls around the island, but I completely understand if you want to take a pass, given the circumstances."

That would be an easy out. She could rent a car herself or just hang out here on the beach with the girls.

But she wasn't a coward. Hadn't she raised two daughters mostly on her own the last five years?

"We're both adults," she said quietly. "I think we can handle a little inconvenient attraction."

Before she realized what he intended, he reached for her hand almost casually, his fingers twining around hers. "Is that what you call this?"

"What else?" she countered, tugging her fingers away.

"To tell you the truth, I'm not really sure."

She knew. Trouble. That's what she would call this attraction that seemed to seethe and eddy around them like the frothy waves on the sand.

"I think I'll go back in the water while I have the chance," she said, escaping the currents tugging between them to head to her own boogie board. "Do you still want to take off about noon?"

"What is that, about an hour and a half? Will that give you enough time?"

"Yes. I'll swim for a minute and then take the girls over to their hula lesson. We'll meet you at our cabana after we clean off."

"Deal."

He grabbed his own board and headed for deeper waters while she waded toward the others.

"EVERY TIME YOU turn a bend in the road, the view becomes more breathtaking. How is that even possible?"

Shane shifted his gaze from driving for just an instant, enjoying Megan's wide-eyed excitement immensely. The craggy, raw green mountains and stunning blue sea seemed even more spectacular when viewed from her perspective.

"I'd forgotten how beautiful it was," he said. "It's the Garden Island. I've been to Oahu, Maui and Hawaii, and I think I'd have to say I still like Kauai best.

If I had to picture the Garden of Eden, this would be the place."

"I love the flowers most," Sarah announced.

"I liked the waterfall. It was *huge,*" Grace said. In the rearview mirror, he saw her hide a yawn after she spoke.

Both girls looked tired, probably still struggling a little with the time change.

"Chicago in January seems like another planet right now. It's tough to think about returning to below-zero temperatures and bitter winds."

He had enjoyed the last few hours with them and hated thinking this magical time had to end.

"Hey, Shane, is that a geyser?"

He looked down where water shot high through huge lava rocks. "No. That's called a *puhi,* or blowhole, like what whales have. Water comes up through a lava tube then shoots out. Pretty cool, isn't it? This one is called Spouting Horn."

He pulled into an overlook and they watched it for a while. Okay, if he were honest with himself, Megan and her daughters watched the blowhole. He mostly watched them.

They, not the beauty of the island, were the real reason he didn't want to return to Chicago. He would treasure the memory of their few hours together always. He loved being with them—Grace with her quiet courage and strength, Sarah with her energy and her inquisitive mind, and Megan, who drew him to her like the moon directing the tides.

All of them were entwining their way around his heart.

"I came here when I was a kid and heard a story about this place. I guess there's some Hawaiian legend about a giant lizard that used to patrol this area and was trapped in the lava tube. According to the legend, that's her breath coming out, and that noise you hear as the water rushes through is her roar."

He wasn't sure where that memory came from, but the girls seemed fascinated by it.

"How old were you when you came here before?" Megan asked, while Sarah and Grace were busy listening for the giant lizard.

"Around eleven or twelve, I think. Cara would have been eight, maybe. Our dad and his third wife brought us here."

"You must have had fun," she said cautiously.

His laugh was rough as memories he'd submerged a long time ago shot to the surface like water through that blowhole. "Not really. They didn't want us along."

"I'm sure that's not true."

"It was another of the endless custody battles in the war my parents waged after their divorce. Dad and Gina had already made arrangements to come here by themselves over the holidays. Then Mom reminded him a few weeks before Christmas break that this was his year to have us for Christmas. She'd already made her own plans that didn't include us, and she wasn't going to change them."

He'd really wanted to like Gina, but it had been

tough when she'd made snide comments throughout the trip about having to bring them along.

He could hear her and his father fighting about it every night of the trip. At least they waited until they thought he and Cara were asleep.

"It wasn't the most pleasant vacation of my life. I was old enough to feel the tension between them and to know we weren't wanted."

Her features softened with sympathy. "How terrible for you."

"Yeah. Let's just say I didn't handle it well. I spent the whole week acting like a little shi— Er, jerk, which didn't make the situation any easier for anyone. Not one of my prouder moments. I think Gina walked out about two months later. I always felt like that one was a little bit my fault."

"That sounds awful. You poor things."

He hadn't wanted her sympathy. Really, he couldn't imagine why he had told her all that in the first place. Something about her warm expression and gentle compassion managed to draw out things he had no intention of telling anyone.

"With that sort of history here, I wonder why Cara wanted to have her own wedding on Kauai."

"She was a few years younger," Shane said. "I'm not sure she understood all the nuances, you know?"

"That makes sense." Megan paused for a moment. "I gather your parents have been around the wedding block a few times."

"An understatement. Five for my dad, four for my mom. I've got enough ex-stepmoms and -stepdads to make a basketball team, complete with manager and a couple bench warmers. What about you?"

She gave a wistful sigh. "I was really blessed. My parents had more than two happy decades together. They were older when they had me—my mom was nearly forty and my dad a few years older. I was an only child. All I remember from growing up was how much we laughed together. Our house was always filled with joy. We loved each other."

He noted her use of the past tense. "What happened to them?"

She focused her gaze on her daughters, who weren't paying any attention to them. "On their twenty-fifth anniversary, they were driving home from dinner when they were T-boned by a drunk driver. Both of them died instantly."

"I'm sorry." On impulse, he reached for her hand and squeezed her fingers.

She looked down at their joined hands and then up at him with a tremulous smile. "That was about a year before I met Nick. My parents would have been crazy about the girls and I know they would have been fantastic grandparents. I still get sad when I think my daughters will never have the chance to know how wonderful their grandparents were."

"They know. I'm sure you tell them. They'll know your parents through the memories you share with them."

Her smile deepened and she squeezed his fingers. "Thank you. You're right. I think I needed that reminder."

"Can we see another waterfall?"

He shifted his gaze to the girls. "I think that can be arranged. Or if you want, we can visit a cookie factory right here on the island."

"Cookies!" Grace said promptly.

"Yay! Cookies!" Sarah added her vote.

"I guess that settles it," he answered, smiling at Megan before he backed out of the viewpoint and they continued on their way.

CHAPTER SIX

SPENDING THE DAY with Shane had been a huge mistake.

That evening, as she dressed carefully for the wedding rehearsal and dinner, Megan wanted to kick herself for ever agreeing to let him give them the tour in the first place.

The afternoon had been filled with priceless moments. Eating delicious coconut shrimp at picnic tables beside a roadside truck with a million-dollar view of the surf. Having her breath snatched away by the sheer wonder of the steep jagged cliffs of the Na Pali Coast. Watching him tenderly carry Grace on his back down a secluded beach to show the girls a sea turtle—a *honu*—that had come out of the water to bask in the sun.

She was falling hard for him.

She pressed a hand to her chest, already aching at the impending loss. Except for when he'd held her hand for a brief time, he'd been careful to keep things between them casual and light. She sensed invisible barriers and had no idea how to breach them—if she even dared.

This was ridiculous, she told herself. What did

it matter if he maintained distance between them? She couldn't be falling in love with the man. She barely knew him. She was letting her heart get carried away by the excitement of an exotic location and the break from her usual life. Vacation crazies. That's what this was.

She only had to make it through tonight and the sunset wedding the next day. In less than forty-eight hours, she would climb back on an airplane that would take her and her girls home, back to their carefully organized life. She'd be able to clear her head once she was away from the trade winds and the palm trees and the endless, seductive murmur of the sea.

She hurried to the other room, where the girls were sitting in the new flowered sundresses she'd bought them that afternoon at a little shop in Princeville. They were entranced with a show on TV, which meant they hadn't had the chance to mess up their clothes yet.

"I'm finally ready," she told them. "Sorry about the wait. Should we go?"

"Yep," Grace said. "The show got over right this minute."

Both of her daughters smiled at her, looking bright and cheerful, and her heart ached with love for them. They were the most important people in her life, she reminded herself. Not a gorgeous police detective with a sweet smile and shoulders big enough for the weight of the world.

She grabbed a couple of delicately scented plumeria blooms from the bouquet on the table and stuck one behind each girl's ear. "There. Now you look like proper Hawaiian princesses."

"You need a flower, Mommy," Grace insisted.

On impulse, she picked another flower from the bouquet and stuck it behind her ear.

Sarah pushed her sister's wheelchair as they took the walkway between the cabanas that led to the area of the beach where the wedding would take place the next evening.

When she arrived, Jean and her daughter, Nick's sister, immediately seized on the girls, asking them all about their day and the things they'd seen.

She was aware of him there, speaking with Cara and a handsome, rather distinguished-looking older man she hadn't met yet. Hanging on the man's arm was an exquisitely dressed woman who didn't look much older than Shane.

She recognized enough similarities between the older man's features and Shane and Cara to realize this must be their father and his new wife.

She thought of the pain she'd heard in Shane's voice that afternoon as he talked about his father's behavior. Even though it happened many years ago, she had to fight the urge to head over to give him a piece of her mind.

She controlled herself, forcing her attention back to the conversation between the twins' grandmother and aunt.

An older woman she also hadn't met yet approached the wedding party, greeting a few of Cara and Shane's other relatives. She was heavily made up and appeared to have had recent Botox injections, judging by her falsely placid expression.

Out of the corner of her eye, Megan watched the woman approach the other group and give Cara a big, overly dramatic hug. Megan didn't miss the scathing look she sent Shane's father and the younger woman with him.

This must be the mother of the bride, she guessed. For Cara's and Nick's sake, she really hoped their parents could manage to keep the peace until the wedding was over.

As she didn't have a direct role in the wedding— of course—during the rehearsal Megan mostly sat on the sidelines and did her best to prompt Grace and Sarah in their responsibilities as flower girls. Grace used her walker and moved with her somewhat labored gait, though she seemed to relish her role, pretending to toss flower petals with abandon.

Megan made a mental note to advise her to pace herself during the real ceremony and not empty her whole basket in the first few feet.

After the rehearsal, the wedding party moved to a small reception room inside the hotel for the catered dinner. Nick's sister and mother took charge of the girls, leaving Megan feeling a little at loose ends.

She was contemplating taking the girls after dinner and returning to their cabana when the mother of the bride approached her, drink in hand.

"I understand you're Nick's first wife," she said without preamble.

She wasn't quite sure what to say or why she'd been singled out for the woman's scrutiny. "Yes," she answered carefully. "I'm Megan McNeil."

The woman's forehead furrowed as much as she could manage and she took a healthy drink.

"I'm Donna Porter, Cara's mother. I have to say, I was stunned—just *stunned*—when my son told me who you were. I can't believe you actually flew to Hawaii for your ex-husband's wedding to my daughter."

She blinked a little at the woman's temerity. What business was it of hers why Megan was there? She didn't have to explain herself to anyone, especially not the half-drunk mother of the bride.

As much as she wanted to bluntly tell the other woman off, Megan decided starting a confrontation would only complicate an already sticky social situation.

"My daughters wanted to see their father get married," she answered. "As you can probably see, one of my twins has special needs. I couldn't just send her to Hawaii on her own."

Donna appeared to digest that, glancing at the girls and then back at her. "Wow, you're a bigger woman than I am. I never would have dragged my kids to one of their father's many weddings. Of course, I would have gone broke trying to make it to all of them. He's on, what, his fifth?"

"I don't know," Megan answered.

"He is. That's him, over there. My delightful first husband, Hal. Have you seen that little tramp he married this time? Ridiculous. She's half his age! Doesn't he know he's making a complete ass of himself?"

Again, Megan didn't quite know how to respond and settled for making a noncommittal sound.

"I've half a mind to go tell him so." Donna picked up her drink and started to slide her chair back. Megan shot a quick look at Cara, busy talking to a couple of other wedding guests. Donna had obviously had a little too much to drink. The last thing the bride needed right now was the stress of her mother causing a scene at the rehearsal dinner.

Megan looked around for someone to help her rescue the situation, but Shane was busy talking to Nick and a couple of Nick's friends, and Cara was distracted with her father and his new wife.

She would have to take things into her own hands, she realized. She quickly placed a hand on Donna's arm. "I love your earrings. Where did you get them?"

"Oh, these? I made them. I took a beading class at the community center in my condo development. Aren't they beautiful?"

"Yes. I'd love to know how to do that."

"It's not hard." Donna launched into an explanation that was mostly over Megan's head. From there, Megan moved on to asking about the Florida community where she lived, what books she liked to read, and interesting people she'd met, all while trying to substitute Donna's drinks for water.

Forty minutes later, Megan's eyes were gritty and sore with fatigue, as if somebody had tossed a handful of beach at her.

She couldn't blame her sudden tiredness on lingering jet lag. Keeping the mother of the bride distracted and happy was more exhausting than dealing with the twins on a sugar high.

People were beginning to leave, and Megan decided she should take the twins back to their lodgings to get some rest. She was just about to make her excuses to Donna when Shane approached them.

As soon as Donna spied him, she jumped up and slipped an arm through his.

"Megan, this is my son, Shane," she said, her voice only slurring a little. "Isn't he a gorgeous one?"

Despite her exhaustion, she had to hide a smile at the embarrassed look in his eyes.

"Absolutely," she answered with total truth.

"Girls started calling him at home when he was twelve years old. Can you believe that? And they haven't stopped for a minute since. He ought to be the one getting married, don't you think?"

This time her smile broke free. "I think that's for Shane to decide."

"Mom, can I walk you back to your cabana?"

She pouted a little. "Already? I was thinking I would hang out at the bar for a while."

"Are you sure?" he pressed. "Tomorrow will be a big day. You don't want to be off your game for Cara's wedding. You know you'll want to look your very best in the pictures. And aren't you spending the day helping her get ready?"

"I guess you're right. It was lovely talking to you, Megan." She gave Megan a rather sloppy hug and kiss on the cheek. Apparently they'd bonded over talk of beads and books.

"You know what my son needs?" Donna said suddenly. "A nice girl like you!"

Shane looked horrified—by his mother's behavior or her words, Megan wasn't sure. She tried not to be hurt by the possibility that he was horrified at the idea of needing someone like her. Still, she couldn't help being annoyed that he obviously didn't appreciate the energy she'd just expended on his and Cara's behalf.

"Come on, Mom. Let's get you home."

"If I have to," Donna huffed, gathering up her purse.

After a long look at Megan—one she couldn't quite analyze—Shane gripped his mother's arm and led her away from the reception room.

Megan sighed and went to gather her daughters, wondering if she would turn out like Donna someday, alone and unhappy.

As was often the case, Megan somehow found an extra measure of energy after she helped the girls through their evening routine—medication, bath, pajamas, story—and settled them into bed.

After they were asleep, she sat out on the lanai with the video monitor and a book, listening to the whispering palm fronds and the soft, soothing sound of the waves.

All the craziness of the evening seemed to fade away out here in the breeze. She drew in a deep breath, relaxing her neck, her shoulders, her trunk. She leaned her head back against the cushions of the settee and closed her eyes, letting the quiet peace seep through.

She might have dozed off. She wasn't sure. But when she opened her eyes, she found Shane standing a few feet away, watching her.

He still wore the dress slacks and the Hawaiian shirt he'd worn to the wedding rehearsal, and he looked strong and handsome in the moonlight.

"I'm sorry I woke you. I saw you up here with your book and thought you were reading."

"I wasn't asleep," she answered, almost sure of it.

"What about the girls?"

She held up the video monitor. "Deep in dreamland. I was worried they might be too excited about the wedding tomorrow to fall asleep easily, but they dropped right off. They're not used to all this excitement."

"Hey, I'm a police officer in one of the most crime-ridden cities in the country and I have to admit that being thrown into the middle of my dysfunctional family is too much excitement for me, too."

She smiled a little. He watched her for a moment, then came over and eased down beside her on the settee.

"I came to apologize."

"Why?" She wondered briefly if he was referring to that stunning kiss again. If so, she might have to smack him.

"My mother. I'm sorry you were saddled with her

all night. I should have stepped in earlier. The truth is, I wasn't paying attention and didn't realize what was going on. She's not a big drinker, since she's smart enough to know it goes straight to her head. Usually she has the sense to stay away from alcohol. I should have been more in tune."

"I handled things."

"I'm guessing you prevented her from causing a scene. Am I right?"

She shrugged, a little astonished at the accuracy of his guess. No wonder he made a good cop, with detective skills like that. "It was no big deal. Turns out, she was easily distractible. Kind of like the girls when they're gearing up for a tantrum."

"Well, thanks. I owe you."

She shifted, uncomfortable with the idea of him feeling obligated to her for anything. "Don't be silly. I didn't do anything. Anyway, it's small payment for the personalized tour of Kauai you gave us today."

"I enjoyed today," he answered. "Sharing the island with you and Grace and Sarah was like seeing it for the first time all over again."

"It's a memory I know I'll never forget."

He said nothing, only continued gazing out to sea. She remained quiet as well. Maybe he needed the quiet calm as much as she did.

The night was seductive, the two of them alone in the soft, warm darkness, and she felt closer to him than ever.

CHAPTER SEVEN

HE SHOULDN'T HAVE come here. It had been sheer impulse. After he'd settled his mother in her cabana, he'd been walking toward his own lodgings along the beach when he'd seen her here on the porch, her features softly lit by a small reading light.

He had been drawn to her, unable to keep away.

Now he didn't know what to do, especially when the only thing he could think about was their stunning kiss that morning—and how badly he wanted another taste.

"Shane," she began.

He didn't know what she intended to say. The sound of his name on her lips, low and beguiling, shivered through him as if she'd trailed a hand through his hair.

Just once more. The night was too perfect, soft and romantic. He had to kiss her.

He shifted on the settee and found her face tilted to his, almost as if she were waiting for him to lower his mouth to hers. He drew in a ragged breath and then he forgot everything except the wonder of her.

Her mouth was warm and sweet and tasted of

chocolate and strawberries, two of his very favorite things.

She gasped a little when he kissed her and he thought for a moment she would push him away, then her mouth softened on his and her arms slid around his neck.

He knew this was crazy, but he couldn't seem to help himself. Kissing her was addictive, all the paradise he could ever need. It was beaches and soaring green mountains and the vast sea, all rolled into one delectable package.

He was vaguely aware anyone walking along the beach could see them, but they were in shadows here that would conceal them from all but the most careful scrutiny. The truth was, he didn't want to stop. He kissed her while the palm fronds rustled on the roof of the lanai, while a frog croaked somewhere nearby, while drums from a distant luau sounded in the night.

He wanted to drag her back to his cabana, to lay her down on the beautiful Hawaiian quilt and make love to her all night long.

Emotions welled up inside him, as tender as they were terrifying.

He was falling for her.

He supposed it had started that day in the hospital, when she'd teased him and smiled at him and distracted him from the pain racing down his arm. Seeing her again, discovering the woman inside the nurse's scrubs, had only deepened his growing feelings.

He had never felt these things before. They scared the hell out of him, left him unsure how to proceed.

Desperate for a little space to catch his breath and his sanity, he eased away from her.

She looked breathtaking in the moonlight and he practically had to dig his nails into his palms to keep from reaching for her again.

"Sorry," he murmured. "I told myself I wouldn't do that again."

Her eyes looked huge in the dim light. He couldn't quite read them, though he had the vague feeling he'd hurt her.

"Yet you did."

"Whenever I'm around you, I just can't seem to help myself."

She was silent, her breathing rapid and her expression veiled by the darkness. "I guess it's a good thing we're all going home in a few days, then, isn't it? Away from the temptation to do things we know aren't good for us?"

She thought *he* wasn't good for her? The thought burned, even though it was the truth.

He rose from the settee. "I should go. I told Nick I would meet him at the bar for drinks, a kind of informal bachelor's party."

"Good night. Thanks again for the memorable day."

He didn't want to go. He wanted to stay right here with her in his arms, but he knew that was the last thing either of them needed right now.

"I DON'T WANT to go swimming." Grace pouted. "It's raining!"

"Hardly at all, Gracie," her sister said. "It's only sprinkling a little. We could still have fun."

"I don't want to."

"How about a movie?" Megan tried.

"No!"

"Should we read more of our book?"

"No." This time, she whimpered the word miserably.

Megan sighed, fighting for patience. Grace had suffered a restless night, waking several times, which, of course, woke everyone else.

Despite a dose of Tylenol this morning, she still radiated unhappiness.

Megan did a quick forehead scan with the thermometer she'd brought. As it had registered earlier, Grace had a low-grade fever. It wasn't high enough to cause major concern, but was still worrisome.

Why did she have to choose today, of all days—the morning of her father's wedding—to come down with something?

It wasn't the girl's fault, Megan reminded herself. Grace was tetchy and miserable and probably felt lousy. She had all the signs of an ear infection.

She grabbed her cell phone and speed-dialed her pediatrician back in Chicago, with whom she had a great relationship.

"Given the circumstances, I'm going to trust your judgment," Dr. Phillips said after Megan explained Grace's symptoms. "If you think it's an ear infection, I'll call in an antibiotic to a pharmacy there in Kauai. You say you'll be home tomorrow night?"

"Yes. Late."

"Just bring her in when you get back so we can check things out."

"Thank you, Anne. I owe you."

As soon as she hung up her phone, she realized she had another issue—transportation. She'd just have to call a taxi, she decided. It would be easier than trying to figure out bus schedules.

She called the pharmacy for directions and had just hung up when someone knocked on the door.

She opened it to see a rippling cascade of vivid tropical flowers—and a particularly gorgeous man holding them.

Her mind instantly replayed their kiss on the lanai the night before, the heat and passion and sheer *romance* of it.

"Hello," she said to Shane, her tone guarded.

"I'm running errands for Cara this morning. These are the flowers for the girls' hair, with an extra lei for you."

"Oh," she said softly. "They're beautiful."

They were the most exquisite flowers she had seen yet, pure white edged with a soft purple that would go beautifully with the girls' dresses. "I'll put them in the refrigerator until tonight. Thank you."

"I really get to wear one of those?" Sarah's eyes were huge.

"Yes. And Grace, too."

"No. I don't want to," she groused from the sofa.

Shane's eyes widened and he gave Megan a careful look. She imagined he wasn't expecting that kind of grumpiness from Grace, who was usually unfailingly cheerful, even when nurses were trying to stick her for an IV.

"We're having a bad day," she murmured to him. "I'm convinced she has an ear infection. She has all the signs. Her pediatrician just prescribed an antibiotic."

"Can you get it filled somewhere here at the resort?"

She shook her head. "We're going to head into town. I was just about to call a cab."

He made a face. "That's crazy. I can pick it up for you. You were the last flower delivery. What pharmacy?"

She gave him the address. "That would be great if you could pick it up. Thank you. Let me find my insurance information."

"No, Sarah," Grace grumped loudly from the sofa. "I *don't* want to play on the iPad. I told you that."

"You don't have to get mad at me," her sister snapped back. "It's not *my* fault you don't feel good."

"Girls, that's enough," Megan said. She worried the antibiotic wouldn't start working in time to help Grace's mood before the wedding.

Shane looked between the girls and then at Megan with an expression of sympathy. "Why don't we all go into town? A change of scenery couldn't hurt. We could run to the pharmacy and then grab a plate lunch somewhere."

She wanted to say no. Spending more time with him didn't seem smart right now. On the other hand, she was at her wits' end with Grace. If a trip to the store would distract her from her cranky mood for a few minutes, Megan would take it.

"Let me put these in the refrigerator," she said after a pause.

When she finished, she found him helping Grace into her wheelchair for the trip into town, making silly jokes the whole way. She found something almost heartbreakingly sweet about watching his care with both of her daughters.

The rain had eased and everything smelled fresh and clean as they walked outside.

"Look at that, girls," Shane said, pointing to something on the wooden side of the simple structure. "It's a gecko."

He pushed Grace closer so she could see, and Sarah stood beside her, entranced by the little reptile. "Will it bite?" Sarah asked, sounding not too concerned at the possibility.

"Not geckos. They're pretty harmless. Cute, aren't they?"

"I want one for a pet," Grace announced. "Can I take him home?"

His low chuckle sent Megan's stomach twirling. "I don't think this little guy would be very happy with our cold Chicago winters," Shane answered. "What do you think?"

Grace pouted a little but seemed to accept the

logic of that as Shane continued pushing her to the small parking lot nearby.

The idea of trying to distract her had been pure genius. Grace's mood improved immensely. Without her bad temper, everyone else's mood did, too.

The drugstore had an aisle filled with souvenirs. Before Megan headed to the pharmacy counter to pick up the antibiotic, she put the girls to work selecting a few items for their friends back in Chicago. When she returned to the aisle, medicine in hand, she found Shane wearing about four wildly colored artificial leis, a funny hat and a pair of sunglasses with pineapple-shaped frames. The twins were laughing uproariously.

"No, let's try this one," Sarah said in a rather bossy voice. She picked up another silly hat, this one fashioned like a coconut. As Shane bent down so the girl could swap out hats, Megan felt a soft warmth seeping through her.

She wasn't sure how, but Shane had become immensely important to all of them. The girls would miss him after all the fun they'd enjoyed together during this trip. Their life in Chicago would seem drab by comparison. She fought down the pang. She didn't have room for him in her life, remember? Things were complicated enough.

She pushed away her sudden melancholy, the wildly hopeless wish that they could stay here forever.

"That is a very good look for you," she said.

He grinned at her, looking so adorable she wanted to stop right there in the aisle and kiss him.

"Thanks. I think the pineapple sunglasses help me pull the whole thing off, don't you?"

"Definitely. You're not really buying all those things, are you?" she said to the girls. "I thought I said something about macadamia nuts."

"We got those already," Sarah said, pointing to a nearby cart. "We just wanted to see how Shane looked."

"I like the hat best of all," Grace offered.

He smiled, pulled it off his head and set it on hers. "Then I'll buy it for you. And Sarah, what do you want?"

After careful consideration, she selected a T-shirt with a cute monkey wearing a hula skirt.

They paid for their purchases and headed out to his Jeep, where Megan gave Grace the first dose of her antibiotic. This was one of the few times she was grateful for her daughter's feeding tube, which helped her get enough nutrition through formula that was pumped all night. Medications went down much easier when Grace didn't have to taste them.

Shane watched the whole thing with interest. "So food and medicine can go right into the stomach?" he asked.

Grace nodded. "Cool, huh? Sarah always has to swallow yucky medicine but if I don't want to, I don't have to."

Megan smoothed a hand down her hair, loving

this little girl who never resented that her twin didn't share her limitations.

They grabbed lunch at a nearby restaurant that featured the ubiquitous Hawaii plate lunch, either chicken, shrimp or beef cooked in a sauce over rice. They ate on picnic tables overlooking the ocean, their napkins anchored with salt and pepper shakers.

Megan had a teriyaki and pineapple chicken that was just about the best thing she'd ever eaten. She tried to savor the moment with Shane, knowing their time together was limited. Soon they'd be back in their separate lives. She likely wouldn't see him again when they returned to Chicago, a prospect that left her feeling bleak.

Within five minutes of leaving the restaurant, both girls fell asleep, cuddled together like puppies in the backseat.

Megan discovered them and winced. "They're out," she said.

"You say that like it's a bad thing. I would think you'd want to celebrate naptime."

"I do. Believe me, I do. It's just that I was hoping to make them have a little quiet time in their beds before we have to start getting them ready for the wedding."

"Want me to drive around for awhile to let them sleep?"

She was conflicted. The girls were both much happier when they were well rested, but that also meant more of this dangerous time with Shane when they were virtually alone.

"Do you mind?" she asked. "We were up and down all night with Grace's earache. I finally sent Sarah into my bed so I could stay in with Grace. Even a half hour would help."

"If you need to sleep, too, I don't mind driving all the McNeil ladies around for awhile."

She smiled. "I should be okay. I'm not tired."

They lapsed into a comfortable silence as he drove, passing fruit stands and beaches and exclusive homes set away from the road. Hawaiian slack-key guitar played on the stereo, quiet and relaxing.

Despite her words, the rough night must have caught up with her. When she blinked her eyes open, they were once more parked at the resort, and Shane was gazing down at her, an unreadable expression in his eyes. She had the oddest feeling, completely comfortable and natural.

"Oh. I feel asleep."

He smiled, white teeth gleaming in his tanned face. "Two minutes after you said you weren't tired."

"I'm sorry. That was a poor trick to play when you were kind enough to play taxi driver."

"I told you I didn't mind if you slept. I had nothing to complain about. Sunshine, gorgeous scenery, great music and a beautiful woman beside me. I would have kept driving, except I knew the girls would need to get ready for tonight."

"Oh. Yes."

She blinked awake a little more. "What time is it?"

When he told her, she straightened quickly. "We

really *do* need to hurry. They're supposed to be there early to take pictures with Nick and Cara."

He helped her wake the girls and transferred a still-sleepy Grace to her wheelchair, then pushed her to their cabana.

"There you go."

"Thanks for the T-shirt," Sarah said. "I love it."

She reached her arms up, and after a startled moment, Shane bent down and hugged her.

"Me, too," Grace insisted.

He hugged her tightly, too. When he straightened, he again had an odd, bemused expression on his face.

"Thanks for your help," Megan said. She wanted to ask for a hug, too, but decided that probably wouldn't be wise.

"You're welcome. I'll see you at the wedding."

He gave her another searching look, then headed for the door.

CHAPTER EIGHT

"I NOW PRONOUNCE you husband and wife. You may kiss the bride."

Just like that, her daughters gained a stepmother.

Megan wiped her eyes, touched by the joy in Nick's and Cara's expressions that was obvious to all the guests.

It truly was a beautiful wedding, at sunset on the beach with the murmur of the sea for background music. The bride was stunning and Megan had never seen Nick so happy.

She felt a little twinge of sorrow that the two of them had never been able to make it work, but she was happy the girls would have such a kind woman as Cara in their lives.

She would have been sorry to miss it, even though she still felt out of place.

After the wedding, the guests mingled as the sun continued to slide below the horizon. Megan kept a close eye on the girls while trying to stay on the sidelines and remain unobtrusive.

Somehow she wasn't surprised when Shane approached her.

"How are you holding up?" he asked.

She really hoped he knew by now that her heart wasn't broken because Nick had found someone else. "They make a beautiful couple. I'm thrilled for them."

He gave her a searching look. "I don't know many ex-wives who would be able to celebrate when their former husband moved on."

"I couldn't ask for a better situation for my daughters. That's the important part."

She would have said more but the twins made their way in their direction, Grace with the walker she had used to go down the aisle. Nick and Cara were close behind.

"Did you see me, Mommy? I threw the petals just like I was supposed to," Grace declared triumphantly. Even after one dose of antibiotic and Tylenol, she was obviously feeling better than she had that morning.

Megan hugged her. "You did a beautiful job, darling. I'm so proud of you."

"And me," Sarah said. "What about me?"

She smiled. "You were both magnificent. Without you, your dad and Cara's special day wouldn't have been nearly as wonderful."

"She's right," Nick said. "Thanks, girls."

He hugged Megan. "Thanks for being here. I know the girls were only able to attend because of you."

"It was a beautiful wedding," she told him, before hugging Cara, too.

"Thank you," Cara said. "Having the girls here made it perfect."

Megan smiled with genuine affection for Shane's sister. She was so sweet-natured and kind. Given what he'd told her about their tumultuous upbringing, it seemed a miracle that she could emerge with such a giving heart.

"I can't wait for the day when you find someone special and can know this kind of happiness," she murmured.

Megan forced herself not to look at Shane as a bittersweet pang pinched at her. Somehow she didn't think a happy ending was in store for her.

"I'm perfectly happy the way things are. Don't worry about me," she assured her.

"We're moving down the beach a little for the reception," Nick said. "Cara has arranged a dance floor and a band and everything. You're coming, right? I want to dance with my girls."

She really wanted to decline the invitation. Grace still wasn't completely herself, and all of them were tired. But they'd come all this way to celebrate the wedding. What were a few more hours?

"Yes. We'll come for a while."

And then she would take her girls back to their cabana, spend their last night in paradise and return to real life.

THE RECEPTION WAS informal, more of a party and buffet meal, really, with music and dancing.

She and the girls found a table and a little food.

The twins watched, starry-eyed, while Nick led Cara out for the first dance.

"Hmm. Three beautiful ladies," Shane said. "Which one do I dance with first? Eeeny, meeny miny, moe. Grace, I guess that's you."

Her daughter giggled, clearly delighted at the idea of dancing with one of her new favorite people.

"Your choice. In the chair or out?"

"Out," she said promptly.

Sarah didn't have time to even summon a pout, as Nick came over at the same moment to dance with her.

Megan's heart warmed, watching both of her girls. Nick moved across the dance floor with Sarah, but Shane stayed close to Megan's table and she had a clear view of the two of them, Shane moving carefully to accommodate Grace's slightly awkward gait.

As she watched them smiling together at something Shane said to this very special child, emotion clogged her throat, tender and soft.

She was in love with him.

The realization washed over her like surf pounding against the reef, battering away all her defenses. She was in love with Shane.

He was an amazing man, good and decent. A man dedicated to his job, to his family. He was kind to Grace, patient with Sarah.

Beyond that, when he kissed her, she felt as if she could take on any challenge, conquer any difficulty. He made her feel things she never thought possible, given the choices she'd made in her life.

How could she help but fall in love with him?

"The girls look like they're having fun."

She jerked her gaze away from Shane and the stunning truth to see Jean, Nick's mother, approaching her.

"Yes." Her voice came out strangled and raw so she tried again. "I think they're having the time of their lives."

"I'll tell you, I wasn't thrilled when Nick and Cara told me they were having this destination wedding. Why did they need to come all the way to Hawaii to get married? I asked myself. We have perfectly good wedding venues in Chicago. I'm not too proud to admit I was wrong. It's turned into a really lovely time. I've loved having the girls here to share it. Thank you for bringing them."

She kissed her former mother-in-law on the cheek. "It's been magical for us."

At that moment, the song ended and she watched while Nick and Shane switched partners.

She chatted with Jean about their travel plans during the next song, all while watching Shane laugh with Sarah.

Her girls loved him, too. Her emotions were a tangled snarl as she envisioned heartache for all three of them when they returned from this warm, sweetly scented paradise to the cold and wind of Chicago, and Shane returned to his own life.

Another song inevitably ended and Shane walked with Sarah back to their table. "Jean, do you mind keeping an eye on the girls while I steal a dance with Megan?"

Her mother-in-law's gaze widened and she looked between the two of them. Megan didn't like the sudden speculative look in her eyes. "No, of course not. They'll be perfectly fine. Take all the time you want."

He slipped his hand into hers and led her out to the moonlit dance floor. The song was a slow, romantic Hawaiian melody she didn't recognize, featuring a slack-key guitar. She fought back the knowledge that this might be the last time she would be in his arms as they began to move slowly in time to the music.

HE COULDN'T SEEM to take his eyes off Megan.

She was stunning in a soft blue, floral-print sleeveless dress, the lei he'd brought her earlier in the day and delicate silver hoops in her ears.

She'd pulled her hair up into a loose, flowing style, and in the flickering glow of the tiki torches, she took his breath away.

The scent of her, like strawberries and cream, drifted to him on the breeze, and though he hadn't had anything but a swallow or two of wine, he felt intoxicated.

She didn't say anything, only settled her cheek against his chest as if she couldn't imagine anywhere else she'd rather be. He closed his eyes and held her, trying to treasure every breath, every moment. He couldn't have said what song they danced to—or, indeed, if any music was playing at all. He was completely absorbed with her.

There must have been music. He was aware when it ended, as everyone but the two of them moved away from the dance floor. He gazed down at her, consumed with the need to wrap her in his arms again and lower his mouth to hers.

He couldn't do it. For one thing, he knew she wouldn't appreciate a big public display of affection in front of her ex-husband's family. Beyond that, he was aware of a melancholy ache in his chest.

This...*thing* between them was impossible. In his heart, he knew it. Whenever he looked at her adorable daughters, reality yanked him back to his senses like an inescapable riptide.

He had sworn a long time ago he wouldn't date a woman with children. He didn't want the girls to have to deal with that kind of complication and chaos. He wanted that increasingly rare beast, the traditional marriage where neither party had previous entanglements.

It was old-fashioned, maybe, even backward. But whenever he might have been tempted to go back on the vow he'd made to himself as an angry, hurt teenager, he only had to look at his parents. Right now, his dad and the new wife—what *was* her name again?—were dancing embarrassingly close, and his mother was flirting with one of the husky Hawaiian bartenders.

All those memories poured back, the nightmare of his childhood when he and Cara had been forced to bounce back and forth between them, not feeling at home or even wanted in either place. Custody and child support issues had been wielded as weapons in the ongoing war between his parents, with him and Cara stuck in the middle.

He refused to do that to any other children.

The ache in his chest intensified, the heartfelt wish that things could be different. He was fully aware of the irony of the situation. Even if he could, he wouldn't have wished a different life for Megan than the one she had. Her daughters were wonderful and he had a feeling she'd become the woman he cared about so much *because* of her daughters, not in spite of them.

Knowing he had to do it, even though it hurt, he walked her back to her table. "Thank you for the dance. And for making this an…unforgettable trip."

"You're welcome," she murmured. She looked as if she wanted to say something else, but didn't.

"What time does your flight leave?" he asked.

"Early. Nine."

"Ah. I don't take off until later. The red-eye."

"I couldn't put the girls through that one."

"Understandable." He had a hundred things he wanted to tell her. A thousand. All of them would have to remain unsaid. It was better that way, for both of them. "Well, have a safe journey."

"Thank you. Same to you."

He kissed her softly on the forehead and turned away, trying to tell himself that emotion in his chest wasn't sorrow or vast, aching regret.

He headed immediately for the bar with the intention of ordering a good, stiff drink. He was waylaid by Cara, in the midst of a crowd of well-wishers, who grabbed his arm as he passed.

"There you are. Dance with me," she ordered.

"You're just as bossy as ever," he complained.

In answer, she tucked her arm through the crook of his elbow, waved at the group she'd been talking with, and tugged him to the dance floor.

"You make a beautiful bride, sis," he said, after they'd been dancing for a few moments. "I don't think I've told you lately how happy I am for you and Nick."

She hugged him. "It's been a beautiful few days, hasn't it? Just like I always dreamed."

"Yes. Everything was perfect."

"I saw you dancing with Megan. She's wonderful, isn't she?"

His emotions felt too raw to talk about this. Yes, Megan was wonderful. The most amazing woman he had ever met. That ache in his chest seemed to ramp up a notch or two.

"The two of you are perfect for each other," Cara went on without waiting for an answer. "Have you made plans to get together when we're all back in Chicago? Nick and I will have the girls every other weekend and every Wednesday night, which means her schedule will be completely clear at those times. Just saying."

A muscle in his jaw flexed, and he didn't know what to say. At his silence, Cara met his gaze. Her expression sharpened and she frowned suddenly.

"You're not planning to ask her out, back in Chicago, are you?"

"What would be the point, really?" he finally asked.

She stared at him, storm clouds gathering. He winced. The last thing he wanted to do was upset his sister on her wedding day.

"The band you hired is really good. How did you find them?" he asked, desperate to distract her. Tonight wasn't about him. It was about his cherished sister marrying the man of her dreams.

"Thanks. I found them on the internet," she answered.

He thought his ploy had been successful, but he should have known better. When she was in a mood, Cara could be like a stubborn pitbull guarding a particularly juicy bone.

"Back to Megan. Seriously, Shane. What is *wrong* with you? She's amazing."

"I agree. She's just not the right amazing woman for *me*."

She stopped dancing altogether now to stare at him. "I don't understand. This is crazy. You care about her. I can see you do. And I could be wrong, but I think she has feelings for you, too. You live in the same city and live only a few L stops away from each other. Why not take her out, see where things could lead?"

"Just drop it, Cara. I don't want to fight with you on your wedding day."

"This isn't a fight," she countered. "This is a heated discussion."

"Only one of us is heated," he pointed out.

"Because the other one is *crazy*." She grabbed his hand and dragged him off the dance floor to a quieter corner. "I've seen the kind of women you date, Shane. They can't hold a candle to Megan. Good heavens, I just married her ex-husband and I already love her like a sister. That should tell you all you need to know about her, shouldn't it? I mean, what's not to love? She's a wonderful mother, a caring nurse, a good friend."

He really didn't need to hear all this. He already knew about all her fabulous qualities. Having his sister reinforce them only tightened the knife in his gut.

"Megan is fantastic. I agree. But things would never work out between us."

"Why not?"

He sighed. "Do we have to talk about this right now? This is your wedding, in case you didn't notice. You've got guests who've come a long way to celebrate with you. We really don't need to hash out my disaster of a love life."

"Fine. Just tell me what the problem is so I can tell you how stupid you're being, then we can both go back to my wedding party."

He knew Cara wouldn't let up. She was the very definition of relentless. "It's no big deal. I like Megan a lot," he said, a glaring understatement, "but our lives are just too different. For one thing, she has two daughters."

She frowned. "What's wrong with the girls?"

"Nothing. Absolutely nothing. They're great. Funny and smart and adorable."

He loved them, too, he realized. He had fallen hard for all three of the McNeil ladies.

"So what's the problem?"

He kissed her on the nose. "I promise, sis, this is nothing you need to concern yourself about on your wedding day. We'll talk about it later."

"Too late. I'm concerned."

At that moment, she spied their father dancing by them with his latest wife locked in a tight clinch. He almost saw a lightbulb switch on above her head like a cartoon.

"Oh. Oh! The girls. You always said you'd never be involved with a woman who had children. That's what this is about, isn't it?"

He really didn't want to bring this up now, to dredge up these rough memories. If he didn't, though, she would keep pushing and pushing at him.

"Cara, you remember what it was like for us." He picked his words carefully. "You know the turmoil we lived through, with people moving in and out of our lives all the time. Just as we came to know a new stepmother or stepfather, the bloom would be off the rose and they would be out of our lives again. I decided a long time ago that I would never put any child through that. I care deeply about Megan—and I care about Sarah and Grace. Because of that, I

won't add more chaos to their lives. End of story.
My mind is made up and I'd really prefer you don't
lecture me about it."

CHAPTER NINE

ON THE OTHER side of the bushy shrub with bright pink flowers, Megan pressed a hand to her stomach at the finality of Shane's words.

I care deeply about Megan—and I care about Sarah and Grace. Because of that, I won't add more chaos to their lives. End of story. My mind is made up.

She had known. Somehow, she'd figured out he had deeply personal reasons for keeping some part of himself distant from her and the twins. Hearing him admit the truth with such stark certainty sliced at her like a machete.

She hadn't meant to eavesdrop, she'd only come here to find the girls' baskets and the cute little Hawaiian dolls Cara had given them as wedding favors. When she heard Shane say her name, she couldn't help but listen.

Finally, everything made a horrible sort of sense—why he seemed drawn to her one moment and pushed her away the next. Why he could wrap his arms around her as they danced as if he never wanted to let her go…and then two seconds later return her to her table with a casual kiss on the forehead, as if they were polite acquaintances.

She stared at the delicate flowers on the shrub. She had a feeling that from this point forward their light, fresh scent would always make her feel vaguely nauseated.

Tears welled up and one spilled over before she could push it away. She angrily wiped her cheek. No. She wouldn't let this devastate her. She couldn't. She had two beautiful daughters who needed a mother who was strong and resolute.

Okay, so she loved a man who wouldn't let himself love her back. Yes, it hurt like hell. Yes, she wanted to curl up out there on the beach and weep and wail and throw handfuls of sand around like the girls in the middle of one of their terrible-two tantrums.

She was tougher than that. Broken hearts eventually mended, right?

On some level, she even understood his point of view. His childhood chaos had left him with a skewed perspective on life. She couldn't blame him for that—nor could she fight and rail and curse reality.

He didn't want her. Or, more accurately, he wanted her and the girls but he wouldn't let himself have what he wanted because of the accompanying complications

She wanted to tell him that life was seldom as clean and whitewashed as a person wanted. It was sloppy and tangled and hard. Grace and her challenges had taught her that. But out of the mess and mud could come something beautiful, if only a person summoned the strength to struggle through it—another lesson Grace had taught her.

Thinking of her daughters gave her the courage she needed to move forward. She wiped away another tear, drew in a shaky breath and gathered up the girls' things.

She needed to focus on Grace and Sarah. It had been a long, exciting day, and Grace still wasn't feeling a hundred percent. The travel day would be long and difficult, and she'd need all her grit to get them home.

Yes, it was time to go back to real life, away from this tropical paradise—this glorious, heady, impossible dream.

BACK AT THE cabana, the girls were subdued. Both of them were tired from all the excitement and Grace was a little fretful.

They went to bed with a minimum of fuss, much to Megan's relief. She wasn't sure she would have been up for a battle with them.

After they were sleeping, Megan gathered up their belongings and packed as much as she could for their return journey.

When that was done, she felt rather at loose ends. She wasn't tired—her heart ached too much for sleep—so on impulse she grabbed the video monitor and headed outside into the warm moonlight.

This time she kicked off her flip-flops—slippahs,

if she wanted to use the Hawaiian term—and walked to the water's edge.

The moon glimmered on the water, dancing a little with each wave, and the heavy air was sweet with the scent of flowers, underscored by the salty, sharp, indescribable scent of sand and sea.

The tears she'd pushed back earlier in the evening threatened to break free. Her heart was broken. She had known both love and loss in a short time. What was the harm in giving in to them a little while she was alone here with the night?

She retreated above the high-tide mark and sat in the sand, hands wrapped around her knees as she cried silent tears—only a few—for what could never be.

Enough self-pity. She still had everything she had known before she arrived in Hawaii. A great job she loved, two beautiful daughters, a warm and comfortable home. She would get through this.

She sat for a long moment more, trying to find the same wonder and magic she'd discovered on their first night in Hawaii. She was just about to get up when she sensed someone approach. Even without looking away from the mesmerizing sea, she knew who she would find.

"Mind some company?" Shane asked.

She wanted to tell him she minded very much. He'd broken her heart. She knew she would eventually heal from it, but she didn't need him coming around to pour seawater on the open wound, thanks very much.

He was still wearing the dress slacks he'd worn to the wedding, rolled up to keep the sand out, and in the moonlight she saw the gleam of his bare feet.

"You left the party before I had the chance to tell you and the girls goodbye. One minute you were there, the next you disappeared. Is everything okay?"

Besides the minor matter of her shattered heart, just fine. "Yes. They were tired and tomorrow will be long and hard. I'm not looking forward to a long flight with Grace having an ear infection."

"That's too much for you to handle on your own. Maybe I can see about changing flights."

"I'll manage. I always do," she murmured. "Thank you, though."

He was quiet for a long moment, then he reached out to enfold her fingers in his. "You handle everything. You're amazing."

Instead of feeling flattered, she was suddenly furious. How many ways did this man have to break her heart?

She yanked her hand away and stood up abruptly, brushing sand off her dress and picking up her flip-flops.

"I should go back in. I've still got packing to do," she lied.

He stood as well, looking big and tough and sexy in the silvery light.

"Wait a minute."

She turned, seeking deep for just a little more strength and hoping he couldn't see her puffy eyes and red nose. A few more moments and then this would be over.

He seemed nervous suddenly, something she wouldn't have expected in the man who could endure a gunshot wound and still flirt with the emergency room nurses.

"Yes?" she finally asked when he remained silent.

"I would like to see you again, when we're back in Chicago. Can I call you? With the real number, this time?"

Fresh pain sliced at her and she wondered what kind of cruel game he was playing with her fragile, shattered heart.

"Why?" she asked, her voice barely a whisper.

He blinked a little, looking even more disconcerted. "I've enjoyed being with you these last few days. I…care about you and the girls. I love spending time with you. When I'm with you, I'm…happy."

She clutched her flip-flops to her chest, not caring about the sand she knew would find its way home in her suitcase. His words fluttered their way to her heart like brilliantly colored butterflies, but she refused to let them settle there.

"Why waste our time?" she finally asked. Her voice sounded ragged and she had to clear it before continuing. "I heard you tonight talking to Cara."

Confusion crossed his strong features for just a moment, followed quickly by chagrin. "You did?"

"I wasn't listening on purpose. I only meant to get the girls' things so we could go. But, yes, I heard all about your hard-and-fast rule. No children. I obviously can't change that about my life, so I don't see the point in seeing you again back in Chicago. I'm not the woman you need and you're not the man I thought you were."

That last was cruel, she knew, but the words were out before she could stop them.

He closed his eyes. When he opened them, they were filled with pain and regret and something else she couldn't identify.

"I can't answer to the last part. But I *can* tell you that you're exactly the woman I need. I lied earlier."

She blinked, not sure what he meant. "You lied about what?"

"I said I cared about you. That's not true."

"It's…not?"

He shook his head and took a step closer. She barely refrained from retreating a step, which probably would have landed her on her behind in the sand.

"Okay, it's not really a lie. More like a ridiculous understatement. Already, my feelings are deeper than that."

Again, those butterflies seemed to clog her chest, her throat, fluttering madly.

"I'm in love with you, Megan," he murmured. "I think I have been since that night at the hospital. I certainly couldn't get you out of my head, and almost went back to the ER just to find you, even though I felt like an idiot."

She drew in a breath at his words, feeling as if

she were on a tiny skiff out on the vast sea, being tossed in every direction by the waves and the wind.

She wanted to believe him, but the memory of the last two hours of pain was too raw. "What…what about the girls?"

"I love the girls, as well. They're wonderful, Megan. Bright and sweet and cheerful. How could I *help* but love them, too?"

"I don't understand. I heard what you said to Cara. You won't let yourself care about a woman with children. You said so."

"How much did you hear of that conversation?"

She rehashed those moments in her memory. "I left right after you said that to Cara."

He smiled a little and reached for her hand. "So you missed the delightful part where the lovely, demure bride told me I was being a raging idiot."

"Apparently so. I'm sorry I didn't hear that."

He laughed softly. "She was quite firm about it. She told me only said raging idiot would let a decision he made as an angry teenager compel him to make the biggest mistake of his life by letting a wonderful woman slip away."

"Did she?"

"Yes. She also informed me quite firmly—I think there might have been yelling by this point—that if I was stupid enough to let our parents and the chaos they created for two innocent children still have that much power over my decisions in life, years later, then I didn't deserve someone as fantastic as you and Grace and Sarah."

"I do love your sister. Have I mentioned that?"

His laugh was as soft and low as the sea, sending shivers sizzling down her spine. "I love her, too, even when she's being a big, annoying smarty-pants."

His smile slid away and he reached for her hand. This time, she left it there.

"She's right, Megan. I've been an idiot. I love you and I want to be with you. In Hawaii, in Chicago, in Antarctica, for all I care. And I love the girls, too. I can't imagine you without them. They are part of the package—the bright, beautiful, perfect package—and I wouldn't have it any other way."

She smiled, unable to believe she could shift so swiftly from despair to this vivid joy. "For the record, I love you, too. These last few days have been magical. I don't want them to end. I've been dreading going back to my cold, gray existence."

He kissed her then, his mouth tender on hers. She wrapped her arms around him, relishing his heat and his strength.

When he finally eased away, both of them were breathing hard and Megan could feel her hair tumbling down her back where his hands had pulled it free.

"I'll change my flight tomorrow," he said when he caught his breath. "I don't want you to have to fly home without me."

"You would give up another day in paradise for me and the girls?"

He shook his head. "No. Wherever you are, that will be all the paradise I need."

Touched beyond words, she rested her cheek against his chest as he pulled her closer. The palm fronds rustled and the warm breeze danced in her hair, and the sea murmured a love song just for them.

* * * * *

To
Leanne and RaeAnne,
with love from the author who,
for the purposes of this
collaboration,
will answer to the name of
Marianne

HAWAIIAN REUNION

Marie Ferrarella

PROLOGUE

She waited until the last minute to leave for O'Hare Airport.

Which, given the fact that this was January in Chicago and there'd been yet *another* snowstorm just yesterday, piling even *more* snow on top of what had already fallen earlier in the week, was risky at best. Snowplows were out in force, trying to make the streets passable and having moderate success.

All this contributed toward making the simple ten-mile trip from her apartment building to the airport something that would have been more easily attempted with a team of huskies in top condition than a mere taxicab with chains on its tires.

Amy Marshall was seriously running the risk of missing her flight—and she knew it

Subconsciously, maybe she actually *wanted* to miss it, even though it was a flight out of this deep freeze, with its discolored snowdrifts, to the inviting, balmy beaches of Kauai.

Six months ago, when Nick McNeil and his fiancée, Cara Russell, had first made the plans for this destination wedding—plans that involved seventy-two hours in Hawaii away from snowplows, galoshes and overcoats—it had sounded like nothing short of pure heaven.

What a difference six months could make.

Now, instead of heaven, flying to Kauai for those seventy-two hours had become Amy's own private hell because she was carrying around not just one major secret but two.

Secrets that weighed as heavily on her shoulders as the fresh snow weighed on the roofs of her neighborhood.

On the way to O'Hare, Amy imagined those roofs sagging with the added weight—and she completely identified with them.

How in heaven's name was she going to carry this off, Amy wondered, if she actually *did* manage to get there in time for the flight? How was she going to be able to smile for the duration of those seventy-two hours and pretend that everything was just wonderful? Pretend that she and Devlin, Nick's fellow firefighter and best friend—not to mention his best man—were as wildly in love now as they'd always been instead of occupying opposite sides of a pending divorce?

She knew that she could have opted to bow out, but that would have meant explaining why to Cara. So far, the very idea of talking about the end of her marriage hurt. And because it did, *none* of their friends knew, or even suspected, that she and Devlin weren't living together anymore, that they hadn't even occupied the same square-mile radius for the past three months.

Other than dealing with her own aching heart, there was the problem generated by the bride-to-be. Even the slightest hint of the word *divorce* had Cara all but freaking out.

Growing up, Cara and her older brother, Shane, had to live through their parents' less than amicable divorce. If that hadn't been traumatic enough, they'd also looked on as both parents married—and divorced—other people with such regularity that it wound up turning the institution of marriage into the punch line of a joke. A least it had for Cara.

Discovering that a divorce was taking place within her private circle could just possibly make Cara call off her own wedding.

Devlin had told Amy he didn't want to risk it, and admittedly, she knew she wouldn't have been able to cope with having that on her conscience.

So Amy had reluctantly agreed to fly out to the wedding as if her own life wasn't going through the major upheaval that it was.

Emphasis on upheaval, she thought, pressing her hand to her abdomen as the taxi inched its way to its final destination.

Amy glanced at her watch. It looked as if she really might not make the flight.

In the scheme of things, she supposed that she could manage pretending she was Devlin's wife for another seventy-two hours. After all, the very thought of being married to him had once filled her with absolutely indescribable joy.

Once, she thought ruefully.

But not anymore.

It was the other secret she was holding back from everyone that *really* concerned her.

But with luck, Amy thought as the taxi finally came to a stop before her terminal, the cab's rear fishtailing rather dangerously, she could pull that off, as well.

After all, she'd played the starring role in her senior-year play in college.

She could do it.

If she somehow did manage to reach the plane before its departure.

"SIR, WE'RE GOING to have to close the doors now," the tall, blonde flight attendant told him. He'd stubbornly refused to move even an inch for the past five minutes.

Devlin was standing at the very edge of the pathway leading to the plane's door. The plane bound for Kauai. The plane that everyone else had already boarded.

Except for Amy.

Damn it, Amy, this isn't the time to play games. I can't believe you'd do this to Nick and Cara—and me. Granted, things had gotten dicey between them and he'd put up with a lot of things even a saint wouldn't have—but he'd always believed that, at heart, Amy was a decent person.

Decent people didn't bail on their friends and their husband, estranged or not, without so much as a word.

"Thirty more seconds," Devlin insisted, tapping his wristwatch. The watch Amy had given him when they'd celebrated their first six months of marriage. Back when she *liked* being married to him. "She's got thirty more seconds."

"Sir, I really don't think that whoever—" The edge to the attendant's voice was beginning to display her impatience.

Just then, he heard the sound of running feet, accompanied by heavy breathing and the clunking of a carry-on suitcase with only one working wheel.

"There she is!" Devlin declared, pointing to the breathless, frazzled woman who was also his wife.

At least for now.

The flight attendant's smile was stretched to its very thinnest. "So I see."

Rushing out to meet Amy, Devlin grabbed her arm and all but dragged her along in his wake. He succeeded in getting her to the plane's still-open door faster than she could have gotten there herself.

Amy was unusually exhausted and far from her best mood right now. She also braced herself for yet another huge argument.

She didn't have long to wait.

"Where the hell have you been?" Devlin ground out between tightly clenched teeth. He still managed to lock them into a smile, no easy feat.

"And hello to you, too," Amy retorted, her voice frostier than the weather outside the terminal.

It was going to be a *long* seventy-two hours, she couldn't help thinking with a deep sigh.

But this, too, would pass, she promised herself. At the moment, that promise was the only thing that kept her going.

CHAPTER ONE

HER STOMACH LURCHED.

Amy was barely aware of nodding in response to the greetings that came their way as they hurried to their seats. Hers was next to Devlin's, Amy realized as the attendant brought them to their row.

Of course it was.

What did she think, that they were going to be put at opposite ends of the plane? Cara had been in charge of booking the flights for everyone and she'd made a point of clustering the wedding party and guests as closely together as she possibly could.

It was only natural to have couples seated next to each other.

Except that they weren't anymore. Weren't a couple, and if she allowed herself to dwell on that fact and not on how they *got* to be this uncoupled couple, Amy knew she'd be more than mildly upset.

She and Devlin were supposed to be the perfect pair.

Ha!

Mercifully, she didn't have to talk to him. Not yet, anyway. The first few minutes were taken up with seat buckling and less-than-heartwarming instructions of what to do in case the plane became a giant flotation device.

The flight attendants said a few more informative things she pretended to listen to.

And then they were taxiing down the runway, moving much too fast in Amy's opinion, or for her liking.

Forward, linear movement was replaced with the very queasy sensation that took hold of her as the plane began to climb.

She'd always hated this part, hated that feeling of climbing up to heights sane people should never be allowed to climb to.

In response to this stimulus, Amy did what she always did. She prayed for it to be over and for the plane to finally level out. And, as usual, she clutched the armrests as hard as she could and focused the powers of her concentration on the pilot being successful in getting their plane to the proper altitude.

It wasn't until Amy saw the seat belt sign turn off that she realized her right hand was clamped onto Devlin's left in what could only be described as a death grip.

Embarrassed, she immediately released his hand.

Devlin looked down. There were small, perfect crescents along his skin where her nails had dug in and left their mark.

He tried to flex his hand a little and pretended that it wasn't easy. Amy was watching from beneath hooded eyes.

"I'm not sure I'll ever be able to make a fist again," he cracked dryly.

And then the eight-year veteran of the Chicago Fire Department looked at the woman beside him. "I didn't think you were coming," he told her honestly. She had always been late to everything, but this had to have been a record, even for her. "I mean, I knew you were *supposed* to come. Cara mentioned while we were all boarding the plane that she'd spoken to you the other day to check if you'd confirmed your plane reservations and you'd told her you couldn't wait for the wedding."

"It had been snowing for two days when Cara called me and it wasn't showing any signs of *ever* letting up." She stared straight ahead. She deliberately avoided eye contact with him. Him, the man who had once lit up her world so brightly she would have needed sunglasses to see anything but him. "At that point, if the devil had turned up with plane tickets to Hawaii, I would have told him I was going— and I would have meant it. *Then.*"

Devlin took a breath. She always knew how to get to him. Sometimes he wondered why he took it and kept coming back for more. Maybe he needed to have his head examined. "So now I'm the devil?"

She slanted one quick glance in his direction before looking away again. And then she shrugged. "You're missing the tail and the horns…" Pulling out the magazine tucked into the back of the seat in front of her, Amy began to thumb through it.

"I haven't told anyone yet," he said, keeping his

voice low. He hadn't said a word because he kept hoping that by some miracle they'd work things out and there'd be no need to tell anyone anything. Despite her irrational outbursts of jealousy, he still loved her. But at times, it wasn't easy—like now.

Her glance was less than warm. "I figured that part out."

Devlin ignored what he perceived to be sarcasm. The last thing he wanted was to get into an argument with her in public. "And I'd appreciate it if you continued to keep this a secret for a while longer," he told her.

This time, Amy did look at him. They'd already agreed on this. Did he think she was an idiot who needed to be constantly reminded so that she wouldn't wind up ruining the wedding?

"I guess that means I'm going to have to cancel the skywriter," she deadpanned. "And he was all set to do his thing the night of the rehearsal, too. He's going to be really disappointed. Think he'll give me back my down payment?"

Absolutely no one could press his buttons the way Amy could. Maybe he should just go through with this divorce, get a fresh start. It was something to seriously consider.

"Is everything a joke to you?" he wanted to know.

Her eyes were flat as she regarded him. "It didn't use to be—until the most important part of my life turned into one."

Her jealousy over the way other women flirted with him had always been a bone of contention for them. What was he supposed to do, wear a bag over his head? Why couldn't she trust him? How many times did he have to go through this? "Nothing happened," Devlin insisted. "You *know* that."

"Yeah, because I turned up."

Devlin struggled to keep from giving in to the urge to shout, *No, because I was faithful. I've always been faithful, damn it!* But Amy hadn't believed him the other times he'd been forced into a position to have to tell her that, why would she suddenly believe him now?

And it was all so hopelessly clichéd and stupid, he couldn't help thinking.

Amy turned her head away from him, blinking back the tears. She'd come home early that night, thinking to surprise him. Like other firefighters, Devlin worked two days and was off two days. This was his downtime and she had great plans for them involving candles, wine, music and the sexiest lingerie she could find.

The plans instantly turned to dust when she walked through the door to discover their neighbor from across the street draped over her husband in the most suggestive, provocative pose *she* had ever seen.

She'd slammed the door behind her. The neighbor, a sexy blonde divorcée named Bonnie, had hardly even looked embarrassed while Amy's about-to-be-cheating husband had looked at her, flustered and speechless.

Not that any words would have changed what she'd seen.

That's what you get when you marry a drop-dead gorgeous man who also happens to be a fireman, a branch of public service that comes with its own sex-starved groupies.

She had thought she knew what she was getting into, that the prewedding couples' therapy that Devlin had insisted on had shown her how to handle her surges of insecurity, but she'd been wrong.

Besides, she'd really been convinced that Devlin was different, far from the cliché. Talk about naive.

She'd tried to get used to women's heads turning whenever Devlin walked by. She'd almost succeeded because, for the most part, he appeared not to even be aware of it. Whenever she brought the matter up, he'd pointed out that he didn't care about other women, that *she* was the only one for him.

And she'd believed him.

But after the Bonnie incident, she knew that every man had his breaking point, and their sexy neighbor was his. She realized that it had been just a matter of time before Devlin was led astray. She felt like a fool.

"I'm not having this argument here," Devlin said in a low voice. What was the point of repeating that Bonnie had rung the doorbell, saying she wanted to drop something off, that when he let her in, it turned out she was dropping off herself? Amy was his wife—she was supposed to believe him, not what she *thought* she saw.

He didn't need this aggravation. Maybe he should just go through with the divorce. God knew his life would be a lot less stressful if he did.

Amy raised her chin, doing her best to look as if she didn't care *what* Devlin did or didn't do.

"Not asking you to," she told him crisply.

"But you turning up just then, that night, had nothing to do with the way I responded. End of story."

Yes, it had, she thought. It *was* the end of the story. Their story.

"We almost took off without you," he told her, changing the subject. "I had to do a lot of fast-talking to keep that flight attendant from closing the door."

"I'm sure she was more than happy to oblige," Amy said with a saccharine smile. "Is she meeting you after the plane lands?"

Three months apart and nothing had changed. Same old song, he thought angrily.

He wasn't even going to dignify that with an answer. Instead, he appealed to her better nature. Appealed to the woman he'd fallen in love with and was fairly sure was still in there, somewhere.

"Look, this means a lot to Nick and Cara, so please, just hang on to this secret for a while longer, all right?"

And what do I do with my other secret, Devlin? How long can I hang on to that?

She knew her emotions were all over the place. She was far from the level-headed, rising ad executive she'd been three months ago.

That, too, was his fault, she thought, glaring at him.

"If you play along and act like you still want to be

my wife," he was whispering, "when we get back, I'll give you that divorce. Uncontested. So is it a deal?" Devlin held out his hand to her.

She looked at him for a long moment. She didn't take giving her word lightly, and he knew that. "It's a deal," she finally told him quietly.

As she shook his hand, Amy felt her stomach lurch again. Lurch and then begin to rise almost up to her mouth. One second she was shaking Devlin's hand, the next she bolted out of her seat and made a beeline for the bathroom, the placement of which she'd had the presence of mind to notice the moment she'd boarded.

When she finally returned to her seat some ten minutes later, after first having consumed half a roll of mint-flavored Life Savers, Devlin looked at her quizzically.

"You all right?" he wanted to know.

She avoided his eyes. Hers still felt a wee bit watery. "Fine."

He seemed skeptical. "You're pale," he observed.

"Had something that didn't agree with me for lunch." She said the first thing that came to mind. "Ate too fast so I could get here on time."

"You weren't on time," Devlin pointed out.

Why was everything an argument with him? "I'm on the plane, aren't I?"

Devlin inclined his head and let it go. Winning arguments with Amy had ceased to interest him when he realized that she was dead serious about filing for divorce. Suddenly, there was a bigger picture involved.

When she wasn't making him crazy—the way she was now—he found himself not wanting to give her more reasons to leave him. He wanted to peel away the ones she felt she had.

"Yes, you are," he agreed.

And just maybe, he added silently, that was a hopeful omen.

CHAPTER TWO

"REALLY GLAD YOU could make it."

Nick McNeil's enthusiasm was directed at Amy. Since the seat belt sign had been off for the past half hour, the groom had begun to make his rounds, greeting the wedding guests on the plane with him and his bride-to-be.

Outgoing and friendly, Nick was setting an informal, laid-back tone for the three-day celebration that was still ahead of them.

"I was starting to have my doubts back there for a while, Amy," Nick admitted with a laugh. Amy liked Nick; she always had. She didn't want what was happening between her and Devlin—Nick's best man— to spoil the guy's wedding. Faced with his genuine concern, she said the first thing that came to mind, seizing on an explanation that was, in part, the truth.

"The taxi got stuck in traffic. The snow made it almost impossible to travel faster than a snail. You know how it is."

"Yeah, I do. Gotta love Chicago weather." Nick laughed and shook his head. "To be honest, in all the excitement, I didn't realize you were missing until I saw the others boarding the plane. How come you didn't arrive with Devlin?" he asked. "I figured the two of you would have been coming in the same cab."

Devlin read her nervousness in her eyes. Amy was talented in many ways, but she definitely wasn't any good at fabricating excuses out of thin air. It was one of the things he'd loved about her. Amy didn't know the first thing about lying.

He came to her rescue. "She had some last-minute things to take care of at the ad agency—and you know Amy. She's not happy until everything's just as perfect as she is."

Then, as if a show of momentary intimacy would help reinforce his words, Devlin gave his wife a quick, one-arm hug and brushed her cheek with what would have looked like an affectionate kiss to anyone who was watching.

As always, her skin felt silky against his lips, reminding him just how much he missed their casual displays of affection now that there weren't any.

Nick leaned over the seats, giving Amy's folded hands a quick squeeze, apparently oblivious to the fact that those hands were actually clenched together.

"Well, bottom line is you made the flight and we're all very happy about that," Nick told her. He grinned at Devlin. "I know that my best man here definitely wouldn't have been himself if you missed the flight for some reason."

Amy forced a smile to her lips. As if she cared whether or not Devlin was himself or the creature from the black lagoon.

"I would have just caught the next flight," she told Nick glibly.

"If there *is* a next one," Nick qualified. "From what I hear, the weather forecast says there's another big storm front moving in. You ask me, I think we got out of the airport *just* in time. Otherwise, Cara and I might be saying our vows in an airplane hangar."

Straightening, Nick glanced to his left. Another couple waved to him a few rows away. "Well, I'll see you at the hotel," Nick said, making it sound more like a vow than something left to chance. He withdrew to talk to the other guests.

Devlin ducked his head down and whispered against her ear, his breath warm.

"You can stop smiling now if you want. Although I have to admit I like you better smiling like that— even if you do look a little like a deer caught in the headlights."

Now he was making her feel self-conscious, Amy thought, annoyed. "Sorry, it's the best I can do under the circumstances."

Devlin spread his hands wide in innocence. "Not complaining," he said.

"Funny, it sure sounded that way to me," she responded, then shrugged carelessly. "But then, I always managed to misunderstand you, didn't I?"

He knew what she was doing. She was trying to goad him into saying something that would make her feel further justified about dissolving their union. But he wasn't going to fall for it, wasn't going to willingly walk into the bear trap she'd set for him. Instead, he leaned in so that, once again, only she could hear the words he whispered into her ear.

"Not all the time. I can remember some really special times when you understood everything I was saying…." The grin on his lips looked positively wicked from where she was sitting. "And intuiting everything I was thinking. There was a time when we were very, very much in sync," he reminded her.

Amy galvanized her inner resolve. She wasn't going to allow herself to think about the references he was making, wasn't going to allow him to trick her into remembering the good times. They were all in the past and she was determined to face the future. Even if she believed him, believed nothing had happened between him and their neighbor, or any of the other women who responded to him, it was only a matter of time before he was enticed by *someone*. He wasn't about to get homely-looking anytime soon and she wasn't exactly a raving beauty. It was better this way. She'd made up her mind, filed for the divorce and she was going to go through with it, no matter what it took.

To accomplish that, she was going to maintain a very tight rein on her emotions so that she wouldn't let her guard down and be overcome by the fact that she missed him like crazy.

Hang tough, she told herself.

"Yes, well, things change," she said out loud to Devlin, doing her best to appear disinterested in anything he might have to say.

   With that, she buried her face in the magazine that offered her all sorts of bargain prices for things she had absolutely no use for.

   Devlin retreated.

   For now.

   He was beating his head against the wall, trying to convince Amy of his innocence in these imagined transgressions—the ones he'd *never* committed, or even wanted to.

   Divorce would have been a hell of a lot easier if he wasn't still in love with her.

THE FLIGHT FROM Chicago to Kauai, including a connection in L.A., took nine hours. And at least once every hour—if not more—Amy found she had to get up and move around the plane, at least for a little bit. She'd always been able to sit for hours on end, concentrating on whatever had captured her attention at the moment, but Amy found that she was currently exceedingly restless and *needed* to stretch her legs and walk around before she could sit down again.

   Consequently, to cover up this new, strange need, she visited with everyone on the plane she knew. Everyone, except for the one person she'd known far longer and definitely more intimately than anyone else here.

   She talked to Cara and Nick, the bride- and groom-to-be. She visited with the groom's brother and even with Nick's ex-wife, Megan. Ordinarily, an ex-wife wouldn't have been included on the guest list for her ex-husband's wedding. But both Megan and

Nick had agreed that their two little girls should be in the wedding party, and not miss out on the festivities.

Nick and Megan's divorce, Amy noted, had apparently been amicable, and they seemed to be, if not friends, at least friendly.

She couldn't help wondering, as she returned back to her seat for the umpteenth time, if she and Devlin would wind up being friendly.

Probably not, she decided. She thought of Megan and wondered how Nick's ex did it, how she looked so calm. Seeing Devlin with someone else, let alone seeing him exchange wedding vows with that person, would kill her.

Not that she had anything to worry about in that department. Once Devlin found out what she was keeping from him, most likely the hard feelings that would spring up would keep him from including her in *anything* that had to do with his life.

Amy lowered herself into her seat as if she was ninety instead of twenty-seven.

"Still searching for a way off the plane?" Devlin asked.

She stared at him, confused. "What are you talking about?

"Well, you've gone off on enough scouting parties in the past nine hours to make it look as if you were. Is something wrong?" he asked, growing serious. "I don't remember you ever being so restless before."

Best defense was a good offense. That was the only sports analogy she ever retained. She put it into play now. "With all those women throwing themselves at you, I'm surprised you remember me at all."

Here we go again, Devlin thought wearily, struggling to hang on to his temper. He waved a hand at her. "Forget I said anything."

"Like it never happened," she answered, staring straight ahead.

The plane's P.A. system crackled. "Ladies and gentlemen, please put your seat belts on. We'll be landing in a few minutes. I'm happy to tell you it's a balmy, clear eighty-three degrees—just another perfect day in paradise."

The pilot went on cheerfully, but Amy tuned him out. She was too busy dealing with yet another overwhelming wave of nausea. When was this going to stop?

She was gripping the armrests again, Devlin noticed.

"You look pale," he observed.

"Just trying to figure out what time it is," she said, frowning as she looked down at her watch. "We've been in transit for nine hours, but there's a time difference…."

Amused, he could afford to be patient with her, at least in this instance.

"You want me to tell you or do you want to struggle with the calculations?" he asked.

"I'll get it," she snapped. She pressed her lips together.

"You always do," he told her. He wasn't about to be pushy and he could afford to wait.

She shot him a dirty look that dissolved into frustration at the speed of light. "Okay, tell me," she retorted. "What time is it?"

Time for you to come to your senses and realize that no one's ever going to love you as much as I do, he thought.

Out loud, he said, "It's 4:00 p.m."

She muttered a grudging "Thank you," as she reset her watch.

CHAPTER THREE

THE THREE AIRPORT shuttles and fleet of cabs that Cara had reserved for the wedding guests who weren't renting cars were waiting to take them to the hotel when they deplaned.

"We'll all meet in the lobby," she announced, waving her friends and family to the shuttles and taxis that were parked at the curb.

"God, the Invasion of Normandy wasn't this organized," Amy noted as she got on the nearest shuttle.

"Well, Nick told me Cara wants everything to be memorable—and perfect—because this is going to be her only wedding," Devlin said, boarding the blue-and-gold vehicle directly behind her.

Overhearing him, the guest who followed Devlin onto the shuttle muttered quietly, "Good luck with that."

"Amen," Amy murmured under her breath. The best-laid plans of mice and men—and women, as well, she couldn't help thinking.

The expression on Devlin's face when he sat down next to her indicated he'd heard her.

"Sometimes things do turn out well," Devlin reminded her.

"Yeah, just look at you two," Shane, Cara's brother, pointed out with a grin as he made his way to the seats behind them. "You guys are going as strong as ever."

"Just lucky, I guess," Devlin answered. Making good use of the opportunity, he glanced at Amy for confirmation. "Right, honey?"

The smile on her lips was almost spasmodic. "Right," she echoed.

"See?" Shane said, his point made.

Amy sank a little lower in her seat and stared out the window to her left.

The shuttle driver took a quick head count. It apparently tallied with the information he'd been given—Cara had divided the wedding guests so that each driver knew how many passengers he'd have on his vehicle.

With a satisfied nod of his bald head, their driver got behind the wheel and set out for the beachfront resort where they were all staying.

The scenery was every bit as gorgeous as she'd anticipated. The road, however, felt almost unnecessarily bumpy. Amy quickly became oblivious to the former as the latter commandeered all of her attention.

She found herself praying the entire trip to the hotel, fiercely telling herself that she was *not* going to throw up no matter what.

"Now you're not just pale, you're turning almost *green*," Devlin commented, growing genuinely concerned. He tried to touch her forehead, but she pulled her head back. "Are you coming down with something?"

"I'm just bus sick," she ground out, waving him away and fervently hoping that she wasn't going to throw up on Devlin. She'd never hear the end of it, and he might insist on dragging her to some walk-in clinic. Her secret wouldn't be long-lived if *that* happened.

"I've known you since our first year in college. Since when do you ever get motion sickness?" he wanted to know.

"Since now," Amy bit off. Why was he harassing her this way? She was here, wasn't she? Now why didn't he just bug off and leave her alone?

Anything else Devlin might have wanted to discuss was placed on hold because she absolutely refused to part her lips until they arrived at the hotel.

The trip seemed to take forever.

In reality, for the wedding guests who weren't battling nausea, traffic was light and it took all of fifteen minutes to get from the airport to the hotel.

When the shuttle finally came to a stop, Amy thought she was going to weep with relief.

Getting off, she discovered she'd stood up too fast, and her legs felt wobbly. Amy stumbled down the shuttle's four steps.

Devlin turned when he heard her suck in air and was just in time to catch Amy with ease, his muscular arms closing around her. Holding her safe.

At least, that was the way *he* saw it. Amy viewed the whole thing differently.

"Well, this is a surprise," he commented, looking down into her flushed face. "Are you throwing yourself at me?" he teased.

"Not hardly." Amy scowled, embarrassed and also wondering how much longer she could keep her queasy stomach in check. She needed to get completely upright before she wound up rewarding her soon-to-be ex with a gift he definitely wouldn't want. "You can let me go now," she prompted.

His eyes met hers. "Not sure I want to."

Her eyes flashed just like they had in the beginning of their marriage. "Trust me," she told him, "you want to."

There was something about the way she said it as well as the expression on her face that had Devlin releasing her and making sure the ground beneath her feet was flat—and steady.

"I'll take your word for it," he answered with an amicable grin.

Inside the hotel, Amy queued up at the front desk only to have Cara cheerfully breeze by with a general announcement for her wedding guests as she handed out keycards.

"You don't have to wait in line. I've already checked you all in," she said. She apparently enjoyed being everywhere at once and multitasking as she went. "Your cabana's next to ours," she said, handing both her and Devlin the corresponding keycards. "Why don't you two take a couple hours to unpack and check out the beach. Nick and some of the guys are having a surfing lesson before dinner, too, if you're interested. We're meeting at the hotel restaurant around eight to go over the agenda," she said, raising her voice so she could be heard by all the wedding guests.

"Agenda?" Amy repeated, confused. She'd thought the only structured event was going to be the wedding itself.

"Yes, the agenda for the next couple of days so that everyone knows where they're supposed to be and what they're supposed to be doing. We'll eat dinner, too, of course." Cara flashed a wide smile, the eternal happy and nervous bride-to-be. "I can't believe this is finally happening," she all but squealed, then looked up at Nick. "Nick and I are about to start our life together—officially." She underscored her words with a loud, contented sigh.

Since Cara's thousand-watt smile seemed to be aimed in her direction, Amy did her best to return the smile before Cara moved on to another couple.

She'd been like that once, Amy couldn't help thinking. Happy, hopeful and wildly, wildly in love.

Now that period of her life seemed like a distant memory.

Except, of course, for the one tangible piece of proof of that love, courtesy of their one last attempt at reconciliation.

Initially, she'd agreed to have him back to the house so they could talk things out over dinner, she remembered ruefully.

But wine and candles had been involved, as well

as vulnerable feelings, and one thing somehow led to another.

Morning came, and with it clarity—and her old insecurities, when Devlin's phone rang and she saw that the call was from Bonnie. He'd sworn he didn't know how the neighbor had gotten his number. She'd filed for divorce that day. When she'd found out she was pregnant a few weeks later, that revelation hadn't changed anything and she hadn't wanted to tell him until the divorce was final.

Amy glanced down at the keycard. The name of their cabana, Blue Paradise, was embossed on it.

The same as on the keycard that Devlin was holding in *his* hand.

"We're sharing the cabana," she said, the reality slowly sinking in. She had no idea why that should come as a surprise to her. After all, in the eyes of their friends, they were still very much married, and married people shared the same room.

And the same bed.

The latter piece of information became glaringly evident as she walked into their assigned cabana— which was a single, large room with a full bath attached to it.

The queen bed seemed to grow in size as she stared at it until it all but took over the room.

"This," she said with finality, staring at the bed, "is going to be a problem."

"It doesn't have to be." Devlin sounded annoyingly cheerful.

Her eyes narrowed as she turned to look at him. "You're right. Thanks for volunteering."

Since she could only be referring to sharing the bed, he pointed out one obvious fact. "We're both adults here, Amy."

"Hence the problem," she insisted.

He laughed, thoroughly enjoying watching her squirm. "Only if you can't keep your hands off me."

She didn't like him having fun at her expense. "I might be the only woman on this island who can," she retorted.

He was not about to get sucked into *that* argument. Instead, he decided it was best to turn his attention to unpacking. For once, he thought, Amy took the hint and fell silent as she put her things away.

Silence became the third occupant in the room. It grew by the minute, seeming to suck up all the oxygen around them.

Devlin had to put an end to this. "Amy—"

He was interrupted by a knock on the door.

"Hey, you two, no dawdling. We're all meeting at the restaurant in fifteen minutes so if you're fooling around in there, make it quick," Nick called through the door. His words were followed by a hearty laugh.

There went her stomach again. She didn't know how much longer she could hold out. "You go on ahead," she said, waving Devlin off. "I just need to freshen up."

How long could that take? In his opinion, she was gorgeous just as she was. Not that she ever thought that herself, which was, he knew, the root of all their trouble. If she could have believed she was beautiful, that he wanted nobody but her, surely she would never have succumbed to her extreme jealousy toward other women.

"I can wait," he told her.

She misinterpreted him. "You don't trust me?"

Were they doomed to a life of eternal sparring? There was no way he was going to be pulled into an argument. "Let's just say I missed being around you and I'm making up for lost time."

Amy rolled her eyes. "Oh, puh-lease."

"That's my story and I'm sticking to it," he informed her.

Especially since it's true, he added silently. *Most of the time.*

CHAPTER FOUR

SHE WAS GOING to throw up at any second and she *really* didn't want Devlin around to hear it. She just knew he'd start asking her all sorts of questions and it wouldn't take him long to put two and two together. The last thing in the world she wanted was for him to tell her they needed to stay together for the baby's sake.

If he was going to stay, determined to make a go of their marriage, she wanted it to be because he loved her. But that boat had obviously sailed. And she'd had a hand in pushing it out of the harbor, she thought ruefully, her emotions spiking again.

"Go. Now. Please. I'll catch up—I promise," she said between gritted teeth. She didn't know how much longer she was going to hold out.

"Okay, fine. But Nick and Cara are expecting to see us as a couple—a loving couple, not a couple of bantam roosters going at each other."

"Right. Couple. Loving," Amy agreed.

Placing both her hands to his back, she pushed him out the door.

The second it was closed and he was gone, she made a dash for the bathroom. She had just enough time to drop to her knees in front of the toilet bowl before she began heaving. Amy closed her eyes for a moment, struggling to pull herself together.

It was getting worse, not better. Morning sickness she could put up with. But this was turning out to be "all-day sickness" and she had absolutely no way of predicting when it was going to strike next. One minute she'd be fine, the next she felt like she'd been spun around like a top.

Maybe if she just didn't eat *anything,* Amy thought, making her way out of the bathroom, she wouldn't have these repeat bouts of nausea. Otherwise, she was fairly certain she wasn't going to be able to hide this from Devlin for the three days they were together.

Amy changed into something a little more suited to the weather on the island, and popped a few mints into her mouth—fervently praying *they* wouldn't lead to another round of nausea—and went to meet the others at the open-air restaurant that looked out onto the beach.

Just as with the flight, Amy was the last of the guests to arrive. Everyone else was already seated.

Glancing around for Devlin, she spotted the dark-haired girl hovering over him first. Whatever he had just said to her had her laughing.

Nothing ever changes, Amy thought angrily. Women were still throwing themselves at Devlin, and now that they were headed for a divorce, he was going to be catching them.

And whose fault is that? a little voice in her head asked.

Amy pivoted on her heel, made a ninety-degree turn and started back to the cabana. She really didn't feel like watching Devlin in action.

She'd hardly taken two strides toward her destination before she felt someone behind her grabbing her arm. She found herself being pulled around and staring up into the face of an exasperated Devlin.

"Where are you going?" If he hadn't looked up just then, he wouldn't have seen Amy storming away. *Now* what was wrong?

"Back to the cabana—to pack," she ground out.

She wasn't making any sense. "Are you out of your mind?" he demanded. "Pack? You just got here. You're supposed to be *un*packing." It took everything he had not to shout at her. *Nobody* could get him angrier faster than Amy.

Forced to stay put because Devlin wasn't releasing her wrist no matter how hard she tugged to get free, she lifted her chin, her eyes shooting tiny, flaming arrows at him.

"Nothing changes with you, does it?" she retorted. "I take five minutes to join you and you're already flirting with some island girl." Her eyes narrowed into accusing slits. "You're incorrigible."

"And you're delusional," he shot back. "That 'island girl' you thought I was 'flirting' with was the waitress, taking our order. I ordered for you," he added abruptly. "I didn't think you'd want seafood on a weak stomach, so I went with something safe—the baked pineapple and ham platter. Comfort food."

Surprise corkscrewed through her anger before Amy could think better of it and cover her reaction. "You ordered for me? Comfort food?"

"Of course I did," he answered, still trying to get a grip on his temper. "Now stop reading hidden meaning into everything and come back before everyone starts asking questions." He was smiling now, broadly in case any of the wedding guests could see him.

Since he still hadn't let go of her wrist, Amy had little choice but to return with him to the restaurant.

Walking in, she flashed a dutiful smile at the others seated along the long table and then slipped into the spot Devlin had saved her.

"Pretend you're having a good time," Devlin whispered into her ear as he sat beside her.

His thigh brushed against hers and she did her best not to notice. But her best was not nearly good enough. The brief contact was like touching a live wire.

Electricity zigzagged through her, leaving none of her untouched—or unaffected.

She damned him for it.

Devlin could *still* make her light up like a Christmas tree, the way no one else ever could, she thought grudgingly.

She was going to have to do something about that, Amy promised herself.

WHEN THE WAITRESS she'd accused Devlin of flirting with returned bearing a tray loaded down with their dinners, Amy was too busy trying to psyche herself up to face her meal to even look at the young woman.

She tried her best.

Subtly holding her breath, she carefully cut up the thick slice of baked ham into bite-size pieces. However, they were bite-size pieces she just couldn't induce herself to bite. The very smell threatened to send her bolting to the ladies' room again.

So, covertly watching everyone else around the table, she carefully palmed, then deposited, each piece of ham into the napkin she had spread out on her lap.

As soon as she could, she was going to donate the booty in her napkin to the first hungry-looking dog or cat she came across. No sense in wasting the meal. And Devlin had been right. It was her favorite kind of comfort food.

Just not right now.

The conversation around the table lasted a long time. The wedding guests caught up on one another's lives and made tentative plans for the next couple of days, right up to the actual wedding ceremony and reception.

"After that," Nick announced, addressing them all, "you're on your own. I don't want to see or hear from any of you." He grinned broadly. "I've got a honeymoon to keep me busy," he told them, punctuating his statement with what amounted to a sexy wink.

While the evening was still young by local stan-

dards, considering that the wedding guests had all
flown in from Chicago, exhaustion was catching up
with the best of them. Some of the guests were going
to stay up for limbo dancing, but Devlin was ready
to call it a night.

"Well, I'm going to turn in early and rest up,"
Devlin said. He was the best man and it was up to
him to keep everything running smoothly for the
bride and groom. "We've got a big two days ahead
of us."

Taking care to fold her napkin tightly, Amy
slipped it into her purse, closing the clutch before
she stood.

"Turning in sounds good to me," she agreed.

"Hey, if I were turning in with the likes of your
husband, it wouldn't just sound 'good' to me, it would
sound downright magnificent," one of the wedding
guests—Jennifer something—cracked with an ap-
preciative laugh as her deep brown eyes skimmed
over Devlin.

"Yeah, well, better luck next time," Amy said
coolly, dismissing the blonde. With that, she left the
table and began to walk back to the cabana.

"Amy, wait up," Devlin called after her. He detached himself from Nick and all but sprinted after
Amy, hurrying to catch up.

She barely slowed. "Don't leave on my account.
Maybe that waitress is waiting to take an extra order
or two from you."

"Give it a rest, Amy," he said flatly. "Waitresses
are supposed to be friendly. They get bigger tips that

way." He matched his gait to hers as he came up beside her. "I've got a question for you."

"What?" she bit off impatiently. She deliberately avoided looking at him as she continued walking back to their quarters.

"Why did you put your dinner in your purse?"

Devlin could see he caught her off guard with that one. She probably thought no one had noticed what she was doing. But he had taken in every detail, thinking it rather odd that she cut up all of her meat in one go-round, rather than as she consumed it.

"You feeding some little animal you smuggled into our room?" It wasn't meant to be a serious guess, but with Amy, he never knew.

"I don't know what you're talking about." She lengthened her stride.

"Sure you do." He hardly had to increase his pace to keep up.

Then, because Amy was obviously not expecting it, he succeeded in grabbing her purse out of her hands.

"Exhibit A," he announced, pulling back the napkin and displaying the pieces of ham that were now scattered inside her clutch purse.

CHAPTER FIVE

"GIVE ME THAT," Amy cried, snatching her purse back from Devlin. She snapped it shut and tucked it under her arm. "I wasn't hungry. Didn't feel like eating and didn't feel like having you badger me with all kinds of questions as to *why* I wasn't eating," she told him, grinding out each word. "Satisfied?"

His eyes on hers, Devlin moved his head deliberately from side to side. "Not even close."

She should have expected as much. "Well, too bad, because that's all you're getting," she informed him as she turned away.

Devlin caught her by the shoulders, forcing her to turn around and look at him again. "Amy, you'd tell me if something was wrong, wouldn't you?"

This time it was her heart that rose up to her throat instead of her stomach.

Did he suspect?

She couldn't tell.

"Like what?" she asked, doing her best to sound disinterested instead of nervous.

"Like if you were sick, if you had some sort of a condition—a disease," he said, frustrated that he was tripping over his own tongue like this. But the kind of illness he was thinking about wasn't easy to discuss, or even broach. "You'd tell me, right? Right?" he demanded when she didn't answer.

For a second, she began to pull free, but the concerned—really concerned—look in his eyes froze her in place.

He was worried, she realized. Seriously worried. As annoyed with him for putting her through this as she was, with her hormones splattered all over the map the way they were, Amy couldn't let him labor under that false impression.

Not when it made him look so haunted.

She blew out a long breath. "Yes, I'd tell you, and no, I don't have any kind of disease, if that's what you're asking me. What I have is jet lag and a bad bout of nerves."

That part was true, as far as it went. What she didn't say was that she was nervous because of him. Because she was afraid he would see right through her. That she was pregnant.

"I don't like lying to people we consider friends," she said, then winced, realizing that she was lying to him.

Was that it—she didn't like lying? Somehow, he wasn't entirely convinced. With Amy, things were never straightforward or simple. There were layers to peel away. But for now, for simplicity's sake, he just went with what she was telling him.

"If it makes you feel any better, you're not lying," he said as they continued to walk back to the cabana. "You're just not expounding on the truth."

Amy rolled her eyes. Now he was just bending the truth to suit his purposes. "That's just a matter of semantics," she pointed out.

"Not really," Devlin maintained. "Nobody asked you if we were still married, or getting a divorce, did they? You weren't forced to tell someone that we were deliriously happy, right?"

"Right, but—"

"No, no 'but,'" he cautioned her. "That's where it stops."

That was okay for now, she allowed. "But what about later?" she asked. "What about after we get the divorce? You don't think our friends are going to be angry at us for deceiving them?"

"Honestly?" he asked her.

She lifted her shoulders and then let them fall. "If you're capable of that."

He ignored the sting of her comment. "I think that'll be one of the last things on their minds when they hear we've split up. Mostly, they'll wonder how they didn't see it coming, and *since* they didn't see it coming, will it happen to them, too, without any warning?"

They'd reached the cabana and Amy slipped in her keycard. The door gave. Amy shrugged in response to his involved answer. "Maybe you're right," she murmured, giving up.

Then, walking inside, Amy moved to close the door behind her. "Well, good night."

Staying one jump ahead of her, Devlin had put his hand in the way, stopping the door from closing.

"This is my cabana, too, remember?" he said mildly.

Yes, she remembered. Remembered all too well. Remembered, too, what had happened the last time they had been in a bedroom together.

Morning sickness.

"Are you really going to make an issue of this?" She instantly went on the offensive. She was beyond exhausted—and that was the way it had been for the past month, as she'd vacillated between complete fatigue and minor surges of energy that came out of nowhere. And she just didn't have any reserve energy on tap for arguing.

"I don't really have a choice, do I?" he asked her. "Not unless you want everyone talking about our situation and how you let your rampaging, *baseless* jealousy ruin a good thing."

"My rampaging, baseless jealousy?" she repeated in complete disbelief. Did he think of himself as the innocent victim here? She stared at him as if he'd lost his mind. "Is *that* how you see it?"

His face was the picture of innocence. "There's no other way *to* see it." She wouldn't be jealous if he didn't give her anything to be jealous about. If he had been just oblivious to these women who devoured him with their eyes and who, given half a chance, would run off with him to some secluded spot and give in to all their secret fantasies.

"You're impossible," she told him.

"No, I'm very, very possible," Devlin replied, looking at her significantly.

He was standing way too close, Amy thought. She could even feel his breath on her skin as he talked—and that was completely unacceptable.

Because she could feel barriers turning from steel to tin foil.

Her bravado was all she had left and she wrapped herself up in it.

"Have it your way," she declared. She pulled a blanket off the bed and held it out to him. "Go sleep in the tub."

Devlin made no effort to take the blanket from her. "Only if I'm a masochist," he said. "I sleep in that tub, my neck's going to be stiff for the next two days."

Okay, she wasn't completely unreasonable. "Fine. Sleep on the floor," she told him. When he began to spread out the blanket next to her bed, she made the instructions more specific. "No, the *bathroom* floor."

"What if you want to use it during the night?" he asked, a wicked look coming into his eyes. "If you don't mind crawling over me to get to the toilet and then having me possibly witness—"

She held up her hands as if to physically push his words back. "Okay, okay, you've made your point. You can sleep on the floor in here," she said in exasperation. "Just as long as you remember to *stay* on the floor," she warned.

"Hey, no problem," he conceded. "You're not as irresistible as you might think."

All right, it was a petty thing to say and he knew it, but the things she was saying were getting to him and he was willing to bet she didn't even know she was inflicting wounds.

Declaring dibs on the bathroom, Amy went in first. For once, she wasn't fighting the urge to throw up. She quickly pulled on a nightgown and deliberately put a robe on over it before she made her way out.

"Bathroom's yours if you— What are you doing?" she demanded, stopping dead.

While she'd been in the bathroom changing, he'd been doing the same. Except that Devlin's "changing" involved stripping his clothes *off*—and putting nothing on in their place.

"Just getting ready for bed," Devlin answered her innocently.

He couldn't be serious. "Put something on," she ordered, immediately turning her head away and focusing on a spider that was making its way across the opposite wall.

"Why?" Devlin made no move to cover himself. "Did you forget that I sleep in the raw?"

Yes, she had. *How* she could have forgotten, now that she thought about it, was completely beyond her. But with all the other logistics involved in pulling this off so that no one suspected the truth for now, which in turn meant Devlin would sign the divorce papers, she'd forgotten this one very salient point.

Forgotten, too, just how magnificent a build Devlin had—and obviously still had. If anything, the quick glimpse she'd just caught told her that not only had he kept in shape, he actually looked to be in even better shape than he had been before.

"Your new girlfriend making you keep in top condition?" she asked, sliding into bed, still careful to keep her eyes on anything *but* him.

"There is no new girlfriend—and before you say it, there is no *old* girlfriend, either," he informed her wearily. There'd never been anyone but Amy since the first day he saw her. For a while, he'd thought he'd actually convinced her of that—but he'd obviously been mistaken.

"Having too much fun playing the field?" she prodded.

"You are impossible to talk to, you know that?" he accused.

She said nothing, turning her head toward the window so that she didn't have to look at him.

And so he couldn't see she was crying. Crying because his accusation reminded her that there had been a time when they'd stay up all night, doing nothing *but* talking. Talking about their hopes, their dreams and, eventually, talking about just how much they loved each other—and always would.

Reflecting back now, it seemed to her as if that had all happened in another lifetime. To someone else. There was nothing left of those two people, she thought—except for maybe an incredibly sculpted, washboard-hard stomach.

CHAPTER SIX

DEVLIN DIDN'T REMEMBER falling asleep. He'd thought that his frustration with the situation was more than enough to keep him up all night.

But it didn't.

Somewhere along the line, his eyes shut and sleep overcame him for at least a little while. What finally woke him was a very strange, muffled sound coming from somewhere outside his cabana window.

No, it wasn't coming from outside, he realized as consciousness got a better hold on him. The noise was coming from the bathroom.

What *was* that?

Propping himself up on his elbow, Devlin was about to ask Amy if she was hearing the same thing when he saw that the bed was empty. He got to his knees and saw a single, thin line of light coming from beneath the bathroom door.

There it was again. That strange sound.

He listened more closely. If he didn't know any better, he would have said that it sounded like—

Retching.

Someone was throwing up.

Amy?

Devlin was about to scramble to his feet and go toward the bathroom when the door to the latter opened. In the predawn light that was wiggling its way into the room through the window, he could just about make out Amy's face.

She looked utterly miserable.

"Amy, are you all right?"

Devlin's voice caught her completely off guard. She'd thought he was still asleep. She gasped, her hand spread out on her chest. She'd been so focused on trying not to make any noise that might wake Devlin, she hadn't realized that he *was* awake.

She took a deep breath to steady her nerves.

"Damn it, Dev—" she glared at him "—you almost gave me a heart attack."

For once, there were no quips. "I heard you throwing up. What's wrong? Are you sick?"

She waved an impatient hand at his question. "Just something bad I ate," she told him. "Probably the seafood."

"When?" Devlin challenged, bewildered. "I didn't see you eat a single thing and we've been together since the flight."

"So now I have to check with you before I put anything into my mouth?" she demanded, deliberately turning the focus away from herself by baiting him into another argument.

How did she do that? he wondered in pure awe. How did Amy manage to twist things around so that the two of them would wind up in some half-baked argument about things that had nothing to do with the initial conversation?

"I didn't say that," he pointed out. "All I said to you was—"

He stopped immediately. Someone was knocking on the door.

The next minute, they heard Nick's voice. "Dev? Amy? Are you guys up? I need to talk to you."

Devlin looked at Amy and he could see she was thinking the same thing as he was. That they were going to have to invite the groom in, and if he saw the blanket and pillow on the floor, they were going to have to tell him about the divorce.

There was no way he was going to rain on his best friend's big day. Making a dash toward the door, Devlin flipped the lock open, kicked the blanket under the bed and grabbed his pillow. He dove under the covers, joining Amy, who had quickly slid into bed as soon as she'd heard Nick's voice.

"What are you doing?" she whispered to Devlin. He was crowding her and she was forced to move to one side or wind up with his completely naked body all but pressed against her.

"Saving Nick's illusion of the institution of marriage," Devlin whispered back. And then he raised his voice and called out, "C'mon in, Nick. The door's open."

The words were hardly out of his mouth before his best friend walked in, closing the door behind him like a fugitive afraid someone was right behind him in hot pursuit.

He was at their bed in two strides. "I'm really sorry to barge in on you like this, guys, but I really need your help."

"This couldn't have waited until breakfast?" Amy asked. Her voice rose slightly on the last word as she felt Devlin snake his hand along her thigh beneath the covers. She did her best to subtly push it away, never taking her eyes off Nick's face. She wasn't very successful.

"By breakfast it might be too late," Nick said honestly. He looked from Amy to his best friend, silently imploring both for help as well as understanding. "Cara just might walk out on me."

Amy and Devlin exchanged looks. Devlin was the first to ask, "What did you do?"

"Nothing," Nick cried with all the righteousness of an innocent man. "It's her father."

"What about him?" Amy asked. And why would anything having to do with Cara's father necessitate Nick bursting into their room so early?

"He's coming to the wedding. Cara's been up half the night, totally beside herself," Nick told them.

So far, this didn't have the earmarks of a crisis. Amy looked at him, trying to read between the lines. "Wasn't he supposed to come?"

The look on Nick's face didn't bode well, Devlin thought. "Yes, but it seems the old man just got married again and he's going to be bringing his new wife with him."

Devlin was already shaking his head. Cara's father had a reputation for trading in his wives for newer, younger models every so often. "How old is this one?"

The look on his friend's face gave him his answer before Nick said a word. "They'll probably check her I.D. before giving her a drink."

Devlin sighed. "Oh, God."

Nick nodded, looking relieved that Devlin and Amy understood the problem. "I need you to keep those two away from Cara until she's actually walking down the aisle—better yet, wait until the minister's giving her the 'repeat after me' portion of the ceremony."

Devlin stared patiently at his best friend. "And just how do you propose we do that? Throw a bag over their heads, drag them into some alley and keep them there until tomorrow afternoon?"

Instead of saying he knew how absurd that sounded, Nick looked at him hopefully. "Could you?"

"You know you don't mean that, Nick," Amy said gently.

He had the look of a desperate man about him. "Try me," he dared. "You know how sensitive Cara is about marriages and the odds against them succeeding. It took me a year and a half to convince her to marry me. She was afraid that the second she said, 'I do,' everything would start to fall apart for us. We've made it this far, and I can't let a confrontation with her dad—or his new wife—ruin everything."

Amy could see why Cara might be a little leery. "You *have* been married before," she pointed out gently.

He and Megan had been too hasty, Amy thought, marrying on impulse when Megan got pregnant. They didn't really know what they were getting into, didn't know each other well enough to see the problems and complications that might arise.

It turned out they were two very different people than they thought they were. But this time, with Cara, it was different.

"Yes, but Cara's my soul mate," Nick insisted. "I can feel it in my gut."

"So what do you and your gut really want us to do?" Devlin asked.

"Mainly I want you to show her how happy you two are," Nick said. "That all marriages aren't destined to end in divorce, like her parents' did. That *some* marriages actually do work and get better with time—like yours," he added with feeling. "I just want you two to be yourselves and be around us as much as possible." It was obvious that his mind was jumping around, because the next thing Nick said was, "Maybe I can bribe the cabana boy to 'accidentally' lock Daddy Dearest and his child bride in their rooms for the next thirty hours or so."

Nick rose from the edge of the bed, running his hand through his hair, looking somewhat calmer than when he'd come bursting in five minutes ago.

"I'm sorry for laying all this on your shoulders so suddenly, but you're honestly the happiest couple I know and I just want Cara to have that right in front of her—so she's less focused on her father and his new wife when they get here."

Guilt had been eating away at Amy from the moment Nick walked into the room, and it had grown exponentially with each second that ticked by. She had to tell him, had to let him know, he'd made the wrong assumption.

"Nick, there's something we have to tell you," she began slowly.

She was going to tell Nick, Devlin suddenly realized. She was going to cut right through the last tether just when his best friend was hanging by a thread.

Nick looked at his best friend's wife. "What?"

"I have to tell you that—"

"—we'd be more than happy to do whatever it takes to ensure that your wedding goes off right on schedule and without a hitch," Devlin said, talking fast and not leaving an iota of space for Amy to get a word in edgewise. "Now, if you could just leave so that we can get ready. We'll have your back all day and at the rehearsal dinner tonight—Scout's honor," Devlin promised.

Nodding, Nick started to leave, then stopped in his tracks and turned around to face Devlin. "Wait, you were never a Scout, were you?"

"Just speaking symbolically," Devlin answered glibly.

The smile was back on Nick's lips, filled out with gratitude. "Thanks, you two. I owe you big," Nick said just before he closed the door behind him.

"What the hell are you thinking, lying to Nick like that?" Amy demanded the second he was gone.

Did he really have to explain himself? "You want to know what I was thinking?"

Her eyes narrowed in exasperation. "I just asked, didn't I?"

Before she knew what was happening or could stop him, Devlin had curled his body around hers— just the way he used to. Parts of her body she'd forgotten she had were madly telegraphing *Mayday!*

"I was just thinking that I miss lying in bed like this with you," he told her, slipping his arm around her waist.

All the feelings she'd been trying so hard to block and ignore came bursting out, wearing party favors. Taking no prisoners.

CHAPTER SEVEN

"You're breaking the rules," she told him, her teeth clenched.

"We didn't set any rules," he pointed out. To that end, they'd hardly talked at all before she'd gone and served him with divorce papers.

"Not in so many words—" she allowed.

But he was more specific than that because it worked in his favor. "Not in *any* words."

"They were implied," she told him indignantly.

"Well, like you always said," he reminded her, "I can't seem to read your mind."

He wasn't exactly holding her down, but the weight of his arm across her waist was pinning her in place. Perhaps too easily, she conceded, but right now, she wasn't up to physically pushing him away with enough force to get free. Besides, he was supposed to let her go of his own accord—if there was a shred of decency left inside him.

"What do you want me to say?" she demanded heatedly. "That I'm still attracted to you? Fine, I'm still physically attracted to you." She glared at him. His face was barely inches away. "That doesn't change anything when we're out of bed."

"All right," he said amicably, "then we'll just stay in bed."

"What, for the rest of our lives?" she demanded. Was he crazy?

He didn't say yes; he didn't say no. He gave her an answer that worked for him under these conditions. "Let's just take it one day at a time."

He sounded as if he had every intention of staying in bed all day today. That was unacceptable. "We just promised Nick to run interference for him, remember?"

Devlin inclined his head, indicating that he forgot nothing. "If we invite him and Cara to our cabana and no one tells her when the father and the child bride arrive, that might solve all the problems."

"Right, and start a whole bunch of others," Amy bit off. They *couldn't* stay in bed all day. What was he thinking?

The corners of his mouth curved in a vague hint of a smile. "I don't see it that way."

She'd had enough. "I'm going to get up, shower and get dressed. You—" she waved at him dismissively "—do what you want."

The next moment, instead of planting her feet on the floor, Amy found herself being pulled back onto the bed. And then there he was, bringing his mouth down on hers. Kissing her.

Initially, she struggled. Or at least told herself that she struggled—and then, suddenly, for the space of a few stretched-out seconds, Amy completely forgot why she was struggling.

Instead, she was melting, melting just the way she always did. Melting into Devlin's kiss, into him.

And just when she was on the brink of losing herself in pleasure, Devlin surprised her by drawing back, away from her.

It took Amy a second to catch her breath, another second before she could form words coherently.

"Why did you just do that?" she asked in a raspy whisper. Was it just to feed his ego? To prove to himself that he could still turn her inside out whenever he wanted? That despite everything, she still wasn't immune to him?

There was a wicked look in his eyes as he answered her question. "You said I should do what I want, and that's what I wanted to do."

Pulling away from him, Amy got out of bed in a huff and marched toward the bathroom. "I don't know why I even bother to try."

"Yes, you do," he called after her.

Amy slammed the door and turned the water on high so that he wouldn't be able to hear her cry.

WHEN SHE FINALLY got out of the shower and stood, wrapped in a towel, drying her hair, she saw the bathroom door opening.

He still wasn't wearing anything.

Amy quickly averted her eyes, staring up at the light fixture that ran along the upper edge of the rectangular mirror. "Will you *please* put something on?" she demanded.

"Okay," Devlin agreed amicably, "but that's going

to make taking a shower pretty useless, not to mention messy. I only came in because we're running out of time," he pointed out. "And Nick did want us to be his wingmen. The sooner we get there, the better."

"Okay, okay, I'll dry my hair in the other room," she told Devlin, gathering the hair dryer, the hairbrush, the hairspray and her makeup bag as best she could. Her arms were filled to overflowing.

"I can help," Devlin volunteered, reaching for the large container that was about to slip from her grasp.

Amy turned her body to the side, out of his immediate reach. "You can help by taking your shower."

"Yes, ma'am," he responded dutifully, saluting her. He was in the shower before she vacated the room.

AMY HAD BARELY finished dressing before Devlin came out of the bathroom, a towel for once modestly wrapped around his waist.

"That was fast, even for you," she commented. He really was serious about hurrying, she thought.

"There's a reason for that," he admitted. "I was afraid you'd leave without me and I don't know if you can be trusted."

Amy spun away from the mirror, her hairbrush raised in her hand. It looked dangerously like a weapon, the way she grasped it.

"Me?" she demanded, more stunned than angry—for the moment. What was he talking about? *He* was the one who couldn't be trusted, not her.

"Not trusted to keep from making a 'confession'

to Nick and really undermine his shaky confidence," Devlin elaborated. "He's counting on us to help him get Cara to the altar without any incident. If you tell him that we're contemplating a divorce—"

"*Getting* a divorce," she corrected.

"*Contemplating* a divorce," he repeated as if she hadn't said anything, "that'll make him feel as if he's on shaky ground, and it certainly won't make Cara feel any better about what she's about to do— especially since both her parents *and* her groom have at least one, if not several, broken unions in their past. Seeing her father with his new wife just might be the legendary straw that broke the camel's back. Knowing our marriage is on the rocks will only make things worse. Promise me you won't say anything," Devlin said seriously. "Those two really belong together."

His words brought echoes from the past back to her. "Funny, that was what someone once said about us," she said ironically.

He came up behind her, placing his hands gently on her shoulders. His breath was warm on the back of her neck as he told her, "Maybe they were right."

She could almost swear that his words were caressing her, but she knew it was just a figment of her imagination. She was determined not to succumb.

Shrugging him off, Amy stepped out of reach. "And maybe you should get dressed so we can go and brainwash Cara."

"You still do have a way with words," he said, shaking his head. "Give me seven minutes."

"Seven minutes," she repeated incredulously. Her tone mocked him as she said, "Not five, not ten, but seven."

"Six now," he said glibly. "You can time me if you like," he told her. There was what seemed like a wicked grin on his lips.

"No, thanks, I'll just check my makeup," she said, turning away. She didn't want to be in the same room with him when the towel hit the floor.

"No need to check it," he called after her. "You look perfect."

Turning, she said, "Flattery isn't going to get you any—oh, damn," she cried abruptly. His towel was on the floor, and for some annoying reason, her libido was in full flower this morning.

She really needed to get her hormones reined in, Amy thought in mounting desperation.

She heard Devlin laugh as she slammed the bathroom door for the second time that morning. Amy only wished that she could close the door on her reactions and her emotions as easily.

It had to be this wedding, she decided. Seeing all those couples coming together to celebrate the union of two more people. Two more *happy* people. It made her feel not just lonely, but alone. Astronaut-stranded-in-outer-space-with-a-broken-tether alone.

Amy knew that this, too, was a result of her hormones running amok, thanks to the tiny hitchhiker she was carrying around with her, but knowing that didn't help at all, didn't negate the terrible feeling that was gnawing away at her.

"You about finished trying to improve on perfection?" Devlin's voice was coming through the door. "Because there's no telling when Cara's father is going to show up and we really need to be there. I was thinking that the four of us should spend the day together until it's time for the rehearsal. That way, we can keep Cara distracted—away from the hotel *and* from seeing her father, the cradle robber."

Finished, Amy threw open the door and came out. "Do you have to keep coming up with all those cute little nicknames to call her father?"

Now she was defending some octogenarian womanizer? "Why? What would you call him?" he wanted to know.

That was easy enough. "A terrible father."

Picking up her purse, Amy remembered that she hadn't emptied it out last night. Trying to look nonchalant, she took it over to the trash, upturned the clutch and emptied the contents—dried-out baked ham—into the trash. She held her breath, afraid that the smell might send her rushing back to the bathroom for another brief communion with the porcelain bowl.

"Maybe he's not a terrible father, maybe he's just a rotten husband," Devlin suggested, watching her dump out her bag.

She snapped the purse closed, avoiding looking in Devlin's direction. "Well, we're agreed on that much," Amy said.

"See, it's a start," he told her cheerfully, opening the door and holding it for her.

"It's a statement, not a start," she corrected, walking past him.

"We'll see," he said under his breath.

But it was loud enough for her to hear.

CHAPTER EIGHT

CLAPPING HIS HANDS together in a gesture that rang of nothing if not enthusiasm, Devlin raised his voice and began talking to Nick and Cara before he ever reached them in the hotel lobby.

"So, where do you two want to spend your last full day as singles?" he asked, looking first at Nick, then at Cara. His intent was to make Cara feel as if the final decision for the day's activities was ultimately in her hands—even if it wasn't.

Her decision took less than thirty seconds to reach. "Oh, I don't know," she told him with a half shrug. "I rethought everything and decided we might just take it easy, lie around the pool all day, rest up for the wedding rehearsal, that kind of thing."

That was *definitely* not what he was shooting for. Cara's father and his wife would be checking in sometime today and the pool would undoubtedly be the first place he would think to look for her.

"No, no, no," Devlin said, shaking his head. "You want to do something memorable, something fun. Go island hopping in a helicopter, look down the mouth of a volcano, go whale watching, swim with dolphins." He glanced over his shoulder toward Amy. "Help me out here, Ames," he coaxed.

Ames.

Devlin hadn't called her that since the early days of their marriage.

Had that been deliberate, to make her feel nostalgic? Or was it just a slip of the tongue on his part? Either way, he'd made it clear that he needed her backing him up on this.

"Devlin's right," she told an indecisive-looking Cara. "You can sit around poolside at any hotel. Heck, you could have stayed back where we were and sat around the pool at a local Holiday Inn—"

"Not in Chicago, I couldn't," Cara interjected, pretending to shiver for good measure. "Not unless I wanted to be a Popsicle."

Amy didn't bother backtracking or correcting herself. Instead, she just followed Devlin's lead and pushed forward.

"Cara, the whole point of having your wedding in Hawaii is to do Hawaiian things. I vote for whale watching," she announced, holding up her hand as if there was an actual vote being taken. Meanwhile, her eyes never left Cara's and continued to coax and plead.

"C'mon, Cara," Nick urged, giving her a quick, persuasive hug. "It'll be fun."

"Wow," Cara said, looking around at all three of the people surrounding her. "Three against one. I can't fight you all." She grinned. "Okay, you win. I'd like to spend some time at the beach this morning, but then let's go out and do something." She turned toward her fiancé, letting him get the final word. "You pick," she told Nick.

Meanwhile, Devlin turned his head so that only Amy could hear what he was about to say.

"Thanks," he told her in a low whisper.

She didn't want him to think he was wearing her down—even though he was. "I didn't do it for you," she whispered back, doing her best to appear casual. "I did it for Cara."

"Whatever," he allowed cavalierly, looking down into her face. "Thanks."

The man just wouldn't stop until he wore her down completely, would he? she thought. Despite her bravado, she knew it was only a matter of time before that happened. Hell, it was *already* happening, she silently admitted.

But she didn't have to act as if he was succeeding, Amy told herself defiantly. She wanted to keep Devlin on his toes and guessing.

It was *not* going to be easy.

THAT AFTERNOON, THEY wound up doing a little bit of everything on Devlin's list. They went island hopping in a helicopter, getting a breathtaking view of some of the bigger islands. After that, they boarded a whale-watching vessel. *That* was followed up with a short stint of scuba diving, mostly by Nick and Cara. The whole outing had taken a little more than four hours, and at that point, with a good portion of the day gone, Cara reminded everyone that they still had the wedding rehearsal ahead of them, not to mention the rehearsal dinner.

Devlin knew that a formal rehearsal dinner with Cara's parents potentially taking verbal swings at each other was something Nick strongly felt should be avoided if at all possible. The look on his face telegraphed as much to his best man.

Devlin went to work. "We could skip the restaurant and just go to McDonald's," Devlin suggested cheerfully. "You know, symbolically letting go of your childhood by *not* ordering a Happy Meal."

"We've got reservations at a very nice restaurant," Cara reminded Nick. "Really, this has all been a blast. If I didn't feel this way before, I would now— life with you is going to be one great big adventure," she told Nick, brushing her lips against his. "But it's time to get back on schedule and be responsible people for a little while," she said with a laugh. "I'm going to the cabana to shower and change into something a little more dressy, and then we'll go to the beach."

"Wait—" Nick fell into step with her "—I'll join you in that shower."

Cara stopped abruptly, putting her hand up and planting it in the center of his chest. "No. From here on forward we can't be alone together until the wedding. It's bad luck," she insisted.

He looked at her in disbelief, then saw that she was serious. "Honey, that's an old superstition," Nick lamented.

But Cara was firm. "With my family's luck, I'm not taking any chances," she said.

Knowing he didn't have a prayer of talking her out of it, he figured he'd find a single friend to crash with that night. Nick turned to Devlin. "I smell like a wet seal. I can't go to the wedding rehearsal like that."

"Agreed," Devlin replied.

"So can I use your cabana?" Nick looked from his best man to Amy.

"Mi casa es su casa," Devlin said with no hesitation.

"That's the extent of Devlin's mastery of the Spanish language so don't ask him anything else," Amy told the groom.

Nodding, Nick was about to dash off with Devlin's keycard in his hand but he stopped for a second, turning around to look at both of them.

"I just want you to know that I'm really glad you two are here, sharing this big day with us." His eyes were almost shining. "I hope Cara and I are lucky enough to be as happy as you two are."

"Oh, happier, I'm sure. You two will definitely be happier," Amy responded with feeling.

At least I really hope you are, she added silently.

"Only if we're really, really lucky," Nick responded before he hurried off.

THE WEDDING REHEARSAL went off without a hitch. Except for one minor detail.

Cara's father wasn't there.

From all indications, he hadn't arrived on the island at all yet. Consequently, Cara decided to walk down the aisle unaccompanied by anything but the organ music.

After it was over, Amy was the first to reach Cara's side. "You looked absolutely terrific, making your way down the aisle."

"My father's not coming, is he?" Cara said. "My own father's not coming to my wedding."

"Maybe it's better that way," Amy suggested kindly. "You won't have to put up with any of the drama. Devlin said your dad likes to take center stage no matter where he is, and tomorrow is your big day, not his. Yours and Nick's," Amy amended.

Cara nodded, doing her best to look cheerful. "You're right. I'm just being silly. I guess not everyone has the perfect set of parents."

"Very few, actually," Amy told her. "Sometimes parents wind up teaching you how to be a good person by having you *not* follow their example."

The rehearsal over, they gathered their things and headed over to the hotel's reception hall for a catered dinner. But as Devlin and Nick joined them, it was obvious that something was bothering Cara.

Despite the encouraging smile Amy flashed at him, Nick asked, "Everything all right, Cara?"

"Everything's perfect," she told him, kissing him lightly. "Just perfect. Let's go eat." She laced her fingers through his. "I don't know about you, Nick, but I'm starving."

"Ditto," Amy chimed in.

"Okay, you heard the ladies, Devlin. Let's go eat," Nick said, leading the way to the hotel.

"I guess McDonald's is out, huh?" Devlin asked, making one last halfhearted pitch to delay any sort of a confrontation between Cara and her father. He wasn't quite ready to believe that the man wasn't coming.

"McDonald's is out," Cara said with a laugh.

THEY MET THE rest of the wedding party in the banquet room and "perfect" lasted for another hour.

And then, as everyone was finishing their main course and looking forward to a variety of desserts, two more wedding guests descended upon the private dining room.

Conversation gradually stopped as their presence became known.

If there was one thing Hal Russell knew how to do, it was make an entrance. For him, each walk through a doorway was an entrance. It was only a matter of if it was a major one or a minor one.

This was definitely a major one. Especially since the tall, slender man who liked to be referred to as the Silver Fox was not alone.

He was impeccably dressed as always and his hands were outstretched as he strode toward his daughter.

"There she is. There's my gorgeous little bride-to-be," he declared in a rich, booming voice. Never missing a step, he glanced over his shoulder toward the statuesque blonde in his wake. "Didn't I tell you she was beautiful, Cherie?" he asked the woman.

"You did, sugar. You most certainly told me how beautiful she was—and she is," Cherie agreed, turning up the wattage on her dazzling smile.

The banquet room became so deadly still you could hear a wedding ring drop.

CHAPTER NINE

THE LAST THING Cara wanted was a scene, so she did her best to rally. "Daddy, you're here," she said, trying very hard to take her father's larger-than-life presence in stride.

Not standing on ceremony, the man came up to her and all but lifted Cara up from her chair with his expansive embrace.

"Of course I'm here," he responded, his voice reaching the rafters. "What kind of a man would I be if I'd stayed away?" His laugh seemed to be at odds with his sincerity. "I wouldn't miss my baby girl's first nuptials."

Because Devlin could see where this was headed—and because he knew that if Nick articulated what Devlin could easily see was going through his best friend's mind, it would cause an estrangement between the groom and his father-in-law that might very well last a lifetime—Devlin stood up. He would take it upon himself to deflect any harm—intentional or unintentional—that Hal Russell's words might cause.

The wedding must go on became Devlin's secret battle cry.

"Her *only* nuptials," Devlin corrected.

Silver eyebrows drew together over a very distinguished nose as Hal turned toward the source of the voice. "Say what, boy?"

Devlin knew the man had heard him and there was no need to repeat the words. But he was determined to lay any fears Cara might have to rest.

"No disrespect intended, sir, but Cara is not her mother, and more important, Nick is not you. They didn't just decide to get married on the spur of the moment because flying to Hawaii seemed like a fun way to spend a long weekend. They searched their hearts long and hard before making this decision.

"They're committed to each other—for the long haul, not the long weekend. Thank God all those divorces you and your first wife have between you haven't affected Cara, haven't driven her away from the institution of marriage because, done right—" he directed a pointed glance at Amy "—with the right person, marriage can be and *is* a beautiful thing. Not perfect," he allowed with yet another look toward Amy, "because nothing is perfect. Even if you're lucky enough to find someone to love who loves you back, there'll be rough spots. But you work them out because you know that what you've got is very precious and worth fighting for."

"Well, I totally agree," Hal finally said after what seemed like an incredibly long pause. The enthusiasm in his voice swelled as he turned to the young woman with him. "Don't I, Cherie?"

The woman nodded vigorously and he turned back

to his daughter and his son-in-law-to-be. "Where are my manners? I'd like you two to meet my own lovely bride, Cherie. We were married almost three weeks ago. I guess that makes us still newlyweds."

Though he'd been quick to judge the young woman with Cara's father, Devlin did note that she had kind eyes.

He watched her now as she came forward. Taking Cara's hands in hers, Cherie said with sincerity, "I hope you and your man are going to be very, very happy together." She lowered her voice to add, "And you don't have to call me Mama if you don't want to. I understand."

Cara looked at her a little uncertainly, still trying to come to terms with having a stepmother who was the same age as she was, if not younger.

"Thank you. Um, Nick—" she turned toward her fiancé "—could you ask the waiter to bring two more chairs and place settings?"

Relief all but radiated from Nick as he leaped to his feet to corner the waiter. "Sure thing."

And the evening continued on the same even keel.

"WELL, THAT WASN'T so bad," Amy acknowledged as she and Devlin walked into their cabana a few hours later. Peace had been maintained throughout the evening and it appeared that it would remain that way for the next twenty-four hours—which was all the parties involved really needed.

Devlin cocked his head as he regarded his wife with a touch of curiosity. "And by 'that' you mean—"

She took the decorative combs out of her hair and it unfurled, falling straight to her shoulders. Amy dragged her fingers through it to loosen it up.

"The appearance of Daddy Dearest, for the most part," she answered. "I think that tomorrow just might be all right."

Devlin grinned. He paused to observe her. He'd always liked to watch her fiddle with her hair. "Yeah, me, too," he agreed.

Amy paused for a moment, debating whether or not to say what was on her mind or just let it go.

But then, she thought, maybe too much had been let go already and there should be at least a few good things to remember about the last time they spent together. It was going to be over soon.

"That was a very nice thing you did."

He'd started to unbutton his shirt, loosening it from his waistband at the same time.

"You're going to have to be more specific," he told her. "I do a lot of nice things."

Yes, she thought, if she was being honest with herself, he did. Wasn't that why she'd married him in the first place? Because he was one of the good guys?

"What you said to Cara's father when he made that thoughtless comment about not wanting to miss her 'first' nuptials. I think you put him in his place and turned the tide of the evening, maybe the whole ceremony. I was watching Cara while you were talking, and even though you were just pointing out the obvious, I know it had an effect on her. You could almost see that it made her feel stronger, more in control of her own destiny. You're pretty good with words when you want to be," she told him. What would it hurt to give him a compliment this one time? They were going to be going their separate ways soon enough.

The thought made her sad.

"So for once I didn't screw up?" he asked her, amusement highlighting his eyes.

Amy inclined her head. "For once you didn't screw up. Nick was right in asking you to be his best man—and to run interference for him. If you hadn't been there for them tonight, we might be packing our bags right now instead of tomorrow after the reception."

His shirt hanging open on either side of his bare chest, Devlin came up behind her, lightly laying his hands on her shoulders while he contemplated the tempting slope of her neck.

"You know," he told her, his voice low, seductive, "we don't have to pack after the reception."

"Why?" she asked, half turning to look at him. "You thinking of leaving your clothes behind and donating them to some charity fund on the island?" Amy deadpanned.

"I'm talking about turning in the return flight airplane tickets, spending a little more time on the island. Maybe like a second honeymoon," he proposed, hoping he could finally make her give up this idea of a divorce. The whole premise was based on quicksand, she had to know that.

"A second honeymoon," she repeated. "By yourself?"

She knew perfectly well he wasn't talking about a solo honeymoon. The idea was beyond ridiculous.

"No," he said evenly, "I mean a second honeymoon with you."

She shook her head, the serious look on her face shutting him out. "Sorry, I have to get back to Chicago. I've got a big meeting set up at the agency for Monday afternoon."

"Can't you reschedule?" he suggested, skimming his fingertips lightly along her shoulders.

She shrugged him off, moving to the side. Her skin continued to feel his touch long after he pulled his hand away. "I have no reason to."

Temporarily blocked, he dropped his hands to his sides. "Right."

She swung around to face him. "Look, just because I can see you're not a complete black-hearted devil doesn't mean anything's changed between us. You're still the same person you were." Still the person women threw themselves at. And if enough women did the throwing, some were bound to be caught. She knew the odds. Devlin was a human, not a saint.

"Yes," he said deliberately, "I am."

She galvanized her courage, holding it up like a shield. "And I don't want to be married to that person anymore, so nothing's changed," she said with finality.

Devlin shrugged, echoing her words. "Nothing's changed."

That should have been the end of it. But it wasn't.

It wasn't, because then, as it had several times in the past three months, it hit her. Hit her when she was least prepared for it. That completely uncontrollable urge to throw up everything she had ever consumed hit her like a mighty, steel-fisted punch to the gut.

In midthought—practically in midword—Amy was forced to spin around on her heel and race to the bathroom. She only had enough time to slam the door behind her.

Somehow, she managed to turn the faucet on in a feeble attempt to mask the sounds she knew were coming.

The sound of her stomach forcing itself up through her throat and mouth.

Amy didn't even remember falling to her knees— the only thing that registered was the pain that reverberated through them as they came in abrupt contact with the hard, ice-blue tile on the floor surrounding the toilet bowl.

After that, she was too busy retching her insides out to notice anything at all.

Including the bathroom door opening again.

CHAPTER TEN

AS THE NAUSEA finally receded, leaving her feeling barely human, Amy sighed with tentative relief. At this point, she was painfully aware that the respite she was experiencing was temporary. She'd be in this exact position again and, most likely, soon.

Were the entire nine months going to be like this? She'd been pregnant for three months and throwing up practically from the very beginning. At the present rate, she certainly wasn't gaining any weight. In fact, Amy thought she might have actually lost a little.

On the bright side, at least no one would know about this baby until she was ready to tell them.

She realized there was perspiration on her brow, gluing her bangs to her forehead. Eyes closed in abject misery, Amy began to wipe the sweat away with the back of her wrist.

Suddenly, she felt a towel against her cheek. Her eyes flew open and she jumped, stifling a yelp.

"It's just me."

Devlin.

Who else?

Grudgingly taking the towel from him, Amy

wiped not just her brow but her face, as well. "How
long have you been standing there?" she wanted to
know.

"Long enough."

His tone gave nothing away. It didn't have to. Amy
was on the defensive immediately.

Devlin put his hand under her arm, trying to help
her to her feet. Amy desperately wanted to wave him
away, but at the moment, she was so worn out by her
latest bout of throwing up, she didn't have the energy
to get up without some sort of aid. After a second's
hesitation, she let him help her up.

Devlin gently guided her to the other room. He
waited until she was sitting on the bed before he
asked, "Why didn't you tell me?"

Amy wouldn't meet his eye. "Tell you what?"

They were playing games now, he thought. But
given the situation, he let her a little leeway. "That
you were pregnant."

Tension that had been teetering on the perimeter
of her consciousness now charged through her like
a race car in the Indianapolis 500. This was *not* the
way she wanted Devlin to find out.

Actually, she *didn't* want him to find out. She
wanted to tell him after the fact, after the baby had
been born and was a living, breathing little person.
She'd feel less vulnerable then.

The lie came to her lips like a reflex. "I'm not
pregnant," she said defiantly.

"I'm a man, Amy, but that doesn't mean I'm completely stupid." Devlin stood looking down at her for

several moments, his arms crossed before his chest. "One of the things I really liked about you when we first met—you had a lot going for you, but this was something that really set you apart for me—was that you didn't lie. Were pretty much incapable of it, actually," he said. "The few times you even attempted to form some sort of little white lie, I would always know." He smiled at her the way an indulgent parent might at a child who had accidentally messed up.

"Oh, because you're so good at seeing through people," she retorted sarcastically.

"No," he said patiently, "because you have a tell." He saw her eyes widen. "When you lie, you squint your right eye just a little, as if you can't bear to look at the lie." The smile faded. He became serious. "Why didn't you tell me?" he repeated.

There was no use even trying to deny it anymore, so she didn't. Instead, she shrugged, looking away again. "You didn't have a need to know."

"No need to know?" he echoed. "It's *my* baby."

"How do you know?" She raised her chin, the way she did just before getting into a fight with him. "Maybe it's not."

She started to rise. Devlin put his hands gently but firmly on her shoulders and kept her where she was. He looked at her for a long moment. The silence stretched out for almost a minute.

"Yes, it is," he said quietly.

Amy wasn't about to give up. She realized that she loved him, would never love anyone as much as she loved Devlin, but she didn't want him in her life out of some sense of obligation. She'd rather go it alone than have him that way.

"Are you so sure of that?" she challenged. "How do you know I didn't fool around with someone else? We weren't together for three months."

"Two months and twenty-nine days," he corrected quietly, then said, "Because I know you and I trust you. It's not in your nature to start an affair with someone until we were actually divorced. We weren't, which means that's our child growing inside of you." He smiled. "I guess the reconciliation attempt took better than I'd thought."

Amy sighed, feeling suddenly hemmed in and hopeless. This wasn't the way she wanted to remain married. "So now what?"

"That," he told her quietly, "is entirely up to you." She looked at him in surprise. "I know what I want to happen. I want us to pick up where we left off—*without* the baseless jealousy," he emphasized. "And go from there." He inclined his head. "But it's not up to me."

Devlin looked at her for a long, long moment. A dozen thoughts and memories collided in his head. "You're the one holding all the cards, Amy, so the next play is yours. But you need to understand one thing."

She hadn't taken her eyes off him since Devlin had begun talking. "And that is?" Amy asked in a low voice.

His eyes held hers intensely, attempting to communicate with her soul. He *needed* her to believe him, once and for all. "All the accusations you've thrown at me are baseless. I never *once* cheated on you."

"Never once," Amy echoed, following the words up with a dismissive laugh.

"Never once," he repeated firmly. "I can't control what you think, Amy, just like I can't control what another woman is capable of doing. If she wants to throw herself at me, I can't stop her. The only thing I *can* control," he said, "is how I react to that. And it's always the same."

"Really?" she asked, silently imploring him to convince her, *really* convince her once and for all.

He pushed on, determined to get through to her for all their sakes. Because it wasn't just about her, or him, anymore. There was now a third person to consider, a third person who was going to need both of them.

"Really," he replied, his tone dead serious. "And you want to know why?"

Underneath her swagger and dismissive expression, Amy wanted, more than anything, to shed the oppressive insecurity that weighed her down. That very nearly ruined what they had.

"Go ahead."

"Because," he told her, his words slow and deliberate, "since the day I said, 'I do,' I had a wife to come home to, a wife I loved more than anything or anyone. Why would I even *think* of risking that for what amounts to a quick thrill at best, a disappointing experience at worst? You know me to be a reasonably intelligent man, Ames. Does that sound like something I would even remotely contemplate doing?"

When Amy didn't answer him, he pressed on. "Does it? Look into your heart and *then* tell me."

An exasperated sigh preceded her answer. She looked down at the floor. "No."

Very gently, he raised her to her feet and took her into his arms. "Then why don't you stop seeing infidelities under every rock, hiding in every shadow, and tear up the divorce papers? I just want to spend the rest of my life with you and little who's-it-what's-it." He drew Amy even closer. "I don't know why you're so insecure, anyway," he told her honestly. "You're always the most beautiful woman in the room."

"No, I'm not," she contradicted. She had never had an inflated sense of self, and vanity had never been her problem.

Devlin's green eyes never left hers. "You are to me," he told her with finality. "And that's all that really counts."

But when he went to kiss her, Amy put her hand up between them. She saw his eyebrows rise in a weary question.

Before he could ask her what was wrong now, she said, "Let me at least brush my teeth first."

Devlin stepped back. He did it mainly because he wanted her to be comfortable. "I've waited this long, I can wait a couple of minutes longer. But just for the record, it doesn't make a difference to me."

He followed her back to the bathroom. "This comes under that heading about loving you 'for better or for worse.' And all things considered, bad breath is really small potatoes."

Amy paused, toothbrush in one hand, tube of toothpaste in the other. "And you seriously have never, even *once* thought about or been tempted to cheat on me?" She turned to look at him as she quickly brushed her teeth.

"I've thought about strangling you when you've pushed me to the end of my patience," he freely admitted. "But cheat on you? No."

She rinsed and turned to face Devlin, the tiled sink counter at her back. "Works for me," she told him.

"Then you'll tear up the papers you signed?" Devlin asked.

"I never really signed them," she admitted. "I just told you I did."

"On the phone," he recalled, taking her back into his arms again. "Which is why I didn't know you were lying to me."

"I'm going to have to work on that tell," she told him.

"I've got something better for you to work on," Devlin countered just before he brought his mouth down on hers.

"Gladly," she murmured.

He really liked the sound of that.

EPILOGUE

THE NEXT DAY, Nick and Cara's wedding went off without a single incident to mar it.

To everyone's surprise, Cara's parents were civil to each other and genuinely moved watching their daughter getting married to a man who obviously adored her. The flower girls actually distributed the petals in their baskets fairly evenly and had a few left to toss down at the altar, while the five-year-old ring-bearer made it up to the altar without dropping the rings even once.

It was as perfect a ceremony as any of the guests could remember—but Devlin and Amy hardly noticed. They hardly noticed anything outside the small circle that they formed around themselves. A circle created out of second chances and making the most of them. And a renewed love that was stronger than ever.

At the reception, when it came time for the best man to make the toast, Devlin rose to his feet holding his glass of champagne in one hand as his other dipped into the pocket of his jacket to retrieve the speech he's written late last night. His fingers came in contact with the silk lining and nothing more.

With an apologetic grin, he told those seated in the room, "I seem to have left my speech in my other jacket." The comment received a smattering of polite laughter. "No, really," he said. "I really did forget it." Taking a breath, he went on, "So I guess I'll have to wing it." He looked at the newlyweds for a moment, reflecting. "I won't bore you with little personal stories about how right these two are for each other— you just have to look at them to see that. And I won't tell you how hard Nick had to work to get Cara to see that they belonged together. The point is, they are, he did, she did and here they are—married and very much in love."

He raised his glass as he looked at the couple. "May you always love each other as much as you do right now and may you always remember exactly how you felt at this moment. And, if I can interject one personal note into this," he said, glancing at his wife, "may you be as happy as Amy and I are right now."

With that, he took a sip of his champagne and everyone else followed suit with their own glasses of champagne.

Except for Amy—who was sipping ginger ale.

As Devlin sat down again, the guests began to tap their silverware against their glasses, signaling their desire to see the bride and groom kiss. Nick and Cara happily obliged.

But they weren't the only ones. Just as they weren't the only ones beginning a brand-new life together. Except that in Devlin and Amy's case, it was their second time. But the second time, Devlin silently promised Amy as he kissed her, was the charm. They were both committed to that—and each other.

* * * * *

This novella is dedicated to Marie Ferrarella,
RaeAnne Thayne and Claire Caldwell.

HAWAIIAN RETREAT

Leanne Banks

CHAPTER ONE

"YOU ARE TRULY insane," Gabi Foster's friend Helen said as they drove to Chicago O'Hare. "Not just insane. A raving lunatic."

Gabi glanced up from the text she was sending to a client. She'd been friends with Helen for many years, and each of them could call each other for just about anything. "I really appreciate your driving me to the airport, especially in this weather," Gabi said as she looked at the falling snow. "I know you think that anyone in their right mind would be happy to trade the frozen tundra of Chicago for Hawaii for a few days, but this is a very critical time for me at work. It's hard having my father for a boss, and I think he's finally starting to see me as a valuable employee instead of just one of the marketing representatives. He has given me some extra opportunities lately. He's let me take the lead on a few things." Gabi knew she was in a unique position since her father was the CEO of the company. The fact that she worked with one of their major accounts, and that major account wanted the organic cosmetics line her father hadn't approved yet, put her future in a trajectory for either success or failure. Gabi was banking on success. "There's a promotion in my near future. I can smell it, taste it—"

"You should be concentrating on smelling Hawaiian flowers and tasting mai tais," Helen said. "Do you know how much every person in Chicago would like to trade places with you right now?"

Gabi sighed, wishing she didn't feel so conflicted about attending her half brother's wedding. Nick was the product of her mother's first marriage. "I do, but it's an interruption. You know how much I love Nick, but the timing is difficult for me. Plus, I still love Nick's first wife, Megan. She's perfect. How could they divorce? Even though they've been split up for years, I still don't understand it."

"Didn't you tell me they have the friendliest divorce ever?" Helen asked as she pulled up to the airport terminal.

"Yes, but I'm still team Megan," Gabi said, even though she knew she sounded ridiculous. That was one of the great things about having a longtime friend like Helen. Gabi could say anything to her. Helen might correct her or even mock her, but Helen would always have her back.

"Even though Megan doesn't want to be married to Nick, either," Helen said.

"Sometimes I think all they need is to come to their senses," Gabi said. "They just seemed so perfect for each other."

Helen shot her a sideways glance. "I hope you're not planning on cooking up anything that would mess up your brother's marriage. You wouldn't try to get Nick back with his ex during a wedding celebration, would you?"

Gabi rolled her eyes. "Of course I wouldn't. I'm not that crazy. I'm just not completely sure about his fiancée, Cara. She seems nice, but what if she's not good with his twins?"

"Do you really think Nick would choose someone who wasn't going to be nice to his daughters?" Helen asked.

Gabi sighed again. "You're right. The truth is, I need to be more supportive about him getting married. I want him to be happy, and he believes this will make him happy."

"Now, you're sounding like the Gabi I've known since sixth grade," Helen said. "Not some crazy, overworked woman who has lost all perspective about what's important."

Gabi smiled at Helen and her friend's burgeoning baby bump. "Ever since you and Frank got married, you've really softened up. I remember hearing you talk about your court cases with blood nearly dripping from your incisors."

"Real love will do that to you," Helen said.

Gabi felt a stab of melancholy at her friend's happiness. She was thrilled for Helen, but sometimes her practically perfect family life made Gabi think about what she was missing. Gabi slammed the door shut on those thoughts. That was all the more reason she should focus on her career. She'd given love more than one try and failed every time.

"Maybe for someone else, but not for me," Gabi muttered as Helen approached the drop-off.

"Just because things didn't work out for you with Bill doesn't mean love has passed you by."

Gabi made a face. That was one more reason she wasn't thrilled about attending this wedding. Her brother's friend Bill Kenyon had dumped Gabi last year, and Bill would be attending the destination wedding with his new, very pregnant wife. Gabi knew her ego was smarting more than anything, but that would be another unpleasant jab. At least she had a friend, Steven Jackson, flying out to accompany her for part of the celebration.

"You never know," Helen continued. "Love could be right around the corner."

"My promotion is right around the corner," Gabi corrected as she pulled her suitcase from the car. "Listen, you are the absolute best friend ever. Thank you for driving me." She whipped around to the driver's side, where Helen had lowered the window, and gave her friend a kiss on the cheek. "Be safe and take care of your hubby and baby."

"Call me when you get back, and drink a mai tai for me," Helen called as Gabi ran back to the curb.

"Will do," Gabi said and strode into the airport.

"It's only a few days," she told herself, her mind whirling a mile a minute. She just needed to stay focused. She just needed to keep her momentum.

AFTER A SLIGHT delay, Gabi boarded her flight. She worked during the first half of it, took a short nap, then awakened and worked until they landed in Los Angeles. She napped and worked again during the second flight until the wheels touched down in the late afternoon. The balmy air hit her the second she exited the terminal and a representative from the resort placed a lei of plumeria around her neck.

"How lovely," she said, admiring the flowers. Gabi had skimmed an article about Hawaiian culture that had said it was bad etiquette to remove the lei in front of the person who had presented it. After the stale air in the plane, however, the scent of the lei was a delicious change and she had no inclination to remove it.

As soon as she slid into the backseat of the car, she pulled out her phone and checked text messages. Her stomach knotted as she read one from the client at her plum account. They were growing impatient with the delays, and wanted the organic cosmetic line for their drugstores now.

She immediately called one of the admins at the office and left a message asking him to send samples of the most recent organic products the company had produced. That should buy her some time, she thought. If only she could get her father to go ahead and push out the line. But he feared there wasn't enough interest for an organic line and wasn't quite ready to invest as fully as Gabi wanted. Research and development had approved several of the products. Her father was the holdup.

Gabi growled under her breath. She would have to work up yet another market research report that would prove the figures to him because he didn't trust her nearly as much as he trusted most of his other young marketing representatives. The knowledge grated on her, but she was determined to make this happen.

The car pulled to a stop, interrupting her train of thought. Gabi glanced up at the parklike setting of the resort. The driver opened her car door and assisted her out of the vehicle, and a sigh slid from deep inside her. The sight of the lush, green landscape seemed to immediately ratchet down her stress level. Gabi had read that plants could do that for a person. She wouldn't know, since she'd killed every plant she'd either bought or been given.

She could enjoy this for a few days, she thought, as she checked in at the registration desk. Especially if she still had time to take care of her work commitments. The clerk handed her the key to her bungalow and she turned around.

"There she is," her half brother, Nick, said with a huge smile on his face, Cara beside him. He pulled

Gabi into his arms. "Glad you're here. Any problems with the flight?"

"A short delay out of Chicago and I had to connect in L.A., but I managed to get some work done on both flights. Hi, Cara," she said to Nick's fiancée. "Are you ready for the big day?"

"Mostly," Cara said, giving Gabi a hug. "Just trying to keep potential craziness down to a dull roar."

"If you need some help, let me know," Gabi said.

"I'm fine, but thanks," Cara replied.

"Well, I'm not," said Nick. "I've got to hit the beach for a group surfing lesson and I signed you up to join in."

"Me?" Gabi squeaked. "But I just got here. I haven't even gone to my room yet."

"Better hurry," he said.

Befuddled, Gabi glanced at Cara. "Is she doing it?"

Nick shook his head. "She's afraid she'll break something before the wedding."

"I have several things on my to-do list that don't include surfing lessons," Cara corrected, then winced. "Okay, I admit it. I'm terrified. I may give it a try after the wedding."

"But you're not scared, are you, Gabi? You're always up for anything," Nick said.

"Well, 'always' and 'anything' might be a slight exaggeration." Gabi's brother and plenty of other guys had attributed far more athletic prowess to her than she actually possessed. Probably because she hadn't inherited her mother's petite frame. Gabi stood five foot ten with big bones and big feet. She worked out and had done her best to keep up with her athletic brother while growing up, but coordination wasn't her strong suit.

"Aw, come on. It'll be fun," Nick said.

Gabi thought of the vacations her family had taken with Nick at the family lake house. She and Nick had competed on water skis every time they'd gotten together. Sad to say, with Nick getting married, he'd be tied up with his new wife, and Gabi might not have as many opportunities to spend time with him as often as in the past. "Okay, I'll do it," she said. "But I need ten minutes."

"Make it five," Nick said with a big smile that brightened her mood.

"Where are the lessons being held?"

"Just follow the path to the beach," he said. "See you there."

Gabi took her rolling bag to her suite, and immediately changed into her swimsuit and slapped on some sunscreen. Pulling on a cover-up, she stepped into a pair of flip-flops and headed out the door. The green plants and the beautiful flowers provided a soothing contrast to the harshness of wintry Chicago. She heard the sound of a bird calling just before she walked into the bright light of the beach.

Oh, this was paradise. She would still do some

work, but maybe this trip would take a few kinks out of her shoulders. Gabi took a deep breath, and another. She walked on the beach toward the small group that included her brother. A tanned, muscular man appeared to be calling out instructions. She studied him for a long moment. He spoke with a natural authority that would make people pay attention to him. He smiled and she felt a tug of attraction. *Who wouldn't?* she thought. With that body and personality, he probably had women falling all over him. Well, he wouldn't look twice at her. He was clearly a surfer guy who probably spent all his time catching waves or in the gym and undoubtedly preferred a woman with a body as chiseled as his.

Gabi tore her attention from the man and noticed three things: she was the only woman in the class, the rest of the men were firemen—Nick's colleagues—and one of them was Bill Kenyon, her ex. Her shoulders immediately tightened up.

"Oh, it looks like you've already started, so I'll sit this one out," she said, lifting her hand and turning away.

"No need," the instructor said and she felt him gently catch her arm. "I was just distributing the boards. I can get one for you."

Gabi met his green-eyed gaze and felt a jiggle of awareness inside her. "I'm Finn Beckett, the instructor," he said, and extended his hand.

Gabi shook his hand while her insides shook at the same time. "Nice to meet you, Mr. Beckett."

"Call me Finn," he said.

"Finn," she echoed, noting a few lines around his eyes. He was a little older than she'd originally thought. That made her curious.

"And you are?" he prompted.

"Gabi," she said. "I'm the sister of the groom."

Finn nodded. "Go fill out your paperwork. There's a form on the counter at the cabana window. I'll get your board. We start on the sand," he said and walked toward a small hut. Seconds later, he brought a surf board and skin to her. "You'll be okay," he said.

"Yes, I will," she said instinctively. "I'm a good water-skier and swimmer."

He gave a slow nod. "Waves are different. But you'll like it."

Finn returned to the front of the group and began his lesson. Gabi tried not to be bothered by seeing her ex again, but she found it incredibly difficult to concentrate. At the same time, it seemed that her mind always drifted to work. The group practiced by lying on the boards, kneeling on the boards, then standing.

If that wasn't enough, there was something about Finn, the instructor, that deeply distracted Gabi. Yes, he was ripped in a major way, but there was something more. He emanated mental and emotional strength, not just physical strength. *Hmm.*

"Okay, now we're going to head out to the ocean," Finn said.

Oops, Gabi thought. She really should have paid more attention. Gabi dragged her board into the water. She hoped she'd at least be able to mount it.

Finn walked toward her. "Everything okay?" he asked.

Gabi nodded. "Of course. I took an overnight flight, so it's taking me a bit to catch up."

"Don't push yourself," he said. "Call me if you need me."

Gabi scoffed. "I'll be fine." She stepped into the ocean and was thankful for the wetsuit. The water was colder than she'd expected.

"We're going to have you start on your stomach. Get used to the motion of the water," Finn said. "Paddle to adjust your position."

Gabi tried to follow his instructions. It had been a long time since she'd been in the ocean, and she realized lake water was different. Wobbling through the next steps of surfing while on her knees, she prepared herself to crouch on the board.

"Hey, Gabi," her brother called. "Remember that time I sent a wake in your direction and you rode on your butt for at least thirty seconds?"

Gabi shot her brother a playful scowl. "Remember that time I sent a wake in your direction and you did a flip in the air and ended up doing a belly flop?"

Nick gave a good-natured laugh. "I'll cut you some slack for the time change."

"I don't need any slack," she grumbled, noting that her ex was laughing with Nick. *Why had she agreed to this?*

Determined, she focused on the instructor's voice. Deep, with just a hint of a rasp, she thought. Sexy…

"Gabi, are you going to get on your board?" he called.

Gabi winced, realizing she'd allowed herself to get distracted again. "I'm fine," she said. "Just fine." She successfully managed to mount the board on her knees, but every time she tried to stand, she fell off. She swore under her breath, refusing to give up.

"Here," Finn said. "Let me hold the board for you."

He was so gentle and encouraging that she immediately relaxed. "Thanks," she said, and although it took two attempts, she stood on the board.

"Good job," he said. "You have a wave coming in a few seconds…"

Gabi didn't hear the rest of what he said because she was so focused on keeping her balance. Suddenly, she felt the water push her board forward and she swallowed a squeal.

"Go, girl, go," Finn called.

Euphoria rushed through her at the sensation of being one with the wave. One second later, the wave shifted and she lost her footing, falling headfirst into the water.

Down, down she went. Her cheek scraped the bottom and she scrambled to rise to the surface, but it felt as if everything was upside down. Panic raced through her. She opened her mouth to scream, gulping in salt water. Her eyes burned, her throat and lungs felt as if they were on fire.

Suddenly, strong arms lifted her to the surface. She spluttered and coughed as she tried to breathe. She blinked to get the stinging sensation from her eyes. "Oh, my—" She convulsed into another hacking fit.

"Shallow breaths," she heard Finn say and Gabi tried to follow his instruction.

She choked her way through several more inhalations and finally took a tiny bit of air without coughing. She felt him lift her above the water.

"Careful," she managed over another cough. "You'll get a hernia."

"You're no trouble," he said.

The next thing she knew, Finn was setting her down on the sand. She couldn't remember much after drinking more than her share of the Pacific.

Gabi looked up to find herself surrounded by her brother and his fireman friends, all staring at her as if she needed to be rescued. "I'm fine," she said before anyone could speak.

"Are you sure?" Nick asked, leaning down beside her. "You don't look too good."

"Thank you," she deadpanned.

"Well, I just mean your face is kinda scratched and red and—"

Embarrassed that all these rescuer-type men were gawking at her, she pushed herself from the ground. She'd spent a lifetime trying to keep up with her brother. Even though she was tired and a little shaken from her spill, she wasn't going to let anyone see that. "I'm ready to go again," she said, looking toward Finn.

She saw a flash of admiration cross his face. "If that's what you want—"

"Hell, no," Nick said. "Mom will kill me. She's already going to be pissed when she sees your face."

"Oh, it can't be that bad," she said and pressed her fingers against her cheek. When she looked at her hand, she saw a little blood. "Nothing a dab of antibiotic ointment can't fix."

"I have that," Finn said. "This is also my last class of the day. Will you take a rain check?"

Relief slid through her. The truth was, a break would do her good. "That'll work."

"I'll give you my card," Finn said. He jogged to the surf hut and brought back a tube of antibiotic cream. "Head up," he said and dabbed her cheek, temple and forehead. "Wouldn't be a bad idea for you to sit in the shade while we finish the class, unless you want to head back to your room."

"No, I'll watch," she said.

"Grab a bottle of water from the fridge in the hut," he told her and gave a loud whistle to the rest of the class. "Let's catch another wave, guys."

Gabi found the water in the fridge and a chair underneath a tree. Sinking into it, she savored the cool liquid as it slid down her parched, scratchy throat. Her gaze followed the movements of the surfing instructor. He was all muscle, and the graceful way he took the waves captured her interest. A combination of strength, control and going with the flow. It could have been a lesson in life. A surfer was making her philosophical? Gabi rolled her eyes at herself and mentally switched gears. He probably had a girlfriend. Or two. With that body, maybe three. Feeling suddenly restless, she rose and decided to go back to her room. She had work to do, and not much time until dinner.

Gabi worked until six. A call from Steven Jackson, the good friend who'd agreed to join her for this circus, interrupted her progress. "Hey," she said. "I thought you would be in the air."

"You haven't looked at the weather, have you?" he asked. "The Midwest got hit by a blizzard. Everything is shut down. Nothing going out of O'Hare for at least twenty-four hours."

Gabi's stomach sank. Even though she and Steven were just friends, she'd counted on having him here as a buffer against any questions about her romantic life. "Oh, no." She immediately clicked on the television and found the weather channel. Video footage featured meteorologists in driving snow. "It looks horrible."

"Yeah, it is. I'm sorry I'm not gonna be able to make it. Trust me. I'd rather be in Kauai than stuck here."

Gabi appreciated his sincerity, but really dreaded having to face questions from her family. "I wish you could be here, too."

"If anyone gives you a hard time, tell them to jump in the ocean. It probably won't be that bad. Everyone usually focuses on the bride and groom. And it's only a few days. Maybe you should try and enjoy yourself," he said.

"Look who's talking. You wrote the book on over-achieving."

He laughed. "Yeah, well, you've been giving me a run for my money, lately. Promise me you'll have a cocktail out on the beach?"

"I'll force myself," she said. "At least this weather shouldn't mess up your work schedule, since you'd already booked the time off."

"I'd made arrangements for video meetings, so nothing will change unless I add some extra calls after the weather clears," he said.

"Sounds like you've got it all under control," she said. "I'll talk to you when I get back."

"Give me a call. Don't forget the meeting for the Chicago Chamber of Commerce is next week."

"It's on my calendar. Another assignment from my dad. He likes the company to keep a high profile whenever possible. Take care," she said and hung up, feeling glum. At least Steven had a good excuse for not coming. Chicago was notorious for its winter weather, and though locals took blizzards in stride, the airports had been known to close down for days when treacherous weather hit. Her brother and his fiancée were lucky everyone else had flown out ahead of time.

Gabi sighed and repeated Steven's advice like a refrain. *Everyone will focus on the bride and groom. It's only a few days.*

CHAPTER TWO

UNABLE TO CONCENTRATE on work anymore, Gabi got
her mai tai as Helen and Steve had instructed and
went to the beach to drink it. She plopped down on
the sand and took a sip. More fun to drink it on the
beach, she thought, and made circles in the sand with
her index fingers. The sound of the ocean soothed
her nerves.

Suddenly, she heard a shriek and sand sprayed
across her lap. She looked up to see a little boy wearing board shorts and a T-shirt waving a stick. "I gotta
stick. Wanna pay tic-tac-toe?"

He was the cutest thing she'd seen all day. She
set down her drink. "Sure," she said. "Why not?"

The boy drew the grid for the game in the sand.
"You go first," he said without enunciating the *r*.

"Thank you very much," she said and put an X
in one of the boxes.

"Kai," a man called from behind them. "How
many times have I told you not to run off?"

Gabi immediately recognized the man as Finn,
her surfing instructor from the morning. He gave
her a nod. "Sorry if he's bothering you."

"Not at all," she said. "I was actually happy for the distraction."

The little boy shifted from one foot to the other. "I only runned a little bit."

Gabi couldn't help noticing that Finn looked just as good dressed in slacks and a shirt as he had half-naked earlier that morning. He cleaned up nicely, she thought.

Finn knelt down and motioned for Kai to look at him. "You know the deal. You're not supposed to run off. It's my job to make sure you're safe. And it's your job to help me."

The little boy gave a solemn nod. "Can I pay tic-tac-toe now?"

Finn sighed. "If Miss Gabi Foster is okay with it," he said, meeting her gaze.

"I'm fine, and now I know your name," she said to the boy. "Kai."

"Kai, say, 'It's nice to meet you, Miss Foster,'" Finn instructed.

"S'nice-to-meet-you," Kai said, rushing his words as he drew an O in the center square.

Gabi smiled and nodded. "Nice strategy." She randomly chose another space for her X.

They continued taking turns until Kai won the game and began to skip in big circles. "You didn't have to let him win," Finn said.

"Who says I let him?" she asked. "It's been a long time since I played."

Finn chuckled and sat down beside her. "Did he give you that sand?" he asked, pointing to the sand on her dress.

"Most unique pickup I've ever experienced," she said. "He's very cute, but I bet he's a handful."

"You've got that right," he said and raked a hand through his hair. "I had to hit the ground running trying to figure out how to be a dad since his real parents—my brother and his wife—died in an accident two years ago."

Sympathy cut through her. "Oh, my goodness, that's terrible. I'm so sorry. For both of you."

Finn shrugged. "Who knows why things like that happen? You just have to make the best of it."

"Well, he certainly looks healthy and happy," she said.

"Yeah, and we're working on his slight speech impediment. When he gets excited, he runs all his words together and it's hard to understand him. Tough for me and his nanny, Alani." He narrowed his eyes and gave a sharp whistle. "Kai, stay out of the water. We'll go swimming tomorrow, not today." He turned back to Gabi. "Always gotta be watching," he said. "But enough about me. How's the wedding going?"

"Great," she said with as much enthusiasm as she could muster.

He nodded toward her cocktail. "Is that why

you're knocking back an umbrella drink on the beach by yourself?"

She glanced at the forgotten mai tai. "I never knew tic-tac-toe could be so distracting," she joked, then sighed. "It's just a little complicated. I work for my father and I'm in the middle of trying to broker a significant deal because I have a relationship with a big drugstore chain. If I succeed, that could make him finally believe in me, so I really need to be working. This is my brother's second marriage, and I think his first wife is amazing. I'm not totally sold on the woman he's marrying. She's fine. She's just not Megan. And then there's the fact that my ex of less than a year is here. I invited a friend to act as a buffer for me, but he had to cancel due to weather. So I may have to endure some pitying looks. And if there's one thing I hate—"

"It's to be pitied," he finished for her. "Yeah, I saw some of that during the lesson. You were ready to drown yourself and go right back out into the ocean." He gave her a thoughtful glance. "If your buffer friend is a romantic interest, can't you just keep bringing him up in conversation?"

She grimaced and shook her head. "No romance there. Zip. Zero."

"Hmm," he said and glanced at Kai. "If you're desperate, I could fill in. What's on the agenda?" he asked, returning his gaze to hers.

The intensity in his green eyes gave her a jolt

that traveled all the way to her toes. She opened her mouth, unsure what to say. She couldn't imagine why he would offer such a thing. Unless...

"You don't have to do me such a big favor. I'm not going to sue you because I almost drowned earlier."

Finn laughed and shook his head. "Besides the fact that you'd have a hard time suing me since you signed the release form, maybe I'm just interested in the free food and the company."

Gabi stared at him in disbelief. "Really? That would be great," her mouth said before she'd thought it all the way through. Gabi blinked at herself. Well, now she'd committed. "Dinner's going to be in about an hour." She grimaced. "With limbo."

He chuckled. "Then I'm assuming I'm dressed okay. I can take Kai over to his nanny's house. She lives pretty close by." He shot her a sly look. "Are you planning to limbo?"

"Not in a dress, and I'm not planning on changing."

"Well, darn," he said. "I would have liked to have seen that."

GABI FRESHENED UP FOR dinner. The scrapes on her face from her tumble in the ocean were still tender, so she applied antibiotic cream in lieu of cosmetics. She walked to the garden patio where several guests were already gathered.

Gabi's mother caught sight of her and waved her over.

"Hi, Mom, you're looking great," Gabi said and extended her hands to embrace her. Her mother, Jean Foster, was a petite beauty with perfectly coiffed blond hair. She wore a pink shift dress with a stylish light bolero jacket and looked, as she often did, as if she'd just stepped off a catalog shoot. Her mother was particular about her appearance, but she was also one of the sweetest women in the world. She was the kind of person who made everyone feel special, and she'd done the same with Gabi throughout her life.

"Oh dear, it's so good to see you, but—" Her mother gasped as she hugged Gabi. "What on earth happened to your face?"

"Oh. My cheek," Gabi said and winced. "A little scuffle. You should see the other guy."

Cara appeared by Jean's side. "And that is one of the reasons I refused to take the surfing lesson this afternoon. Nick thought I was being silly, but he doesn't now."

Her mother shot Gabi a look of exasperation. "Did Nick put you up to this? I wouldn't be surprised." She gave a clucking sound and looked at her future daughter-in-law. "Gabi's been trying to keep up with Nick since the day she was born. It's a wonder she didn't become a fireman, too."

"I considered it," Gabi said. "But I decided I didn't like the way the fireman's uniform looked on me," she said and quickly changed the subject. "Have you seen the twins?" she asked, speaking of her brother's daughters from his previous marriage.

"Yes, they're just getting ready," her mother said. "They were great on the plane, but I'm sure they're exhausted."

"Megan is such a trouper to bring them. She should be up for best mom and great human being awards," Gabi said, thinking about how hard it must have been for Megan to bring both girls on such a long flight.

"I agree," her mother said. "We're all lucky that Megan is so devoted."

Gabi met Cara's gaze, then Cara looked down and nodded. "She's a wonderful, wonderful mother. Nick and I both appreciate the sacrifice she's making so that the girls can be here."

"We just need to make sure she gets a break while she's here. She's one of those self-sacrificing types who may not tell us when she's tired," Gabi said.

"That's a good point." Cara looked as if she were at a loss.

"Oh, I plan to take the girls whenever I can," her mother said.

"Thank you. That's very generous of you," Cara said, looking relieved.

"It's my pleasure. I adore them, as I'm sure you do," Jean replied.

"I do. I'm just going to have to work on the mother part. Megan seems so perfect at it," Cara confessed.

Gabi felt a sliver of sympathy for her brother's fiancée. It was the first time she'd seen her exhibit a lack of confidence about anything, and Gabi felt herself liking the woman more for it.

Her mother patted Cara on the arm. "You've got time."

Another young woman, stunningly beautiful and glowing with pregnancy, stepped into the group. "I was afraid I was late. Did I hear something about motherhood?" she asked Cara, smiling as she patted her belly. "Do you have some special news?"

Cara gave a laugh that bordered on hysterical. "Oh, no. I'm not pregnant. We were talking about Nick's—" She broke off and took a breath. "Nick's and my girls."

"Oh," the woman said, appearing confused.

Gabi's mother extended her hand to the pregnant woman. "I don't believe we've met. I'm Jean Foster, Nick's mother."

The woman nodded and shook her hand. "It's very nice to meet you. I'm Candace Kenyon, Bill Kenyon's wife."

Oh, goody, Gabi thought. Between the trouble with the account she was trying to bag, her disastrous surfing lesson, and her faux boyfriend getting stuck in Chicago, her day was rounding out to be one hot mess.

"I'm Gabi," she said, because it was the polite thing to do. "I'm Nick's sister." *The woman your new hubby dumped as soon as he met you.*

AN HOUR AND a half after leaving the beach with Kai, Finn returned to the resort, looking for Gabi. He had surprised himself by volunteering. He was fascinated by both her drive for success and her more tender side. He'd never be able to forget the image of her playing the game with his nephew...his son.

Women hit on Finn every other day. He rarely offered to attend any sort of wedding events. Those parties were nonstop on Kauai, and he'd tasted too many in the last two years. But Gabi seemed different, and he couldn't resist spending some extra time with her.

His life had changed drastically since he'd lived in Manhattan. Wall Street had been his game until his brother and sister-in-law died. Although there'd been plenty of his sister-in-law's family in Hawaii ready to help with Kai, there must have been a reason that his brother and sister-in-law had chosen him as Kai's guardian. Goodbye, Manhattan. Hello, Kauai. He'd been a businessman and turned himself into a surfing instructor.

He spotted Gabi at a table on the opposite side of the patio talking to a gray-haired man and walked toward her. She smiled and waved at him. Finn arrived at her side. "Sorry if I'm late," he said.

"No problem," Gabi said. "Please meet my father, Preston Foster. This is Finn Beckett."

Preston nodded. "Pleasure to meet you. How did you meet my daughter?"

"He saved me from drowning when I was taking the surfing lesson this afternoon," Gabi said.

"An exaggeration," Finn added quickly.

Preston's eyes glinted with laughter. "My daughter has been known to push herself when challenged."

"I'm wondering if that's a learned trait from her father," Finn ventured.

Preston smiled proudly and extended his hand. "I can tell you're a smart man."

"Just observant," Finn said and shook the man's hand.

Preston glanced at the other side of the party. "My wife is calling me. Enjoy the party."

"Thank you," Finn said and felt Gabi's gaze on him.

"Very well done," she said.

"You think?" he asked.

"Thank you," she said. "Food and cocktails. What's your pleasure?"

"Lead me to the food. I'm starving," he said.

Laughing, she flagged a waitress.

Finn stuffed himself, then slugged down several glasses of water. He'd be driving Kai home after this shindig, so he had to stay sober. Several people came over to introduce themselves, including a tall man and a pregnant woman.

Finn felt Gabi stiffen even though he wasn't touching her.

"Hey, Gabi. I wanted to come over and say hi," the man said and turned to Finn. "I'm Bill Kenyon and this is my wife, Candace."

"I met her earlier tonight. Congratulations to both of you," Gabi said.

"Thank you," Candace said. "How did you two meet?"

"Earlier today, when he was teaching a surfing class," Bill said and chuckled. "Gabi drank some ocean water and Finn had to pull her out."

"Yeah," Finn said. "I'm the lucky one. I understand her original date couldn't make it due to weather, so I asked her right away. No-brainer."

Bill stared at both of them. "Yeah. Have a nice night," he said and led his wife away.

Gabi looked at Finn in surprise. "Wow. That's two in one night. I don't know what to say."

"Too easy," he said. "You wanna dance?"

Her eyes softened. "That sounds wonderful."

He pulled her against him. She was warm and oh, so feminine. Finn hadn't let himself go in this way in several months. Once he'd taken custody of his brother's son, Kai had become his priority. Gabi reminded him that he was a man...with his own needs. But he could tell she was very focused on her career. He'd have to treat this time with her as a temporary pleasure.

"So, what made you take pity on me?" she asked.

He shook his head. "It wasn't pity," he said. "It was curiosity. The woman who tried to win at surfing then played tic-tac-toe with my nephew."

"I'm a weirdo," she said.

He spun her around and drew her close. "I like your kind of weird."

She laughed and the sound filled him up. The last two years had been full of crazy adjustments. A move from Manhattan to Kauai. A new career that had demanded all kinds of changes. No more hedging on physical fitness. Becoming not just an expert at surfing, but at teaching it. Managing it all like a businessman.

"You don't need to feel like less because of your ex or your father," he said. "You've got way too much going for you."

"You're the first person who's said that to me," she said.

"That's because I'm incredibly perceptive."

She met his gaze for a long moment. "In another situation, I'd think you were trying to seduce me, but you and I know you don't have to work this hard. So, thank you. You're more than I thought you were."

"What did you think I was?"

"Surfer dude, until I saw you with Kai. Then I

decided you were a surfer dude with character and a great kid?"

He nodded. "Good assessment."

Finn wanted to dance with her longer. He liked the way she felt in his arms. But then the DJ announced the limbo competition was starting.

"You don't have to do this," Gabi said.

He chuckled and shrugged. "It could be fun," he said and headed across the patio.

He felt Gabi watching him as he surpassed her brother and several of his friends. The duel came down to Finn and her ex, Bill. He busted his abs and back lowering himself under the bar that last time after Bill failed.

The crowd roared, but he was looking for Gabi. Finally, he spotted her clapping. Then she gave him a thumbs-up, and he felt a crazy rush of exhilaration. Finn walked toward her.

"They love you and hate you. Firemen are crazy fit, so they expect to be the winners in athletic contests," Gabi said.

He rolled his shoulders, working out the kinks. "Always best not to be overconfident."

"Have you ever been overconfident?" she asked.

"Oh, yeah," he said. "And becoming an instant parent will give you instant humility."

"What did you do before you became a father?" she asked.

"I was an East Coast city man. It was a big change to move here."

"I would have never suspected that. You seem like the total surfer dude," she said.

"You can't hit thirty without twenty-nine years of living," he said.

She nodded. "You have a much different life than mine, that's for sure. I'm working twelve hours a day and trying to get my father to take me seriously."

"You like that?" he asked.

She shrugged. "It's what I've got to do right now. The same way you have to do what you've got to do."

Finn remembered when a few of his years of hard work had been so intense they'd been a blur to him. He'd had to be attuned to tiny changes in the market, fluctuations in the economy and trends. He'd always felt as if he had one foot in the present and one foot in the future. He'd often been in a detached, clinically observant state. Not anymore. Now, he had to stay on top of a little boy's emotions and needs, past, present and future. It was a messier, more absorbing challenge, but he was adjusting. It was like surfing. Sometimes he stayed on top of the wave. Other times, he got thrown into the water. The important part was getting up and continuing to try.

"Yeah," he said and the differences between them hit him hard. In another situation, he would have pulled back and avoided Gabi. In this case, however, he'd already committed. He had told her he would be her escort for the wedding weekend. A rare impulsive act for him.

"Do you need to head back to your cell phone or would you like a walk on the beach?" he asked.

She shot him a look of indecision, then shrugged. "Walk on the beach. I won't be able to do that next week."

He took her hand and led her toward the sand. "Good choice," he said, knowing everything about Gabi was temporary.

The breeze blew over them.

"Cooler than I expected," she said, shivering.

"You want to go back?" Finn asked.

"No. I'll warm up. Or remember Chicago," she said with a laugh. "You said you lived in the east. Did you ever live anywhere where it was cold in winter?"

"Just Boston and Manhattan," he said.

She winced. "Ouch. Boston?"

"Manhattan was just as bad. You expected it in Boston," he said.

"How did you manage the transition to Kauai?" she asked.

"The temperature change was a lot easier than Boston or Manhattan," he said.

"I can see that," she said.

"The change in responsibility," he said. "Not so much."

They walked a bit before talking.

"So, what made you become a surfer guy? I imagine you didn't teach surfing on the East Coast."

Finn nodded. "I had to figure out my potential skills," he said. "I'd learned to surf when visiting my brother here several years ago. I decided to turn it into a business because it would give me flexibility in taking care of Kai. I realized I couldn't maintain the hours I worked while raising a little boy on my own. On top of that, Kai's mother was Hawaiian and many of her relatives live her. I wanted Kai to grow up with a sense of his culture and I knew it would be a lot easier to do it here than in New York. My father passed away a few years ago, and my mother lives in Florida with her new husband, so the choice seemed clear."

"Impressive," Gabi said. "But how did you win over the resorts? After all, you're not a native."

"I busted my ass and gave them a cut."

Gabi smiled. "And we like that about you," she said with a big laugh.

Finn liked her big laugh. He hadn't met a woman like her in a long time, if ever.

Acting on impulse, he pulled her closer and pressed his mouth against hers. He tasted a combination of surprise and pleasure. She pulled back.

"You don't have to do that," she said. "It was nice of you to volunteer to help me out during the wedding celebration. But you don't have to kiss me."

"What if I want to?" he asked.

She opened her mouth but appeared confused. "It might not be a good idea. It's not as if I'm going to be here very long."

"Carpe diem," he said and took her hand to lead her back to the resort.

GABI WENT TO BED, but not before she checked both her email and cell phone. At the same time, she couldn't stop thinking about Finn. She responded to her messages, but her mind was spinning. She couldn't remember meeting a man like him, a man as passionate for life as Finn seemed to be.

But it was early days. She'd learned the hard way that the first stages of a relationship didn't predict how things would turn out.

Gabi forced herself to close her eyes and tried to fall asleep. She took several deep breaths and counted backward from one hundred. That didn't stop Finn's face from sneaking through her mind. She finally fell into a restless sleep.

Gabi awakened to the sound of someone knocking on the door. She sat up and brushed sleep from her eyes. From the slivers of light peeking through the curtains, she glimpsed a sheet of paper on the floor. She pushed aside her covers and picked it up. *Wedding activities for the day: Morning on your own then hula dancing before lunch.*

Gabi groaned. Well aware of the fact that she wasn't the most graceful and coordinated woman in the world, she'd learned years ago to stick to a side-to-side shuffle when dancing. She decided it would be best for her to miss this little event…until she saw a handwritten note on the bottom of the page. *Megan tells me Grace and Sarah can't wait to learn hula with Aunt Gabi. Hugs, Cara.*

Well, darn. If her sweet nieces were determined to hula, then the least she could do was show up and wiggle her hips with them. Since Grace and Sarah had been born prematurely, they still had some lingering problems. Grace used a walker and sometimes needed a wheelchair, and Sarah had some vision issues. This was one more example of what a good job Megan had done with the girls. They were game to try just about anything. Even though this could be one more source of humiliation for her, there was no way Gabi could turn down her nieces.

FINN HAD GIVEN several group surfing lessons at both resort beach locations, but up till now, no one had captured his imagination the way Gabi had. When she'd pulled back after he kissed her, he'd wondered if she was rethinking his offer to escort her to the rest of the wedding activities. Although the words would have to be yanked from his throat, he knew he would be disappointed.

Taking a quick break for an early lunch, Finn headed toward the resort snack bar. On his way, he heard Hawaiian music and lots of laughter. Peeking past the beach where he gave lessons, he saw a group of women and children taking a hula lesson.

The sight of a little girl gyrating while hanging onto a walker tugged at his heart. Next to her, a woman stood waving her arms and wiggling her hips in a way that was somehow both amusing and inviting. Finn immediately identified the tall, big-boned woman as Gabi. Another little girl on her other side was giggling and pointing at Gabi.

He shook his head. *Damn, that woman was a good sport.* He waited until the end of the song and jogged toward her. "Looks like you're ready to entertain at the luau tonight," he said from behind her.

Gabi whipped around and shot him a mocking glare. "Easy for you to say. Don't you want to join in?"

He lifted his hand. "Lunch break for me. Kai's pretty good, though—it's a shame he's not here. Are these your nieces?" he asked, nodding at the children.

"Yes, they are. This is Grace," she said of the little girl with the walker. "And this is Sarah. Girls, this is Mr. Beckett. He's a surfing instructor."

"Hi," they chorused shyly.

"You girls are great hula dancers. Are you sure you haven't done this before?"

Sarah shook her head. "This is our first time. It's Aunt Gabi's first time, too." She laughed. "She's so funny."

"Thanks," Gabi teased, and ruffled her niece's hair. "It's lunchtime for us, too. We'd better go. Any near-drownings this morning?"

"No. Boring after yesterday," he returned.

"I'm sure you were glad you didn't have to drag anyone out of the ocean and practically give mouth-to-mouth."

"Sorry to say we don't do mouth-to-mouth anymore. It's all compression. A shame, isn't it?" he said.

"Stop the flirting. It won't get you anywhere," she said.

"Then how about a tour this afternoon? I'll do a much better job than the tour guide assigned to the wedding party, and you can escape the wedding mania for a while."

"I really should do some work," she said, clearly torn.

"Speed text, then. I've got another class after I grab a bite to eat. I'll pick you up in an hour and a half."

"That sounds more like an instruction than a request," she said.

"Are you saying no?" he challenged her.

"Well," she said. "No, but—"

"I'll take that as a yes. Wear your swimsuit under your shorts and T-shirt," he said, and jogged away.

CHAPTER THREE

GABI LOST HERSELF in work, studying new market reports and touching base with clients. She put together a proposal for the release of a limited number of organic cosmetic products since her father was reluctant to launch the entire line at once. Gabi was lucky because the admins were overly conscientious about pleasing her, seeing as her father was head of the company. She tried not to pull rank, but her name caused people to act. Lost in thought, she jumped when a knock sounded at her door.

She glanced at the time and winced. Rushing to the door, she opened it to Finn. "I'm sorry. I'm not ready and I really have too much—"

"I can wait for you to get ready. It would be wrong for you to come to Kauai and not see some scenery. Think of it as a unique opportunity for inspiration in the future. I'll give you five minutes. I'll be in the yellow Jeep in the parking lot. Going top down today."

"But," she said, but something in his eyes stopped her. Some sort of wisdom and knowledge bigger than the dozens of emails to which she felt obliged to respond this moment. "You're right. It's not as if I'll be here next week."

"Exactly," he said. "See you in five."

Gabi closed the door after he left and reconsidered for three seconds before she saved her work on her laptop and changed her clothes. Finn was right. It would be pretty sad if she didn't at least get a peek at the island, and she'd much rather go with him than a formal tour group. After applying sunscreen, she grabbed a cap, a towel and her bag with her cell phone, of course. Her phone was her security blanket. She could check messages and respond anytime.

She jogged to the parking lot and spotted Finn leaning against the yellow Jeep. Her heart took a little dip at how naturally appealing he was, and she immediately chastised herself. Sure, he was good-looking and charming, but nothing important was going to develop between them. She was just a woman who had nearly drowned in his arms, and he was just a nice guy who'd agreed to step in and help her out as an escort. That was it.

He helped her into the vehicle and buzzed out of the parking lot. It didn't seem possible, but once they left the landscaped setting of the resort, the scenery became even more thick and lush.

"I can't believe how green it is," she mused. "It's almost like a jungle."

"You would understand if you lived here," he said. "We get our share of rain. We may even get some

today. But we also get more than our share of rain-
bows."

"Oh, that must be wonderful. I can't remember
the last time I saw a rainbow. Winter hit early this
year, so most of what I've seen is snow. Not unusual
for Chicago, and I'm not complaining," she said, but
she thought it sure was nice not having to dress in
wool and multiple layers. The breeze felt heavenly
on her face.

"Do you ever get tired of living in paradise?" she
asked him.

"I've felt a little claustrophobic every now and
then, but I have a good reason to be here, and I may
take Kai back east for a visit next year. I want him
to feel safe and secure before we make that kind of
trip. It changed my perspective when I realized it's
not all about me."

She admired and envied the fact that he seemed so
at peace with himself. Gabi seemed to struggle with
her sense of well-being on a regular basis. She felt
a watery mist and looked upward. "What is that?"

He chuckled. "Rain, the soft kind. We get some
hard storms, too, though."

"But it feels so light," she said. "Not even as intense as a sprinkler."

He nodded. "Happens all the time. You must have
been inside when it misted earlier this afternoon."

"I bet it can really wreck your hairstyle," she said,
rubbing her hand over her slightly damp hair.

"That's why a lot of women have wash-and-wear styles or put their hair on top of their heads. Hold on. We're headed up a steep hill," he said and turned onto a narrow road.

Gabi grabbed the door strap to secure herself for the bumpy road as she gawked at the landscape. They continued riding for several more moments, then Finn took a sharp turn.

"This is one of the reasons you couldn't stay in your hotel room all afternoon," he said, pulling next to a breathtaking waterfall.

Gabi shivered at the beauty. "Oh, wow," she said and nodded. "It's just beautiful."

"And it's one of many," he said.

Gabi glanced upward from the falls. "Look, a rainbow."

"We see those many times a month," he said. "That was one of the reasons I could adjust to living here. The sight of a rainbow brought me a sense of peace, especially when I first moved here."

Feeling a sense of peace herself, Gabi nodded. "I can see how you'd feel that way." She looked at Finn and felt the connection between them snap and sizzle. The sensation was so strong it took her off guard.

Suddenly a pouring rain descended on them.

Finn laughed. "Oops. Guess we'd better cover up," he said and raced outside the car to put the convertible top in place. Gabi scrambled to help him, but there wasn't much she could do, so she climbed back in. Finn returned to the driver's side and smiled at her. "Ready for your next Kauai super sight?"

"Sure," she said, even though she was drenched.

For the next couple of hours, Finn drove past beautiful jungles and more waterfalls. She gasped every time she saw the falls. It seemed every other time she saw a waterfall, she also glimpsed a rainbow. The sights were so beautiful they took her breath away.

"Do you see these falls every day?" she asked.

"Pretty often. It's great, but remember we also have a rainy season, so there can be flooding" he said.

"Do you live close to here?"

He glanced at her. "As a matter of fact, I do. Would you like to visit Hale Beckett?"

"Does Hale mean house?"

"It does," he said.

She smiled at him. "I most certainly would."

He made a turn worthy of a superhero and roared away. "As the lady wishes."

He took several turns and pulled into a clearing surrounded by trees next to a beach. A house stood in the middle of the greenery. No sooner had Finn stopped than Kai opened the door and stood on the landing, waving his arms.

"Daddy-Finn," Kai yelled at the top of his lungs.

Finn laughed, stepped out of the Jeep and pulled Kai into his arms. "Have you had a good day?"

"Yes," Kai said. "But you promised a swim today."

"So I did," Finn said. "Look who I brought with me."

Kai glanced toward the Jeep and his eyes lit up. "Gabi!"

"Miss Foster," Finn corrected.

"Miss Gabi," Kai said, and ran to her side of the car.

Flattered by the boy's enthusiasm, Gabi got out of the car and opened her arms. Kai immediately hugged her. "Will you go swimming?"

"Soon," she said. "I should check my cell phone first."

Kai frowned and turned to Finn. "Let's go swimming."

"We have a guest," Finn said. "Let's show Gabi our house first. She may want some water and a snack."

Kai shifted from one foot to the other. "Do we have to?" he asked.

Finn ran one of his hands through Kai's hair. "Yes, we do."

He led Kai and Gabi to the house. A slightly plump Polynesian woman sat in the kitchen, her hair pulled back into a bun.

"We have four bedrooms, just in case Nanny Alani wants to stay overnight and we have a guest," Finn mentioned. "How are you feeling, Alani?"

The woman slowly fluttered her eyes. "I'm just a little tired."

"Have you made an appointment with the doctor?" Finn asked. "You've been tired often, lately."

Alani nodded. "I have an appointment in a few days. Introduce me to this lovely woman."

Gabi couldn't help smiling at her graciousness.

"Gabi Foster, this is Nanny Alani," Finn said.

"So nice to meet you," Gabi said.

"And you," Alani said. "Welcome to Hale Beckett."

Finn led Gabi through the living room, dining room and bedrooms. She noticed that toys were scattered across Kai's bedroom floor. The house was filled with windows and Finn finally led her to a lanai that afforded a gorgeous view of the forest surrounding the house.

"It's beautiful," she said.

"Thank you," Finn said. "I had some work done on it, and since this is an island, getting anything done takes some time." He led her and Kai outside of the screened porch to two swings attached to strong trees. "They work for adults, too," he said.

Gabi gazed at the swings longingly. "They couldn't hold me."

"Bet they could," he said. "I built them for grown-ups."

She narrowed her eyes at him. "Will you take me to the hospital if they fail?"

He chuckled. "Yes, but you overestimate your weight."

"You're too kind," she said.

"Try it. I dare you," he said.

Gabi took a deep breath. "You know, I almost drowned the first time I took suggestions from you."

"And I saved you," he said.

She groaned. "I hope I don't end up in the hospital," she muttered and headed toward the swing. After setting her purse aside, she plopped onto the rubber seat, pushed off and began to pump. Surprisingly enough, she didn't fall and the swing didn't break. Gabi simply soared. She felt like a child again. It was the most freeing feeling she'd experienced in ages.

The breeze flew through her hair and she devoured the experience. She pumped for several moments, wishing she could swing forever, but she could tell that Kai was growing impatient. He'd been waiting for a swim since yesterday. She couldn't deprive him, she thought, and slowed.

Skimming her feet on the ground, she came to a stop. "That was the most fun I've had in years," she confessed to Finn.

"Then you should do it more often," he said, and she saw a mix of emotions in his eyes that fascinated her.

"Time to swim," Kai yelled.

"He's right," Gabi said. "He's been waiting since yesterday at least."

"Let's go, then," Finn said and extended his hand to her. She ran along with Finn and Kai to the beach.

Kai ran right into the surf.

"Kai, you know the rules. Wait for me," he called and swore under his breath.

Finn ran toward his nephew and swooped the boy into his arms before he was swallowed by a wave. Gabi followed into the edge of the water.

Kai laughed with joy and kicked. "I want the waves," he said.

"Not when you run in without me," Finn said. "Back to the beach."

Finn carried him back to the sand. "Now show me the right way to go into the ocean."

Kai gave a heavy sigh. "Take me with you into the ocean, Daddy Finn," he said and offered his hand.

Finn nodded and took Kai's hand. "Let's go."

Gabi watched as the two of them plunged into the surf. Finn lifted Kai as the waves plunged over them. Kai chortled with glee and pleasure. He was clearly a water child.

Gabi couldn't help enjoying watching his fun with the waves. He was a natural.

Finn lifted Kai over and over, and only allowed him to experience a dunking now and then. Finally, Finn dragged Kai ashore. Kai looked water-logged, but, oh, so happy.

Finn tossed the boy up into the air and both laughed. The sound and sensation was so infectious she couldn't stop herself from laughing, too. The joy of the moment was too much. Everything inside her bubbled up to overflowing. She couldn't remember ever feeling this way.

When Finn set Kai down, Gabi instinctively extended her arms and the boy rushed toward her and hugged her. She relished the sensation of his sweet, warm, little-boy body.

Kai pulled away then rolled in the sand.

Finn winced. "Kai, now you're going to need a shower before you can even go in the house."

Kai jumped up and down. "When can we go into the waves again?" he asked.

"In a day or two," Finn said. "You wear me out. Let's get something to eat." He pulled Kai into his arms and walked toward the house.

Gabi followed them inside. Nanny Alani still sat in the kitchen.

"I fixed some poi," she said. "And I can stay over tonight."

"Are you sure?" Finn asked. "You said you were more tired than usual."

She shrugged. "Like I said, I have an appointment next week. It will help that I'm here instead of going back and forth to my house."

"If you're sure," Finn said.

Gabi sat down to eat with Finn and Kai. The meal was different, but delicious. She enjoyed chatting with Finn and Kai.

Suddenly, she realized she hadn't checked her phone in quite a while. She reached for her small purse, but her cell was missing.

Finn must have read the expression on her face. "What's wrong?"

"I can't find my cell phone. It's missing," she said, checking her purse another time.

"Are you sure?" he asked. "Let me check the car."

They looked everywhere—the car, the kitchen—but it was nowhere.

Gabi panicked. Her mind reeled with anxiety. What if she'd lost it? What if she couldn't respond to her clients? She and Finn looked for another half-hour and she grew more frantic.

"I don't know what to do," she said. "I must have my phone. I *must* have it."

Finn stared at her, his expression filled with understanding and a shade of disappointment. "Take it easy. We haven't finished looking."

"Take it easy?" she echoed. "I've spent the past year trying to work this deal, and it could blow up in my face right now."

"It's next to the swing," Kai admitted. His sweet face was sheepish. "I didn't want you talking while we swimmed."

Relief rushed through her, and she and Finn rushed to the swing. Gabi spotted her phone and picked it up, seeing the message light blinking. She took a deep breath. "This could have been a full-blown disaster," she said. "I don't know what I would've done if my phone was actually lost."

Finn patted her shoulder. "Hey, no one's life was in danger. It's not that big of a deal."

"It is to me," she said. "I'm sorry if you don't understand that."

Finn paused for a long moment, his easygoing nature suddenly gone. "Okay. I'm going to take a shower and get ready for the event tonight." Though Gabi wasn't part of the wedding rehearsal, the reception hall would be opened up to all the guests after dinner wound down.

"Thank you. I would appreciate it," Gabi said, still tense. "I may not have much time to spruce up, but you'll look great as usual."

"That's my job," he muttered. "Looking great for you."

IT DIDN'T TAKE Finn long to shower and get dressed. He escorted Gabi into the Jeep and drove down the mountain toward the resort.

During the drive, Finn struggled with his emotions. He knew that Gabi was an amazing woman, but her reaction to Kai hiding her cell phone bothered him. At the same time, he understood it. Years ago, he would have gone over the edge if someone had swiped his cell. Communication was too important to lose. Her response, however, just pointed to a huge reason why he'd better not fall for her. The only thing he could say in her favor was that she hadn't taken out her frustration on Kai. Still, he could tell she'd had to rein in her emotions.

"Any important messages?" he forced himself to ask.

"Just a couple," she said, and pushed her hair from her face.

It was obvious she was still upset. "Have you responded?" he asked.

"I'm working on it," she said.

He paused and took another approach. "Can I help you?"

He felt her silent surprise.

"Maybe," she said quietly. "Thank you for the offer."

"Don't make excuses. Just tell them you'll take care of them as soon as you can," he suggested.

"Do you think I should mention that I'm attending my brother's wedding?" she asked.

"It depends if you want to keep your job and personal life separate. Sometimes when you draw your clients into your private life, they become more invested, but it's a tricky road. Some clients like having the inside information," he said, although he usually preferred to draw a line between his business and personal lives.

She frowned. "I don't think my clients need to know everything about me."

"Good for you," he said and shot her a glance.

"Then why did you suggest it?" she asked.

"Just in case," he said.

"In case what?" she demanded. "In case I want to share everything with my clients?"

He smiled. "You proved my point."

"What point?"

"That you know how to set important boundaries. Sometimes when you're working a hard deal, it's tough to do that." He knew that Gabi was trying to prove herself to everyone in the world through her career. He wished he could help her make the leap to understanding that there were so many things in life more important than a job.

She frowned again. "Sometimes it sucks to be on call this much."

"That's something worth thinking about," he said. Although he had a strong feeling Gabi might one day value people and relationships over her job, he was pretty sure it wasn't going to happen now. With him.

As soon as Finn pulled into a parking space, Gabi tore off toward her room. "I'll see you as soon as I can," she said. "I won't be beauty-pageant beautiful."

"No worries. What kind of drink can I get you?" he asked.

"Could you wait fifteen minutes, then order a glass of white wine for me? I have a feeling my father may quiz me about work," she said.

"I can help with that," he said, but Gabi was already running.

Out of breath, she strode into her room and immediately turned on the shower and stripped. She took three and a half minutes to quick-wash her body, shampoo, condition and rinse. Outside the shower, she toweled off and plastered her hair into a messy bun at the back of her head.

She put on some of the organic tinted moisturizer, blush and lip gloss. Then she curled her eyelashes and colored them with mascara. Gabi refused to over-study the finished product as she pulled on her undergarments and a long sundress.

Taking several calming breaths, she grabbed her room key and stepped outside her door to find Finn leaning against the wall with a glass of wine. Her heart jolted.

"Well done," she said

"I was thinking the same thing," he said, and put a flower in her hair.

"Thanks." She was touched both by the flower and the wine. She took a sip. "How does the party look?"

"I don't know everyone, but it looks like things are a little chaotic," he said.

"What do you mean?" she asked as they walked toward the reception hall.

"I don't know. There's a weird vibe," he said.

"Really?" she said, curious. "What makes you say that?"

"The bride seems a little out of whack. Plus, her parents are here and apparently her father has brought his latest babe. She looks to be the same age as the bride," he said.

Gabi's heart sank. "Oh, no. That can't be easy for Cara."

"I thought you didn't like her," he said.

"I never said that. I just said I wasn't sure about how she would do with Nick's daughters." Gabi felt a stab of guilt. "But I wouldn't have wished this on her and Nick. Nick mentioned something about her parents' multiple marriages. This can't make her feel good."

"There you go, being thoughtful again," Finn said with a chuckle.

"I'm really not that thoughtful," she said.

"Agreed. You're a total wench," he said dryly.

She couldn't help smiling. "We'll see about that," she muttered as they walked toward the banquet room.

She stepped inside. The tables were dressed in fine linens, with flowers adorning the tops. Wedding guests milled about sipping cocktails and wine. A half beat later, her brother appeared in front of her.

"Have you seen Cara?" he asked, looking worried.

Gabi shook her head. "I just got here. Is there a problem?"

Nick raked his hand through his hair in obvious frustration. "She left the party a few moments ago. She's upset because of her father."

"He brought a teenager with him," Gabi said.

Nick managed a half smile. "Not quite, but close. And Cara's mother is wigging out."

"Because it's all about them instead of her. Right?" she said.

Nick sighed. "Yeah. I need to find her. If you see her, let me know. Right now, I'm not sure this wedding is going to happen. And Gabi, I really need her in my life."

CHAPTER FOUR

"WELL, THAT STINKS," Gabi said after Nick left.

Finn nodded. "I can see why the bride would be upset."

"Me, too," she said, frowning at him and taking a small sip of her wine. "I wonder if I should try to find Cara."

Finn shrugged. "I don't know. What does your gut tell you?" he asked.

"Hmm," she said. Her gut was twisting with regret. "I'll look for her. Keep your cell phone handy."

Gabi turned away from the party and walked to the beach. Following her instincts, she headed east across the sand. Gabi spotted a figure in the distance and walked in that direction.

Several steps later, she saw that the figure was a woman. Her future sister-in-law was sobbing. Gabi rushed forward.

Cara looked up and met her gaze. "Why are you here?" she asked almost defiantly.

"I'm just taking a walk on the beach," Gabi said with a shrug. She was lying, but she tried not to overthink it.

"Oh," Cara said, and looked as if someone had popped her balloon.

"What are you doing here?" Gabi asked.

Cara sighed. "Escaping my parents. They're both drama queens. I don't know who's worse, my mother or father. My father brought a woman—or is she a girl? The fact that she's so young is driving my mother crazy."

"It just makes him look like a fool. It has nothing to do with your mother or you," Gabi said.

"You think so?" Cara asked.

"I know so," Gabi said and sat down beside Cara.

With the breeze blowing over them, Gabi and Cara breathed in the sea air.

"Sometimes I wonder if I can be a good wife," Cara said. "I wonder if I can stay married."

"Because of your parents?" Gabi asked.

Cara nodded. "My father is a complete disaster and my mother isn't much better."

"Just because your parents are a disaster doesn't mean you are, too," Gabi said.

Cara slid her a glance. "Are you sure you believe that?"

Gabi took a deep breath and answered honestly. "In the beginning, I was afraid you wouldn't love Nick's girls the way they needed to be loved."

"And now?" Cara asked.

"Well, the truth is I think I've underestimated

you. I'm very impressed that you're taking a class, to learn to help parent the girls."

Cara sighed. "I'm actually terrified. I want to be good, but Megan is so incredibly perfect. At the same time, she's encouraging me to marry Nick. How can someone be so perfect?"

"I guess she can't help it," Gabi said, and they both laughed. "But I know my brother wants and needs you in his life. I hope you'll stay."

Cara's expression softened. "Thank you for coming to see me."

"Go see Nick. He's desperate for you," Gabi said.

Cara's eyes filled with tears. "I hate to make him feel sad."

"Then go make him feel happy. You're very good at it."

Cara gave her a long, deep hug then stood. "Thank you. I always thought you didn't like me."

"I think I was afraid to like you, but I don't feel that way now." Gabi stood and gave Cara another hug. "Happy wedding and marriage to my fabulous brother. He's a lucky guy."

"Thank you," Cara said. "Thank you so much."

Gabi and Cara walked back toward the resort. Just as they approached the sidewalk, Nick appeared, out of breath.

He stopped directly in front of Cara, his gaze totally fixed on her. "Are you okay?"

Cara took a deep breath. "I'm fine. I just needed to escape from my parents for a little while."

Nick took her hands in his and his expression was so full of longing that Gabi felt as if she shouldn't be watching the moment take place. It was so private, so emotional. "Next time you need to escape, let me run away with you," he said.

"Oh, Nick, I love you," Cara said and flew into his arms.

Gabi felt her eyes grow misty at the sight of them. "I, uh, need to go to the restroom," she muttered and quickly walked away. She was pretty sure her brother and his bride-to-be had been unaware of her during that moment. Gabi supposed that was the way it should be if one was truly in love.

She walked toward the party and immediately spotted Finn chatting with her mother and father. Her stomach clenched. *Oh, goody. One potential disaster after another.*

Mentally girding herself, she walked toward her parents and Finn. "There she is," Finn said, and opened his arms to her.

She walked into his safe embrace. "Hi. Are you having a good time?" she asked, nodding toward Finn and her parents.

"Mostly," her mother said and frowned. "Nick and Cara have been missing."

"I think they'll be back soon," Gabi said.

"What do you know?" her mother demanded.

"Nothing really," Gabi said. "They'll be here soon enough."

"It's about Cara's father," her mother said. "Isn't it?"

Gabi stifled a sigh. "This whole celebration should focus on Cara and Nick, not anyone else," Gabi said.

Her mother nodded. "You're completely right."

"Speaking of priorities, have you been in touch with your clients?" her father asked.

Gabi clenched her teeth. "I sure have. One of our best clients is begging for the organic products."

Her father frowned. "You know that kind of thing takes time. It's very expensive to deliver a new line."

"Then why have we been teasing them?" Gabi asked.

"We're not teasing," he said. "We just don't want to do anything unprofitable at this point."

"Well, I've sent samples to the drugstore buyers and I'm waiting to hear back. I think if we don't step up soon they'll choose someone else. I've done what I can do," Gabi said. "You're going to have to make a decision. I can't stall much longer."

Gabi met her father's gaze and felt the tension between them. Something about the last few days had made her stronger and bolder. Was it Finn?

"Don't take too long," she said, and turned to Finn. "I'd like to dance."

"Works for me," he said and nodded toward her parents. "Excuse us." He led her onto the dance floor.

"Your father's mouth is hanging wide open. He's still trying to figure out how to respond to you and what you said about your new line."

"It's not my new line," she said. "But I wish it was. The research and development department sent me over a dozen samples. They're over-motivated because my dad's the CEO."

"Maybe you should share them tomorrow and ask people to give their opinions. It can't hurt," he said, spinning her around.

Gabi stared at him. "You're right. Perfect. But that means I need to go back to my room to figure out the distribution." She winced. "Maybe I should bow out of this dinner."

"Maybe I could help."

She looked at him in surprise. "Really?"

He chuckled. "Yeah. Really."

Finn followed Gabi to her room and helped compose a quick survey while she divided the samples into bags for members of the wedding party.

"Are we leaving this stuff at the front desk?" Finn asked.

"That's probably best," she said, then frowned. "We just need to make sure the samples are delivered right away."

"I've been told that I always deliver," he joked.

Surprised, she shot a sideways glance at him. Her heart skipped several beats at the sensuality in his tone. She wagged her finger. "You really shouldn't tease like that. What if I believed you really—" She cleared her throat and shrugged.

He snagged her hand. "If you believed I really what?" he asked.

She felt a flood of self-consciousness and shrugged again. "I don't know. What if I believed you really wanted me?" she asked, as if the notion was ridiculous.

"Maybe I do," he said, so seriously it scared her.

She locked eyes with him for a long moment then forced a laugh. "Oh, stop," she said.

Finn pulled her toward him. "You underestimate your appeal."

Still unwilling to take him seriously, she smiled. "You think so?"

"I do," he said, and lowered his mouth to hers.

His lips caressed hers and she couldn't make herself pull away. The kiss pulled her up, over and under. She was dizzy from it. Dizzy from him. He slid his strong arms around her and she only wanted more, more, more.

Her want started in her belly and spread throughout her body, throughout her blood. He lifted her hands to cradle his face while he made love to her with his mouth. During the next few minutes, everything turned into a sensual blur. He slid one of his hands down to her breast, another between her legs...

He pushed his thigh between her legs, and she felt

his hardness against her. One of his hands cupped her bottom and guided her against him.

"You feel so good. I can't get enough of you. I wanted you from the first time I saw you," Finn murmured.

"I don't understand why you want me so much," she said, as he made her dizzier with each caress and kiss.

"How could I not want you?" he asked, and moved against the apex of her thighs.

Gabi could hardly breathe from how her desire roiled inside her. She couldn't keep her train of thought. She felt Finn tug at her dress, and it seemed to dissolve in a pool at her feet.

He held her against him so that she knew unmistakably how much he wanted her. He kissed her deeply then pulled back. "Do you want me to stop?"

"No," she said. "No. Don't stop."

The heated kisses and arousing touches continued. She gasped. He growled. He put on protection and thrust inside her.

Gabi gasped again. "Oh."

"Good or bad?" he asked, studying her face, his muscular body taut above hers.

"Good," she said, wriggling to adjust to him. "It's just been a while."

Finn swore under his breath. "Stop. I won't be able to control it."

She wriggled again. "If I can't control it, why should you?"

Then the thrusting and riding and loving began. Gabi held on for all she was worth.

"Can't wait much longer," he said.

She gave herself over to her sensations. "Don't. Wait," she said, and tumbled over the edge.

Seconds later she felt Finn reach his climax, but she was still shuddering from her own experience. Finally, she took a breath. "Oh, wow."

Finn rolled over to his side and pulled her with him. "You're pretty amazing, Gabi Foster," he said.

She laughed, still recovering from her orgasm. "Tell me that when I'm not naked."

"Done," he said. "Although, I won't complain any time you decide to get naked."

Finn kissed her sweetly and hugged her. Gabi couldn't resist the sensation of his arms around her.

"You make it hard for me to go home," Finn said, rubbing his cheek against hers.

Gabi thought of Kai and felt a sliver of guilt. "Oh, no," she said. "You really should leave. Kai is waiting for you."

"His nanny is taking care of him," he said. "But I do try to get home every night."

Images of all the women Finn could have filled her mind. She clenched her eyes shut. "You probably want to make sure you don't make the nanny stay overnight too often."

She felt his hand on her chin. "What do you mean by that?"

Gabi opened her eyes but looked downward. "I'm sure you meet a lot of women. A lot of desirable women."

"Not necessarily desirable to me," Finn said. "Look at me, Gabi."

Taking a breath, she met his gaze.

"I don't meet a lot of women that I want the same way I want you. You struck me the first time I saw you. Even before you nearly drowned," he said with a chuckle, then he turned solemn. "You're different."

Those two words made her feel a little better. *You're different.* Gabi could believe that. She couldn't believe she was the most beautiful, sexiest woman in the world. But she could believe she was different.

"Well, I don't know what to say," she said.

"How about you say that you'll see me every day until you leave?" he said more than asked.

Her stomach clenched at the reality that she'd be leaving. "That's only two more days," she said, and her heart filled with terrible sadness.

They helped each other dress, then they brought the cosmetic samples to the front desk with urgent instructions for delivery. Finn escorted her back to her room and kissed her good-night.

Gabi sank onto her bed, hoping for sleep. She tossed and turned, wondering if she should have given herself to Finn. Everything between them was happening so quickly.

She wondered how she could possibly make such an impression on him. She was an average woman, not the usual beach babe he must encounter. She was a young woman with an imperfect body and more than a few insecurities. Why would he want her? She wished she knew.

She finally fell asleep, and her dreams were filled with Finn and Kai. When Gabi woke, she felt exhausted. This was ridiculous. She needed to remain focused, she told herself, and checked her emails.

Gabi felt a half-dozen regrets about making love with Finn. Had she done the right thing? She closed her eyes and struggled with her thoughts. Perhaps she should have turned away. Perhaps that would have been better for her mind and heart.

After she'd spent the early morning on business, she heard a knock at her door. Her stomach took a dip. Heaven help her if it was Finn. Hopefully, it was the cleaning crew.

Gabi rushed to the door and looked through the peephole. Her heart stuttered. It was Finn. She flung open the door. "What are you doing here?"

"I can't imagine anywhere I'd rather be," he said. "Can't imagine anywhere else I should be."

She pursed her lips to keep from crying. "We probably shouldn't have—"

Finn covered her lips with his fingers. "Hush. Don't spoil the memory of such a beautiful night."

"You're such a flatterer. I never know when you're flirting," she said.

"There are different kinds of flirting," he said. "But I'm careful about the way I flirt."

She lifted her head. "What does that mean?"

"It means I don't flirt when I don't mean business with a woman," he said.

She squished her eyes closed. "You can't mean business with me. I'm leaving tomorrow afternoon."

"I don't want to miss this time with you," he said. "I can't really explain it, but it feels important."

She opened her eyes to meet his gaze, feeling confused but totally identifying with what Finn was saying. "I hadn't thought of it that way."

He shrugged his broad shoulders.

"I don't want to miss you, either," she realized.

"So, let's make the best of the time we have together," he said.

She nodded slowly. "Suggestions?"

"Yeah," he said. "Let's go back to my house."

"That sounds good to me," she said.

"Bathing suit," Finn said.

"I hear you." She headed for the bathroom. She emerged moments later, showered and lathered with sunscreen. She grabbed a hat and extra clothes. "Ready to go," she said.

She found Finn lying on her bed snoozing.

"Finn," she said, and then repeated his name again.

He awakened with a start. "What. What?"

Gabi walked closer to him and looked down at him. "Do you need a few extra winks?"

He slowly met her gaze and sat up, sliding his hand through hers. "An extra cup of coffee will keep me going. You were pretty amazing last night."

She shook her head. "There you go, flattering me again."

He shook his head. "Wrong, wrong, wrong. You *are* amazing."

"Stop. You're making me blush."

He gave a low chuckle. "Oh, darlin'. I can do better things to make you blush."

Gabi felt a twist deep, where he made her weak and needy. She took a deep breath. "Shut up, Finn. I'm trying to function here."

He leaned toward her and took her mouth in a kiss that spun her upside down and around the world. "Oh, Finn," she said against his lips. "How am I supposed to be sane with you?"

He chuckled and the sound rippled throughout her body. "I like the idea of keeping you a little crazy. Crazy looks good on you."

Somehow, her clothes disappeared, as did his. Somehow, they made love to each other even though she'd thought they shouldn't.

With their kisses and bodies joined in pleasure, they sighed in ecstasy.

"I've never met a woman like you."

"I don't understand," she said. "I'm not the most beautiful. I'm not the thinnest. I'm not amazing."

"Well, you're wrong about the amazing part…and the most beautiful…." He slid his fingers through her hair and stared deep into her eyes. "You're all in," he said. "I've never met a woman who was more *all in* than you are."

"All in?" she repeated.

He laughed at her lack of understanding. "All in means you'll do anything to make it happen. You'll put yourself out there to make it happen."

Gabi blinked. "Is there any other way?"

He grinned and pulled her against him. "Not in your world. I like that about you."

Finn led Gabi to his Jeep and drove toward his home. "I'll take you past another waterfall since you like them so much," he said and took a turn onto a dirt road. Her teeth jangled as he drove down the bumpy road. After a couple moments, Finn took another turn and she spotted the waterfall.

She gasped at the beauty. "It's just amazing."

"Want to swim in the pool?" he asked.

She glanced at Finn. "Can we?"

"I know the guy who owns the land," he said.

Gabi again looked at the waterfall and the pool. "Bet it's cold."

"Yep," Finn said.

She shuddered at the idea of drenching herself in chilly water.

"But you can't do this next week if you're not here."

A huge sense of longing and sadness stabbed at her. "You're right. Let's go," she said. "But be prepared to turn on the heat in your Jeep."

"The heat doesn't work that well." Finn laughed, following her out of his vehicle.

"Don't tell me that," she said, covering her ears. "Lalalalala…" She stopped at the edge of the pool.

"It's not that bad," he coaxed. "How many times have you been swimming near a waterfall?"

"Never," she said and took off everything except her bathing suit. She extended her hand to him. "Go with me."

He nodded. "I'm in." He stripped down to his trunks.

"I'm gonna freeze, aren't I? Don't answer that," she said, clutching his hand and dragging him into the chilly pool with her. She stepped into a sudden drop-off and plunged into water above her head.

Gabi bobbed to the surface and shrieked. She could feel Finn pulling her against him.

"I swear I can swim," she said breathlessly, waiting for her body to adjust to the cold water. "I thought Hawaii was supposed to be warm."

"It is. Chicago is much colder," Finn said.

She wrapped her legs around him instinctively. "I'm usually wearing a coat and tights and long underwear in Chicago. I'm never almost naked in a pool of water." Her teeth chattered.

"Well, if you want to get the rest of the way naked…" Finn suggested with a devilish grin.

"You are a very bad influence," she said. "Very bad."

"I dare you." He grinned.

Gabi closed her eyes. She just couldn't resist him, she thought, and ditched her swimsuit.

CHAPTER FIVE

AFTER THE SWIM, Finn dried off both Gabi and himself. They hopped into the Jeep and Finn drove to his home. Pulling into the driveway, he spotted Kai running out of the house. This always alarmed him. He'd told Kai many times not to run into the driveway.

Finn braked quickly and swore under his breath. Kai ran and jumped toward his side of the car.

Finn opened his car door and immediately hugged his nephew. "Kai, I love you, but I want you to go back in the house and wait for me to give you our sign. Show me the sign."

Kai lifted three fingers and wiggled them. "Good job. Now go back to the house and we'll try this again. Don't leave the porch until I give you our sign."

"But, Dad—" Kai protested.

"Go," he said.

Kai skittered to the side door.

Finn saw his sweet face staring out the window. Finn lifted three fingers and wiggled them.

Kai immediately ran to Finn's side of the car with

a questioning smile on his face. "I do okay?" the boy asked

Finn nodded. "You did perfect. Do it that way next time. The first time." Finn got out of the car and gathered Kai into his arms. "Right?"

"All 'ight," Kai said, dropping his R. She remembered Finn mentioning the speech impediment the first time she'd met the little boy. "Can we go swimming?"

Finn laughed. "Sure."

Kai looked toward Gabi. "Can she come, too?"

"Yes," Finn said. "Miss Gabi can come, too."

Finn motioned to Gabi, and she got out of the car.

"Hi, Miss Gabi," Kai said with his childish exuberance.

Her heart dipped at his sweetness. "Hi, Kai."

"We're going swimming again," he said, practically dancing from one foot to the other.

Gabi glanced at Finn. "You bet we are."

The three of them went into the house and found Nanny Alani at the kitchen table looking very weary.

"Are you sure you're okay?" Finn asked Alani.

"I'm seeing the doctor tomorrow afternoon," the nanny said. "I don't know why I've been so tired lately. Maybe I just need some vitamins." She took a deep swig from her bottle of water.

Finn nodded, but Gabi still saw the concern on his face.

"Maybe you could lie down while we go out for a swim," Gabi suggested.

The woman smiled. "It may take both of you to keep up with him."

Gabi felt a strange mix of emotions. Alani's weakness worried Gabi. She also worried that the nanny might not be strong enough to take care of Kai.

"I'm sure I'll be better after a rest. Don't trouble yourself about me," Alani said. "Go enjoy the ocean."

"As long as you promise to rest," Finn said.

"I will. Now go," Alani insisted.

Finn smeared Kai with sunscreen. Gabi added some more of her own sun protection, then the three of them trotted down to the beach.

Finn took Kai into the ocean with a surfboard and helped him take on the waves. Gabi watched the guys for several moments then checked her cell phone. She wished she didn't feel the compulsion to stay in touch with her business colleagues. But it was necessary. She had too much to lose if she didn't stay on top of work right now.

She returned several messages then tossed her cell into her tote bag and tried to focus on her surroundings. She looked at Finn and Kai in the ocean.

The boys laughed at the top of their lungs. Gabi smiled and waved.

Finn and Kai waved in return.

Gabi couldn't help wishing she could be with Finn for longer than a day. Longer than a month.

She didn't want to think about how long she wanted
to be with him, because it was far longer than today.

Gabi ran toward Finn and Kai to join them in
the ocean. Kai jumped up and down. "Miss Gabi is
here," he said.

Finn and Kai ditched their boards, and Gabi
jumped in the waves. The feeling of Kai's sweet little hand clinging to hers did something to her heart.

Eventually, she and Finn successfully wore out
Kai. The boy collapsed on the sand next to Gabi,
and she pulled him onto her lap. Soon enough, he
fell asleep. Gabi didn't want to awaken him, so she
sat very still, even when she started to feel pins and
needles in her feet.

"Why don't you just wake him up?" Finn asked.

"Because he's sleeping. He feels safe," she said,
stroking Kai's dark hair.

Finn studied her for a long moment. "How do you
know he feels safe?"

"Because he's so relaxed," she said, and lifted
his limp hand.

Finn couldn't help wondering if Kai was longing for a mother figure. Although his nanny filled
many needs, Finn suspected Kai needed more. He
was surprised that Kai had attached himself to Gabi
so quickly. It made him curious, but it bothered him
for some reason, too.

After a half-hour nap on Gabi's lap, Finn lifted
his hand. "Isn't this enough?"

Gabi glanced down at Kai and stroked his forehead. "I'm not sure it is."

Finn struggled with conflicting emotions. He was glad that Kai could feel safe with Gabi. At the same time, he knew Kai couldn't count on her. She was leaving soon. The knowledge twisted inside him.

"Let's let him sleep in his bed," he said to Gabi and lifted Kai against his chest. Kai wiggled and sighed.

Finn took his nephew inside, changed his clothes, and laid him down, then walked from the bedroom to the den.

"Did I do something wrong?" Gabi asked, standing in the den.

Finn shook his head. "Not a thing," he said. "I just realized that Kai is growing attached to you and you're leaving soon. I need to protect him."

Gabi's face fell. "Should I have done something different? Should I have distanced myself from him? Not allowed him to go to sleep in my lap?"

Troubled, Finn shrugged. "No. It's just that—" He broke off because it was hard to explain.

"You say you like me because I'm *all in*," she said. "But you want me to pull back with Kai. I'm confused."

Finn sighed. "It's different with Kai. I have to protect him. With me, I'll just have to handle the memories when you leave." He met her gaze. "I've dealt with loss before. I'm older. Kai has already experienced too much loss already."

His words hurt, but Gabi not only understood Finn's need to protect Kai, she admired it. A terrible lump of emotion formed in her throat and she swallowed hard so she could speak. "I think you should take me back to the resort now," she managed.

He gave a slow nod. "I can do that," he said reluctantly.

Less than two minutes later, she and Finn got into his Jeep and backed out of the driveway. During the drive, he didn't speak. Neither did she. But the emotions flowed like fireworks between them.

She felt too much and she suspected he did, too. The ride felt interminable. Finally, he pulled into the resort parking lot.

Finn turned toward her, but she didn't want to hear what he had to say. She lifted her hand and drew his head toward hers, then kissed him full on the lips. The sensation made her dizzy and she pulled away.

"Thank you for everything," she said. "You've been wonderful. And Kai is the sweetest, most adorable kid in the world. I will never forget you," she said, and kissed him again. Then she raced out of the Jeep.

Her heart hurt and her eyes burned with tears. It shouldn't be this way, she thought. This should have been a little vacation fling. An insignificant destination affair. If that was true, then why did she feel as if her heart was being torn from her chest?

Gabi had clearly made a huge mistake.

GABI LAY DOWN on her hotel bed for a few moments to try to clear her mind and relax. It didn't work, so she got up and took a shower. She wanted to wash away her volatile feelings. But the shower wasn't the cure she'd hoped for.

Swearing under her breath, she decided she'd have to put herself together physically and hope for the best. She fixed her hair, put makeup on her face and then pulled on a Spanx, followed by her dress for the wedding.

She looked in a full-length mirror and deemed her appearance acceptable, then put her cell phone, room key, lip gloss and powder into her small purse. She was ready to face the world, and heaven help anyone who shot her a pitying glance.

Gabi walked toward the beach for the wedding. She immediately ran into her ex and his beaming wife.

"Gabi," Bill said. "Good to see you. You look great."

Gabi smiled. "Thank you, and congratulations again on the upcoming birth of your child," she said to both of them. "I'm sure you're excited for the baby to come."

Candace smiled. "I can't wait," she said. "It was a surprise, but a good one."

"Yeah," Bill said with less enthusiasm. "Definitely a surprise."

Gabi bit back a laugh. *Oh, well. That was telling.* Bill wasn't nearly as enthusiastic about becoming a father as she'd thought he'd be.

"Where's your surfer guy?" Candace asked.

"He has a little boy and has to take care of him today. I'm sure you'll learn about that yourselves, soon enough," she said

"Very soon," Candace said, linking her arm with Bill's. She smiled up at him and he gave a vague nod.

"Yep," he said. "Guess we should go to the main event."

"I think we should," Gabi said and walked ahead of them.

She walked toward the chairs set up on the beach and sat a row behind the seat where her mother would be. It was a perfect late afternoon. There was a slight breeze. The beautiful sunset wedding was a romantic feast for the senses for the wedding party and guests. Gabi sighed, and the thought she didn't want to think crept into her mind. She wondered if she would ever have a wedding. She quickly shut it down. This wasn't about her, she told herself. It was about her brother and his bride.

She watched as her mother and father were escorted to the row in front of her. Gabi's mom turned around and whispered, "You look beautiful, sweet-heart."

"You're the perfect mother of the groom," Gabi said in return.

Gabi's mother squeezed her hand and turned around. The rest of the ceremony proceeded with sweet beauty. Her nieces wore pretty dresses and they stood with smiles on their faces. Cara's mother and father, seated apart from each other, appeared at peace.

Cara was clearly filled with joy and love. Gabi saw the same expression on her brother's face and couldn't keep tears from her eyes. Nick looked at Cara as if she were the answer to happiness in his life. Gabi could only hope that his marriage to Cara would be everything he wanted and needed. She dabbed at her eyes with a tissue as the sun set over the beautiful wedding.

The couple exited and the rest of the guests fol-lowed. Gabi took her time. She didn't want to have to answer any more questions about Finn. She didn't want to even think about him or Kai. She felt as if her heart had been hijacked by both of them. Gabi couldn't help wondering if she would ever find the same kind of love her brother had found.

Strolling toward the reception site, she saw her mother and father, and considered avoiding them, but her mother raised her hand. "Gabi, sweetie, come over here."

Her mother was the dearest person in the world and she couldn't imagine that anyone could refuse her. Gabi went to her mother and embraced her. "Hi, Mom, how are you feeling?" Gabi asked.

"Emotional," her mother said and slid her hands into Gabi's. "I so want this to work for Nick."

"I think they have a good shot," Gabi said. "Cara clearly loves him and she wants to be good with Nick's girls. She's actually taking a course on how to deal with special-needs children."

"Really?" her mother said, and dabbed at her moist eyes. "That's very impressive and gives me a lot of hope."

Gabi gave her mother another hug. "I think they love each other. I guess that means we need to support them. That's what you've always taught me."

"You're the best daughter ever. Speaking of which, I tried the green cosmetics and I love them. Preston," she said, nudging her husband. "Tell Gabi about the green cosmetics."

Her father leaned toward her. "Everyone has been hounding the hell out of me about these products. I couldn't figure out how they knew I was connected until one of them handed me a survey they'd been given." He pulled it out of his pocket and showed it to her. She read the telling line at the bottom of the document. *Tell Preston Foster what you think of these products. He wants to know.*

"Why in hell did you do this?" he demanded.

Her stomach knotted. "I, uh—I didn't. But it was a great idea." She laughed.

"What do you mean you didn't do this?" her father asked with a frown.

"I didn't put together the survey. Finn did," she said. "But, like I said, it was a great idea, wasn't it?"

Preston gave a grudging nod. "It's a limited sampling."

Gabi groaned. "Whatever." She stepped away from her parents. A waiter moved toward her, offering a glass of champagne from the tray he carried. Gabi accepted, and because she was feeling edgy and out of place, she turned on her phone and checked her messages. One caught her interest. The drugstore company she'd been wrangling with over the new line wanted in. Several people had tried the products and they wanted to move on the line now.

Adrenaline raced through her and she pulled her father aside. "I love you, Dad, but in terms of the organic line, it's time to put up or shut up. The drug company is ready to go to contract now."

Preston scratched his chin and looked down his nose at his daughter. "That's some nerve bringing this up at your brother's wedding."

Gabi felt a pang of guilt, but worked past it. "You would do the same," she said.

Preston stared at her for a long moment then shrugged. "You must be a chip off the old block. You want the green line, you've got it." He hugged her.

She felt the tiniest bit of excitement, but it quickly evaporated. Gabi didn't feel her father's embrace on the inside. Her win felt incredibly superficial. Did she want to be a chip off the old block? "Thanks, Dad," she managed, but pulled away from her father.

She should be filled with exhilaration. She waited for the thrill, but it didn't come. Perplexed, she walked to the edge of the crowd and took a sip of her champagne. Why wasn't she turning cartwheels? Why wasn't she over the moon?

Suddenly, she felt a nudge against her arm and looked beside her. Finn. Her heart leaped. "What are you doing here? I thought you weren't coming."

"I never said I wasn't coming, but I had to take some extra time with Kai. I'm not so sure about Alani. She doesn't seem well at all."

"I thought the same thing. What made you leave him tonight?" she asked.

"I left him with another cousin. I'll leave him with Alani tomorrow morning, but she's going to the doctor tomorrow afternoon. I'm hoping we'll get straight after that."

Gabi gave a slow nod. "Good," she said.

'Yeah," Finn said. "How's the wedding going?"

Gabi smiled. "Great, so far. Very sweet. I'm crossing my fingers and toes that everything will work out for Nick and Cara."

A band began to play a slow, romantic song.

Finn looked into Gabi's eyes. "Wanna dance?"

Gabi took a deep breath, knowing this might be her last opportunity to dance with Finn. "Of course," she said, and he led her onto the dance floor.

"How's Kai?" she asked, treasuring the feel of Finn's strong, hard body swaying against hers.

"He's good. Like I told you, Kai's mother had a lot of relatives here. I wanted him to have a chance to experience that family. His cousins are usually more than happy to look after him when I need a break."

"He's such a sweet, happy boy. You've done a good job," Gabi said.

"I can't take all the credit," he said.

Gabi laughed under her breath. "Now you're getting humble. That's not right."

He lifted his mouth in a slow grin and spun her around. "I can be humble."

"But it's not your regular nature," she said.

His face grew serious. "I've learned humility since I took on Kai. This fathering thing isn't all that easy."

"Don't underestimate yourself the way you say I underestimated myself. I'm betting Kai would say you're pretty amazing."

"Kai is very forgiving."

He spun her around, adding to her lightheadedness.

"You look beautiful tonight," he said. "But you looked beautiful when you tried to surf."

Gabi laughed. "I'm going to miss your flattery,

Finn. I know what I looked like when I tried to surf. I looked like a sputtering sea creature."

"Mermaid," he suggested.

She laughed again. "Yeah, right."

"You know, you really should give surfing another try. You'll love it eventually."

Her heart tightened. "I'm leaving tomorrow. There's no time," she said, regret burning through her.

"You could change your flight," he said.

What a tempting idea. Gabi considered it for a moment. She played with the appeal of it. What if she were completely free? Would she stay with Finn to see what could happen between them? The connection she felt with him was far more than that of a holiday flirtation. As it was, she didn't know how she would feel once she returned to Chicago.

She closed her eyes and sighed. "You're making it hard to leave."

"Is that a bad thing?" he asked, pulling her against him.

She took a deep breath and opened her eyes. "I have to go. My life is in Chicago. The deal I've been working on has just come through. Everything is finally coming together for me in my career."

He gave a slow nod. "I knew you'd have to go. I just can't remember feeling this way about a woman."

A knot formed in her throat. "I feel the same way about you," she said. "And Kai." Tears burned at the back of her eyes. "This is so hard. Maybe I could visit."

"Yeah. When you can fit it into your schedule," Finn said. "But you didn't even want to come here for your brother's wedding. How much harder will it be if there's no real family obligation?" With a sad smile, he lifted his hand to her head and stroked her hair. "You're *all in* with your career right now. Maybe that's the way it should be."

"Then why does leaving feel so wrong?" she asked, her voice breaking.

"You have to be the one to answer that," he said, and gave her a warm and wonderful hug. "I wish I could stay tonight, but I can't. I have to take Kai home." He pulled back slightly and looked deeply into her eyes. "This will have to be goodbye."

Goodbye. The word tore at her. "I didn't expect to feel this way." She shook her head. "Or maybe I just put off how I thought I would feel." She looked up at him. "I wish there was another way."

She watched him take a deep breath and narrow his eyes for a second as if he were mentally girding himself. "I'm glad I met you," he said. "I wouldn't change that."

"I wouldn't change it, either. I've never met anyone quite like you, and I'm pretty sure I never will again."

Finn pulled her close and she rested her head on his shoulder. She put her hand on his chest and felt his heartbeat. Closing her eyes, she treasured the quiet moment. In some ways, this was more intimate than sex. They'd both bared their feelings— their hearts—to each other. She was torn between deep gratitude for the short time they'd had together and the loss she was already beginning to feel.

"It's time," he whispered. She lifted her head and he kissed her. The kiss was full of everything they both felt—gratitude, longing, passion and something deeper....

He finally pulled back. "Take care," he said, and she watched him walk away.

It was on the tip of Gabi's tongue to call him back, to blurt out three impossible words, but she stopped herself. Barely.

Then she cried.

CHAPTER SIX

GABI FORCED HERSELF to return for the rest of the wedding festivities. She watched her brother and his new wife cut the cake and gently feed each other bites. She watched her mother and father sway together in a romantic dance. Everyone seemed to be wearing a lovey-dovey glow. Except her. Her mind was whirling with images of Finn. She couldn't understand how he'd made such an impact on her in such a short time.

Frowning, she tried to focus on her brother's celebration, but her heart just wasn't in it. Gabi successfully hid behind a bush as Cara tossed her bouquet. Soon after, she joined the crowd as they gave a bubbly send-off to the bride and groom. Ready to disappear from the whole scene, she raced to her room and changed into comfortable pajamas.

After scrubbing her face clean and brushing her teeth, she packed her suitcase so she'd be ready to go, even though her flight didn't depart until the afternoon. She'd had a full day. She could only hope she would sleep like the dead.

Turning off the light and sliding under the covers,

she closed her eyes. Her body was tired. She could feel the weariness in her feet and legs, even the muscles in her shoulders. She took several deep breaths, willing herself to relax, willing her body to sleep.

Her mind kept turning to Finn and Kai. She tried all her regular tricks to fall asleep, but none of them worked. Finally, she drifted off. But she kept waking up in a panic. Her heart raced and her mouth was dry. What was going on?

At 5:00 a.m., Gabi gave up any chance at sleep and showered and dressed. By six, she could've been ready to go to the airport. An earlier flight? Her mind shut that down in a millisecond.

Unable to stand being in her room with herself one more second, she decided to head for the beach. Maybe the sound of the ocean would calm her. Besides, she may as well steal one more glance, since she was headed back to the frozen tundra of Chicago. No ocean or balmy breezes there.

Gabi headed down the path, took off her shoes and relished the sensation of sand between her toes. She walked a ways down the beach and plopped down to stare at the ocean. The sound was soothing, but her heart still hurt. She absently grabbed a little stick and drew in the sand. The action reminded her of Kai and his excitement about playing tic-tac-toe. She smiled at the memory. She looked at the ocean and remembered the first time she'd laid eyes on Finn.

She'd thought he was a typical surfer guy, but she'd been so wrong.

Sighing, she pulled her cell phone from her pocket. The deal with the drugstore chain was all but inked. She should feel exhilarated, over the moon. When she returned to Chicago, she was assured a promotion. Her future at her father's company was better than ever.

Gabi made a face at her phone and turned it off. Too restless to sit for a moment longer, she walked toward the ocean still holding the phone in her hand. For one wild moment, she pictured herself throwing it in.

Shock raced through her.

Throw her phone in the ocean? The notion was ridiculous. She'd sooner rob a bank.

But the image must have rattled something loose in her brain because she started thinking crazy thoughts. What if she decided not to go back to Chicago? What if she got a different job so that she could stay here with Finn and Kai?

Would Finn want her to stay? She sensed he would, but they'd just met. How could she possibly give up the promotion she knew she'd receive after knowing him such a short time? She'd told herself he was just a temporary fling. She'd told him she had to return to Chicago. Anything else was impossible.

Gabi wondered how he would feel if she showed up at his house and said *Hey, I've decided to stay.*

Aren't you glad? The idea terrified her—putting herself on the line like that, when the results were nothing near a sure thing.

She closed her eyes and told herself to settle down. This was ridiculous. She'd just gotten a little more emotionally involved than she'd planned. It was the environment. A beautiful island and the romance of her brother's wedding. That's what it was, she told herself and started walking.

The devil of doubt rode her shoulder. What if she'd told Finn she loved him instead of just letting him walk away?

How could she possibly love someone, really love someone, she'd known less than a week?

"Impossible," she muttered under her breath. "It's just impossible."

But her heart was screaming now. Perhaps it was due to her lack of sleep, but she felt her denial fading and other questions scorching her brain.

What if Finn was *the one?* What if she never met another man like him again? What if she went the rest of her life and everyone she met was second-best?

Her heart thumped in her chest. She tried again to deny it, but she knew what she had to do. She had to see Finn one more time.

GABI RENTED A car through the resort and prayed she remembered the way to Finn's house. She considered making a U-turn at least ten times during the journey. What was she thinking? How would he respond? What if he thought she was crazy? Maybe she was. Despite her lack of directions, she found her way to Finn's and pulled into the driveway.

Cutting the engine, she took a deep breath and tried to rehearse what she planned to say. Everything sounded crazy. Gabi thought about leaving before she made a fool of herself, but then she remembered what Finn had said he liked about her. *All in*. Well, heaven help her, she was in up to her earlobes now.

Taking her courage in her hands, she went to the side door and knocked. No response. She tried again and still got no answer. Gabi frowned and glanced at the driveway again. Finn's car was gone. She almost slapped her forehead as she remembered he'd said he'd be busy this morning.

Still, she thought the nanny should come to the door. She tried the handle and it was unlocked. "Alani?" she called as she pushed open the door. "Alani?" She paused. "Kai?"

No answer, again. Her instincts told her something was off, and she walked farther into the house. She spotted Alani on the floor of the den.

Alarm rippled through her and she rushed to Alani's side. "Alani," she said, gently shaking the woman. "Alani, are you okay?"

The woman didn't respond and Gabi's fear ratcheted up another notch. "Kai," she called. "Kai, are you here?"

The silence frightened her even more. She quickly walked through the house and saw no sign of the boy. Returning to Alani, she tried to rouse the woman, to no avail. Alani was taking shallow breaths and was drenched in sweat. Gabi called emergency and had to search for the house's address. She was assured an ambulance was on the way. Gabi tried to call Finn, but there was no answer. She suspected he was in the middle of a surfing class.

Gabi was torn between looking for Kai and staying with Alani. What if Kai was in danger? Every minute that passed felt like an hour. She wished she knew what to do for Alani. She wished she knew where Kai was.

Finally, the ambulance arrived and the paramedics began to treat Alani.

"There's a child," she told the medics. "I have to go look for him. I don't know where he is."

One of the paramedics glanced up at her. "This looks like diabetes. We need to stabilize her."

Gabi recalled how tired Alani had seemed. "That makes sense." She bit her lip. "I have to look for Kai," she said and ran out the door. Gabi ran toward the swing and slide, but didn't see him. She dreaded the possibility that he could be in the ocean. Even though she knew Finn was making Kai as water-safe as possible, she didn't want Kai alone out there.

Gabi raced toward the beach and looked from one side to the other. At first glance, she saw nothing. Then she spotted Kai with a stick, close to the edge of the shore.

"Oh, thank God," she said to herself. "Kai," she called. "Kai, come here."

Kai glanced up and bounded toward her. "Miss Gabi," he said. "Can we pay tic-tac-toe?"

Gabi gathered Kai against her. "Not right now," she said. "Why did you come out to the beach alone?"

Kai stuck out his lower lip in a pout. "Alani was napping again. I wanted to play."

Gabi was still recovering from the fact that Kai had been missing. "You are never to go to the beach alone. Never. Do you hear me?"

Kai appeared frightened by her tone. "Okay."

"How would your father feel if he knew you were out here?"

Kai hung his head. "Daddy Finn doesn't want me on the beach without him," he said in a muffled tone. "He be mad?"

"He'll be relieved you're okay," she said and pulled Kai up into her arms. "Let's go back to the house. Alani is sick, but the doctors can make her better."

"Nanny is sick?" Kai repeated, clearly worried.

"Yes, but the doctors can make her better," Gabi reassured him. When she and Kai arrived at the house, it was clear that the paramedics had just loaded Alani into the ambulance.

"Go play in your room. I'll get you a snack in a few minutes," she said to Kai as she set him down on the ground.

"Lots of lights," he said.

"They have flashing lights so they can drive fast," Gabi told him.

"Can I go?" he asked.

She shook her head. "No. Go to your room. I'll come see you in just a sec."

Gabi ran toward the back of the ambulance and caught up with one of the paramedics. "How is she?"

"It looks like diabetes. I think it was caught in time, but she'll need to be hospitalized. It's a good thing you showed up when you did."

Gabi felt a chill rush over her. What if she hadn't given in to her instinct to see Finn again? What if she'd chickened out one of the many times she'd thought she couldn't go through with her plan?

She rubbed her arms. "We just want her to be okay."

The paramedic nodded and closed the door. "We'll take care of her now."

Gabi returned to the house. "Kai," she called.

He came running, holding a little truck in his hand. "Is Nanny okay?"

"She is," Gabi said. "Now, what do you want for a snack?"

Kai paused and a sly expression crossed his face. "Cookies and soda."

Gabi shook her head. "What would Nanny give you?"

Kai heaved a big sigh. "Cheese, c'ackers and juice."

"Then, that's what you'll have," she said and went to the fridge. Kai ate his snack and Gabi read several books to him. He grew restless, so she took him outside. Gabi wondered when Finn would check his messages. Surely it wouldn't be more than an hour. As soon as the thought crossed her mind, his Jeep pulled into the driveway and he dashed out of the vehicle.

"Gabi," he called. "Kai."

His voice was sharp with tension. Gabi could only imagine how upset he was.

She took Kai by the hand and walked from the play area. "We're here."

Finn ran toward them. "You're okay," he said to both of them. "What about Alani?"

"The paramedics think it's diabetes. They said it may take a few days to stabilize her," Gabi told him.

Finn nodded. "I wish she'd seen a doctor sooner. She's been so tired lately."

"That's what I thought," Gabi said.

"I'm hungry. I wanna eat," Kai said.

Finn smiled and lifted Kai into his arms. "We can take care of that. Lunch."

"Lunch," Kai echoed and rubbed his tummy.

Gabi was entranced by the interaction between them. There was so much humor, camaraderie and trust.

"You want some lunch?" Finn asked Gabi.

"Sure," she said, even though she should be leaving now if she wanted to make her flight.

Finn fixed peanut butter and jelly sandwiches with cheese crackers and fruit on the side for all. Gabi nibbled as she considered what she was going to say to Finn. He called the hospital to check on Alani, and learned that she was under expert medical care. Kai grew sleepy, and since Finn was tied up on the phone, Gabi took the little boy to his room and rocked him. He fell asleep quickly, and she laid him down on his bed.

Gabi gently closed the door behind her and nearly walked into Finn. "Oh," she said, caught off guard.

He put his hands on her waist. "Okay?"

She took a deep breath. "It's been an interesting day."

He nodded. "Sounds like it. Want to sit on the lanai?"

She took another deep breath, mentally preparing herself for whatever she was going to say. At the moment, she wasn't sure exactly what that would be. "Yes, thank you."

He led her to the small but beautiful lanai that

looked over the woods. The sound of the ocean in the background soothed her just a bit.

"You want something to drink? I could fix you a mai tai. It sounds like you've earned it."

She smiled, thinking she wanted to be completely sober. "Water's fine."

"Done," he said and disappeared. A moment later, he returned carrying two glasses of filtered water with ice and lime.

"Perfect," she said and took a sip.

Finn dragged a chair closer to her and sat down. He guzzled from his glass. "I didn't expect to get that call from you. I really didn't expect to find you here," he said.

She nodded, still searching for the right words.

"Pretty crazy," he said, looking at her. "It's a damn good thing you showed up when you did."

"That's what the paramedics said." She took another sip of water because her mouth seemed to be growing dryer by the moment.

"So, why did you come? I thought you were headed back to Chicago. You won your account. Everything's going your way," he said.

"Exactly," she said. "Everything was going my way until you entered my life."

Surprise widened his eyes. "Me? What did I do?"

"You turned my plans upside down," she said.

He straightened, looking confused. "Me? How did I do that?"

"By being you," she said, unable to keep an accusing tone from her voice.

Finn scrubbed his face and shook his head. "You're going to have to help me out here."

Gabi took her heart in her hands and went *all in*. "I love you."

He gaped at her and dipped his head. "Excuse me?"

"I said I love you." Her nerves got the best of her and she couldn't sit a moment longer, so she stood and began to pace. "I really didn't count on loving you, and it doesn't make any sense. I mean, we haven't known each other long enough. Right? It's not possible," she said, shaking. "Not at all possible. But I do." She took a breath and turned to look at him. "I love you. I didn't plan it. I can't totally explain it, but I do."

Finn stood, staring at her in disbelief. "You just said you loved me."

"More than once," she managed as he walked toward her.

"I think my brain stopped after the first time," he said and searched her gaze. "I'm a package deal. Kai will always be a part of me."

"I know," she said. "I think that's part of the reason I love you."

He closed his eyes as if she'd answered a prayer. "What does this mean?"

Her throat knotted with emotion. "I don't know.

You tell me. This is me being *all in*. I hope I'm not the only one who feels this way."

Finn immediately pulled her against him. "Oh, sweetheart, you're not alone, trust me. I would ask you to marry me, but I don't have a diamond."

His words both shocked and comforted her. She took a deep breath. "Well, if you had a diamond, what would you say? Here and now?"

Finn took a long moment then dropped to one knee.

"Oh, my goodness," she whispered.

He took her hand in his. "Gabi, I love you. I never thought I'd meet a woman like you. I want to spend the rest of my life with you. Will you be my wife and Kai's mother?"

Her heart overflowing, Gabi didn't need a second to answer. Without knowing it, she'd been waiting for Finn and Kai her entire life. "Yes," she said. "Oh, yes."

She helped pull him to his feet, and he took her mouth in a deep, passionate kiss. Gabi clung to him with all her might. She didn't know what the future held, but she didn't care as long as she and Finn and Kai were together.

He finally pulled his mouth away, his chest heaving. "Your father's gonna kill me, isn't he?"

Gabi laughed. "Probably."

AN HOUR LATER, after Kai woke up from his nap, the three of them piled into Gabi's rental car and headed for the resort. "We going?" Kai asked as he drank some water.

"We're going to meet Gabi's daddy," Finn said a bit grimly, restlessly pumping his leg in the passenger seat.

"Gabi daddy?" he said and smiled.

Gabi smiled in return, but kept her eyes on the road. "That's right. Did you have a good nap?"

Kai nodded and sipped on his water. "Can we go swimming?"

"Maybe later," Finn said. "We need to check on Alani, too."

"Nanny okay?"

"So far," Finn said and turned on the radio. "Music distracts him," he said to Gabi and put his hand on her knee.

"Are you okay?" she asked Finn.

He nodded. "I'm good. I just don't want Preston to come down too hard on you."

"Give me a couple minutes with him before you bring Kai to meet him," she said.

"How do you think he'll react?" Finn asked.

"No idea. He's accustomed to being in control and he's about to lose it," she said.

She continued the drive to the resort with Finn jiggling his leg in time to the music on the radio. Kai wobbled his head back and forth in the backseat.

Pulling into the resort parking lot, she spotted her father escorting a bellman as he delivered the luggage to a limo. Her father wasn't the type to use a passenger van. She parked the rental car several spots away and exited the car. "Wish me luck," she said to Finn.

"No worries," Finn said. "You can handle him. You can handle anything."

His words sank deep inside her and she pulled her strength around her tightly as she walked toward her father, the man who had always demanded perfection from her. "Hey, Dad," she said. "How's it going?"

Her father turned to her. "I'm surprised to see you here. I thought your flight left earlier."

She shrugged. "Things happen. Is Mom okay about the wedding?"

"She's very happy, and so am I. I think Nick and Cara will make a very nice match. Your mother was also happy to have some time with her grand-girls. She can't get enough of them. I have to confess they're very sweet," he said with a grin.

"It's good to see they've won over crusty Preston," she said.

"I'm not sure I like that description," he huffed.

"I'm just teasing about the crusty part. You're a great dad," she said. "The best dad I could have possibly had."

Her father blinked. "Well, thank you, Gabrielle. You've turned out to be a wonderful daughter."

"Partly your fault," she said.

Her father smiled.

She bit the inside of her lip because she knew she was about to displease her father, and she really hated displeasing or disappointing him. "I have something I need to tell you."

He dipped his head and tipped the bellman. "I'm betting the drugstore chain is ready to sign on the dotted line," he said.

"Right, but that's not all," she said, feeling her mouth go dry. She felt like a little kid again, wanting more than anything for her father to approve of her. She deliberately glanced toward the rental car and saw Finn occupying Kai next to the foliage. Her heart calmed. She knew her purpose.

"I'm resigning from my position. I still want to work for you, but I want to change my job and work here, from Kauai," she said. "I'm staying here."

Her father stared at her in shock, speechless.

"I'm not going back to Chicago." She felt she needed to make it perfectly clear.

Her father moved his mouth a few times, then he finally spoke. "Is this temporary?"

"I don't think so," she said. "I've fallen in love."

Realization crossed her father's face. "It's the surfing instructor. Honey, you can't make a long-term decision based on a short-term affair."

"Normally, I wouldn't," she said. "But I learned something about myself during this trip. And it's partly a quality I got from you, I think. When I'm *all in*, you can't stop me. *I* can't stop me. Tell me you don't understand that, Daddy. Tell me you don't understand being *all in*."

Her father was fighting what she was saying. She could see it. Gabi turned and motioned for Finn and Kai to join her. Kai ran ahead of Finn and looked at her father.

"You Gabi's daddy?" he asked.

Gabi saw her father's expression soften. "Yes, I am. And you are?"

"I'm Kai," the boy said, beaming.

"And I'm Finn," Finn said, extending his hand to her father. "We've met."

Her father frowned and reluctantly accepted Finn's hand. "How are you going to take care of my daughter on a surfer's salary?" Preston was revealing what a protective father he was.

"I haven't always been a surfer. I have a little in the bank," Finn said.

Her father lifted his eyebrow. "Is that so?"

"Yes, it is," Finn said.

Her father looked from Gabi to Finn to Kai and raked his hand through his hair. "I don't know what to say," he said. He glanced at Kai and gave a half-smile. "The only thing I know is that your mother is going to love having another grandchild."

CHAPTER SEVEN

"I GOTTA GO to the bathroom," Kai said in a stage whisper for the fifth time.

Finn shot Gabi a sideways glance and she smiled. "Here we go," Finn said, unfastening Kai's seat belt and walking him down the aisle of the jet that was taking them to Chicago.

Gabi leaned her head back against her seat. A lot had happened during the past four weeks. While Gabi had gotten into the groove of taking care of Kai, doctors had helped Alani stabilize her diabetes. Now they could leave Kai with his nanny again, though they made sure to check in with her frequently.

Kai and Finn returned from the restroom. Kai turned to her. "I can't wait to play in the snow."

"You need to remember that it's very cold," Gabi warned.

Kai nodded. "I can't wait."

Gabi grinned at Finn and he returned her smile. They'd taken an extra day in California so they could buy Kai a coat and boots.

"We've got a ways to go, guy," Finn said to Kai. "Try to take a nap."

"Can I have a snack?"

Gabi pulled out some dry cereal and fruit. Kai munched on it and took a few sips of water, then fell asleep, his head resting against Gabi.

Finn stretched his hand across the top of the seats and squeezed her shoulder. She looked at him and felt her heart squeeze at the love that rushed through her. It was amazing how much her feelings and commitment had grown in the short time she'd known Finn. Her priorities had turned upside down. Although she'd expected her father to let her go, he'd allowed her to continue working in a different, unofficial position. She was determined to continue, she had to continue to wear him down for the ultimate position she wanted. A consultant with the ability to manage her own time.

Although she was very responsive to work issues, things had changed greatly. Before Finn and Kai, she'd been glued to her cell phone, determined to make the ultimate deal—the deal that would win over her father and shut down anyone who said she couldn't be a success. But something amazing had happened since she'd gone to Kauai. She'd learned what was truly important to her. She glanced at Kai and Finn and closed her eyes. They were most important to her these days.

During this trip to Chicago, she planned to attend a baby shower for her friend Helen, and she wanted to visit her nieces, her brother and his new wife, and of course, her mother and father. But there was still this never-ending flight.

Luckily, no sooner had she closed her eyes than it seemed the attendants were announcing preparations for landing. Gabi yawned and glanced down at Kai. He was kicking his seat in anticipation. "Awmost there," he said in an excited stage whisper.

Gabi and Finn had worked with him to keep his voice lowered in public, and he was doing his best. Her heart twisted at his effort.

The jet landed and they made their way to the baggage claim. "Here's your coat," Gabi said, helping Kai into the garment he'd never worn. "I don't want you to get cold."

She and Finn put on their own parkas and caught a cab to her apartment. Gabi's parents were dying to have the three of them stay at their house, but Gabi wanted to give Kai a chance to acclimate to his new surroundings before adding her parents to the mix. They would have to cram in several visits during the next few days.

When they arrived at her apartment, Finn hauled in the luggage while Kai begged to go outside. "Give us a few minutes," Gabi said. "Daddy Finn will take you out soon."

Finn bundled up both of them again, then took Kai into the yard. Gabi watched from the window as the two of them ran in the snow and Finn taught

Kai how to throw snowballs. It wasn't long, however, before both returned to her apartment.

"Brrr," Finn said as they burst through the door. "My skin has gotten way too thin for this kind of winter."

Kai shivered. "Too cold."

"I warned you," she said, pulling off the boy's mitts and rubbing his chilly little hands. "We'll put on more layers when you go sledding. My dad will take you. There's a hill behind his house."

Kai's eyes widened. "Swedding? Can we go now?"

Gabi laughed. "No. We'll go visit my mom and dad tomorrow. Tonight we're going to have my favorite comfort meal. Tomato soup and grilled cheese sandwiches."

Kai wrinkled his nose. "Soup?"

Gabi smiled. They didn't eat soup very often. "It's hot," she said. "You'll like it."

It took a while for the apartment to warm up, so they kept their coats on. When she served the food, they ditched the extra layers and dug in. Even Kai. He stuck out his tongue at first, but then he slurped down the warm soup. He devoured half of the sandwich, then laid his head down on the table.

Finn put him to bed then returned to the kitchen nook. "He's out. I just hope he doesn't wake up at three in the morning and want to go sledding."

Gabi chuckled. "I'm hoping the flight and your time in the snow wore him out."

"Me, too," he said and tugged her away from the table to the couch in the den. "Sometimes I wonder if you realize you've gotten in over your head with Kai and me. I mean, he's not really your kid."

She shot him an indignant look. "Oh, yes, he is," she said.

He met her gaze for a moment then laughed and pulled her against him. "How'd I get so lucky?"

"I could say the same," she said. "It may sound crazy, but my life felt like it all came together when I met you."

"Same for me," he said. "When are we visiting your parents?"

"Tomorrow afternoon. Preston Foster always works in the morning," she said.

"I'll bear that in mind. I need to run an errand first thing. Do you mind covering Kai?"

"Not if we go to bed now."

"No objections from me," he said.

THE NEXT MORNING, Gabi woke to Kai jumping on the bed beside her. "Where's Daddy Finn?" he demanded.

Gabi struggled to open her sleepy eyes. "He's gone out for a little while. Don't you want to sleep a little longer?"

"No," he said. "Want to swed."

"Sled," she corrected. "Try to make the L sound."

Kai clearly made an effort to correct his speech. "I want to *sled*."

"We're not sledding until after we visit my parents this afternoon, but I can fix you some breakfast. Do you like that idea?"

Kai nodded and jumped off the bed.

Gabi sometimes wondered where he got his energy. She sure didn't have nearly as much get-up-and-go as he did. Dragging herself from bed, she scrubbed her face and brushed her teeth, then scrounged in her cabinets and made Kai some pancakes. He scarfed them down, then planted himself in front of the television to watch a cartoon.

No sooner had she cleaned up the dishes than Finn walked through the door. "I don't see how you lived here so long," he said, shuddering. "Too cold."

She walked toward him and rubbed his arms. "We're only here for a few days," she reminded him.

"Good thing." He sniffed the air. "Smells like pancakes."

"All gone," she said. "Kai had a hole in his leg. He ate four, and I had the rest."

"Four?" he said, looking at Kai. "How did you do that?"

Kai rubbed his tummy. "Good pancakes."

"I'd like to shower, if that's okay," she said.

"Take your time," Finn said. "Your boys are chilling."

Gabi showered and dressed then tiptoed into the den. Both Finn and Kai were napping. Her heart turned over at the sight of them. She couldn't imagine her life without them.

Later that day, her father played in the snow with Kai and her mother made hot chocolate for everyone. After her father brought Kai inside, he invited her and Finn into the formal parlor.

"I was reluctant about the two of you getting together so quickly," he told both of them. "I thought it was a rash move for Gabi to move to Kauai for a surfing instructor and his little boy. But I'm pretty sure there's more to you than meets the eye," he said to Finn.

Finn shrugged and Gabi said nothing. If Finn wanted to keep his secrets, then she wouldn't fight him. She'd been willing to take a low-wage job to be with him and she was still willing to do that.

"My problem is that one of my clients is, well, distraught, that Gabi is no longer a full-time marketing representative with my company. I would like to offer you a consultant position. You would only need to come to Chicago every three or four months. You can work from Kauai."

Gabi gasped and looked at Finn. "What do you think?"

"I think it sounds perfect," he said and grinned. "Much better than a cabana girl, although I'm sure you'd do well at that."

"Dad, thank you," she said, throwing her arms around her father.

"This isn't nepotism," he protested, although he squeezed her tight. "I'm just protecting my business."

"Of course you are," she said, smiling at him.

That night, after they returned from her parents' and Kai fell asleep, Finn took Gabi onto the balcony of her apartment, even though it was freezing. Gabi shivered. "I thought you didn't like this cold weather."

"I don't. But I want the good luck from the stars looking down on us when I do this," he said. "I didn't do this the way I wanted to the first time."

"What do you mean?"

Pulling a jeweler's box from his pocket, he knelt down and took her hand. "I love you, Gabi. You make my life complete in ways I never dreamed. Will you marry me?" he asked. He opened the box to reveal a large, stunning diamond ring.

"That's big," she said. "Are you sure you can afford it?" She couldn't help asking.

"That wasn't the response I was expecting," he said.

"Yes. Yes, a thousand times over. I just don't want you to go into debt for me."

"I'll let you in on a little secret. I did pretty well in my days on Wall Street," he said, and put the ring on her finger. It fit perfectly.

"You didn't have to do this," she said. "Your love is enough."

"All the more reason why I want to do it," he said, and rose to his feet. "I don't want a long engagement. I want you to be my bride as soon as possible."

Gabi felt as if all her dreams were coming true.

* * * * *

REQUEST YOUR
FREE BOOKS!

2 FREE NOVELS
FROM THE ROMANCE COLLECTION
PLUS 2 FREE GIFTS!

YES! Please send me 2 FREE novels from the Romance Collection and my 2 FREE gifts (gifts are worth about $10). After receiving them, if I don't wish to receive any more books, I can return the shipping statement marked "cancel." If I don't cancel, I will receive 4 brand-new novels every month and be billed just $6.24 per book in the U.S. or $6.74 per book in Canada. That's a savings of at least 22% off the cover price. It's quite a bargain! Shipping and handling is just 50¢ per book in the U.S. and 75¢ per book in Canada.* I understand that accepting the 2 free books and gifts places me under no obligation to buy anything. I can always return a shipment and cancel at any time. Even if I never buy another book, the two free books and gifts are mine to keep forever.

194/394 MDN F4XY

Name	(PLEASE PRINT)	
Address		Apt. #
City	State/Prov.	Zip/Postal Code

Signature (if under 18, a parent or guardian must sign)

Mail to the Harlequin® Reader Service:
IN U.S.A.: P.O. Box 1867, Buffalo, NY 14240-1867
IN CANADA: P.O. Box 609, Fort Erie, Ontario L2A 5X3

Want to try two free books from another line?
Call 1-800-873-8635 or visit www.ReaderService.com.

* Terms and prices subject to change without notice. Prices do not include applicable taxes. Sales tax applicable in N.Y. Canadian residents will be charged applicable taxes. Offer not valid in Quebec. This offer is limited to one order per household. Not valid for current subscribers to the Romance Collection or the Romance/Suspense Collection. All orders subject to credit approval. Credit or debit balances in a customer's account(s) may be offset by any other outstanding balance owed by or to the customer. Please allow 4 to 6 weeks for delivery. Offer available while quantities last.

Your Privacy—The Harlequin® Reader Service is committed to protecting your privacy. Our Privacy Policy is available online at www.ReaderService.com or upon request from the Harlequin Reader Service.

We make a portion of our mailing list available to reputable third parties that offer products we believe may interest you. If you prefer that we not exchange your name with third parties, or if you wish to clarify or modify your communication preferences, please visit us at www.ReaderService.com/consumerchoice or write to us at Harlequin Reader Service Preference Service, P.O. Box 9062, Buffalo, NY 14269. Include your complete name and address.

ROM13R

Don't miss the final chapter of the Celebrations, Inc.
miniseries by reader-favorite author
Nancy Robards Thompson!

Widower Dr. Liam Thayer isn't looking for romance—
least of all at a charity bachelor auction, where
Kate Macintyre bids a hefty sum on the single dad.
As Liam and Kate begin to fall in love, she begins
to wonder whether she can ever truly be a part
of his family.

*Look for CELEBRATION'S FAMILY
next month from Harlequin® Special Edition®,
wherever books and ebooks are sold!*

When in the city of love...

Moonlight in Paris
by Pamela Hearon

Tara O'Malley has traveled across the ocean to find her biological father—and maybe rediscover who she is. The last thing she's looking for is romance.

Nothing is quite what she expected, and the only friend she's found in France is her neighbor Dylan, who happens to be six years old. And his father, Garrett Hughes, who is so standoffish that it hardly matters how insanely gorgeous he is. Tara knows she's falling hard for everything about this man, including his sweet little boy. What will happen when she has to go back home and leave them behind?

It's definitely not the best time to fall in love, but when in Paris...

HARLEQUIN®

super romance

More Story...More Romance

www.Harlequin.com

HSR71905

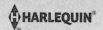

American Romance®

From Minor League Pitcher to Major League Dad?

After the injury that sidelined his pro baseball career, Travis Oak became a Little League coach. Now a kid in danger of being expelled needs his help—and Travis has the perfect solution. He just needs to get the boy's widowed mom on board.

After her sports-star husband's betrayal, Courtney Smith wants nothing to do with baseball. She brought her kids to Cocoa Village, Florida, to make a fresh start. But how can she resist the sexy coach who's fast becoming a hero to her boy?

Don't miss
Second Chance Family

by LEIGH DUNCAN

Available February 2014, from
Harlequin® American Romance®
wherever books and ebooks are sold.